Coming of Age Song

Coming of Age Song

Katherine Hon

Coming of Age Song

Published by Hon Con Publishing
2226 Dwight Street
San Diego, California 92104

This is a work of fiction. Names, characters, places, and incidents are either the product of the author's imagination or are used fictitiously. Any resemblance to actual persons, living or dead, business establishments, agencies, events, or locales is entirely coincidental.

First edition 2009

Library of Congress Control Number: 2009909277

ISBN 978-0-9795005-1-0

Printed in the United States of America

10 9 8 7 6 5 4 3 2 1

The publisher does not have any control over and does not assume any responsibility for third-party Web sites or their content.

Dedicated to Mary Savage, my irrepressible mother

Acknowledgments

Writing this novel has been an exhilarating journey. I would like to thank everyone who joined me on the ride, whether they meant to or not, especially the following supportive souls.

I am deeply grateful to my husband, Steve Hon, for his reality-check questions and dialogue suggestions, even when my reaction was, "If you want a character to say that, you'll have to write your own book."

Thank you to my first readers and editors, my sister Merry Carson, cousin Kerin Forsyth, and dear friend Bari Zwirn, for their thorough review and eagle eyes.

I appreciate the sage advice from experts in the book world, especially Margaret Mannatt, Jennifer Redmond, Jo Carpenter, and Vicki Garcia. I also appreciate the printing expertise of Rose Martinez and Chris Merz at Wholesale Reprographics.

Warm thanks go to two talented North Park neighbors: photographer Roni Galgano for the author's portrait, and graphic designer Ellen Goodwin for the cover and book design.

Another thank you goes to Steve Willard with the San Diego Police Historical Association for crucial information about historical mayhem.

I extend special appreciation to the women of the Old West (and the authors who write about them) for the opportunity to distill their stories as part of this novel. I recommend and acknowledge the following books for the true accounts: *The Gentle Tamers* by Dee Brown, *Those Strenuous Dames of the Colorado Prairie* by Nell Brown Propst, *Cultivating Hope* by Linda K. Hubalek, and any book by Anne Seagraves, particularly *Soiled Doves: Prostitution in the Early West.*

This novel was inspired by and named after a beautiful art piece by sculptor Brad Burkhart. The clay relief depicts a warrior goddess at the moment she realizes her purpose in life. It is one of my most treasured possessions, and I appreciate my friend's permission to use the name of his work for mine.

Finally, a caveat to anyone who might read a snippet of conversation or fragment of a name and think, "Hey, that's me!" or "How dare you!" Relax. Everyone in this book is a figment of my imagination and solely a reflection of what I see in my own mirror.

1

"Oh my god, Packard, listen to this. It's so sad." Catlin's eyes brimmed and her voice shook as she read aloud from the small book, tracing the words with a slender index finger.

"Many respectable citizens in the developing West would not accept a woman who was a 'soiled dove.' Catherine Porter came to Denver from the East Coast in the early 1870s and joined her cousin at a lavish, well-run parlor house. A wealthy rancher fell in love with this beautiful prostitute and she with him. He begged her to marry him and leave her life as a 'fancy lady' behind. But she knew they could never marry because it would ruin his social position. Finally, in distress over the hopeless situation, she took poison and died. When the rancher learned of her suicide, he was inconsolable and blamed himself. Standing at her grave, he shot himself in his grief-stricken heart and joined his lover in death."

Catlin sighed. "Isn't it tragic?"

Packard gazed upward with gentle, honey-colored eyes and barked.

"I knew you'd agree," she said, blowing delicately into a tissue as the phone rang. "Hello?"

"Hey babe, what're you doing?" came the smooth male voice on the line. "Catlin. You're not crying, are you? Have you been reading another sad book?"

"No, no." She dashed at her tears. "I was just, um, in the garden and the pollen got to me a little."

"Oh, that's good. I hate it when you're upset; you know it spoils my whole day."

"And how is your day going, John? Will you be able to leave early enough for our anniversary dinner?"

"That's why I called, babe. Getting ready for that big case—there's too much to get done. I've got to work late and come in early for the next few days. I probably won't be able to see you at all for the rest of the week." John McKenzie, Esq. (he insisted on the "Esquire") leaned back in his towering black leather executive chair and raised a peremptory finger to his secretary as she walked in with several files. "I'll just be a minute, Angela, wait," he said, quickly pushing the mute button on and off again. "So we'll have to do the dinner thing later," he continued into the phone.

"It's not just a dinner 'thing,' John. It's the second anniversary of our engagement. Remember? It's special because it's the last one? We'll be married by this time next year. I was hoping . . ."

"Babe, I hate to interrupt, but I gotta go. We'll talk later, okay? Bye." He rolled his eyes as he hung up. "What a hassle being engaged is sometimes."

"If you think so, I wonder why you still are, John," Angela said. She placed the files in his outstretched hand. "Do you really plan to go through with the wedding?"

"Angela, how many times do I have to explain this to you? Getting married to Catlin is incredibly important to my life plan. She'll inherit the trust fund her grandmother set up when she turns thirty, right after we tie the knot. I'll carefully manage the money and make it grow, as a good husband should. Within five years, I'll have diverted a bundle to my own name, and she'll never know. When I sadly decide we've drifted apart and divorce her, I'll have all I need to set up my own practice and leave everyone in this hellhole behind. Except you, of course." He flashed a smile and grasped her hand.

"Five years is a long time. How am I supposed to wait?"

"Wait for what? Why would anything change between us because I'm getting married? Believe me, I fully intend to keep working late, even weekends. Close the door a minute, would you?" John rose from behind his polished mahogany desk. "Just like the hard-charging attorney I am now, baby," he continued, hauling her roughly into his arms as the lock clicked. "You keep being my indispensable assistant, and I'll make sure you get the perks you deserve." He slid his hands down and rocked sharply against her. "*All* the perks you're getting now." His gray eyes narrowed. "Are we on the same page here?"

"Of course we are." She tilted her head back and surrendered to a brutal kiss.

"Good. Now go get the Wilson file. I need that one too. Shit, all these distractions, now I actually am going to have to work late."

Angela smirked and straightened her dress. "I can stay as long as you need me, John."

"Fine, just get the file." He turned back to his desk and started arranging his notes.

"It looks like it's just us again." Catlin sniffed as she hung up the phone. "I wonder sometimes if I'm cut out to be a successful attorney's wife. There're so many long hours, so much stress. I wonder if I'm being supportive enough. Maybe I should bake a chocolate cake and take it to his office. What do you think?"

Packard whined and lowered his head between his paws.

"What, bad idea? You're probably right. He gets in these states and nothing I do is right. Okay, deep breath, release the negativity." Catlin flapped her arms and exhaled in a whoosh. "I'll use the time to write that Old West article I've been planning. And take you to the park for Frisbee, right, boy?"

She laughed as the big dog bounded up at the word *Frisbee*. She grabbed the backpack, ready with toys and water, and followed Packard to the door. He leapt into his leash and scratched on the door when she fumbled with her keys.

"We'll get there, we'll get there," she assured him as he surged forward, yanking her off the front steps. They settled into a hurried but steady pace once they rounded the block and had the expansive lawns and towering eucalyptus trees of the city park in sight.

"We're lucky to have such a great place you can be off leash so close," she reminded him when they reached the dog park area behind the tennis courts. "Look! All your buds are here. There's Bosco, and Shelby, and Zoe too. Go say hi." She gave Packard a push, but he jumped in her face and barked for the Frisbee. "You are such a jock. Don't you want to see your friends?"

She shook her head and whipped out the Frisbee, flicking it expertly down an open space on the grassy field. Packard took off like a bullet, gauging the trajectory and timing his leap to snatch the disk out of the air three feet above the ground. He trotted back, victorious again, dropped the Frisbee, and danced back for the next throw.

"Yeah, yeah, just fifty more times, right, big guy?" She laughed and continued tossing.

The stroll back home was at a considerably slower pace. *Thank goodness for my beautiful little neighborhood*, Catlin thought as they passed the eclectic mix of Spanish and Craftsman homes built in the 1910s and '20s with their welcoming porches and varied architecture. It was a point of pride to her that friends visiting from newer neighborhoods would exclaim, "Every house is different. That's so amazing." She waved to Ted Graystone, who was watering the abundant fuchsias in his front planter, one hand gripping his walker while the other held the hose.

"It's so quiet and peaceful here," she commented, then jumped at the harsh roar of a diesel engine from a yellow tractor that clattered around the corner.

Packard growled and barked furiously. Hackles raised, he strained at the leash as the machine passed.

"Hey, hey, relax. It's okay." She reined him in and stroked behind his ear. "What's going on over there? C'mon, let's go see."

The next block was a flurry of men and machines. Workers in orange vests and white hard hats swarmed over a flatbed trailer, tossing chains aside to free an enormous excavator on thick steel tracks.

Catlin stopped halfway down the block to watch. "Sit. This looks interesting." She scratched Packard's broad head absently.

"Hey, Neil! Where do you want the sign?" called out a voice behind a large, white board with a blue city border.

"On the far corner—yeah, that's good, Francisco."

Catlin edged closer to make out the bold letters. "City of San Diego. Working to Improve Your Neighborhood in 2005. Sewer Replacement Project 569," she read to Packard. "Well, the view is certainly improving, huh, boy?" She scanned the crew and allowed herself a feminine smirk at the confusion of tanned forearms, straining biceps, and heavy boots.

"Looks like we've got our first spectator, boss," Francisco said, wiping the dirt from his hands on his jeans. He jerked his head in Catlin's direction.

"What?" Neil looked up from his clipboard.

"I said, Foreman Prescott, we've got our first spectator."

"Oh. Uh huh." Neil glanced carelessly toward the trim young woman and massive brown dog down the street watching them. "Damn it, where's the equipment trailer? It should've been here an hour ago. I wanted that set up first."

"Beats me. That's Bill's job."

"He better get here soon if he wants to keep it." Neil stalked off, whipping his cell phone out while he tossed the clipboard through the open window of a white Ford pickup and headed to the group unloading the excavator.

"He's intense," Catlin said. "Looks like we'll have some new sights on our morning walks." She tweaked Packard's leash and turned toward home.

2

The next morning, Catlin rose with an unexplained sense of anticipation. "Hey, Fishbreath, have a good night's sleep? What's going on today? You going to watch Oprah when I go to work? I know it's your favorite show." She laughed and rubbed Packard's ears. "How about breakfast?" She padded into the kitchen and started coffee, then scooped out kibble into a metal dish. "Enjoy," she said, watching the food disappear.

Dressing for their morning stroll through the neighborhood, she couldn't shake the feeling that something exciting was going to happen. "Maybe we'll see your new friend, the tractor," she told Packard as she slipped into slim jeans and a cut-off gray sweatshirt. "Let's rock and roll."

She rubbed her hand against the fragrant rosemary bushes in the front yard and took a deep breath, enjoying the earthy scent that always reminded her of comfort food. *I'll have to call Mom this weekend and tell her about the work going on*, she thought.

After a meandering walk through the park, they approached the corner with the construction sign. She read the big red letters on the side of a storage trailer now squatting nearby. "Altman Construction. There's an attractive addition to the neighborhood. I wonder what the Turners think about having that in their front window. But then look what comes along with it."

She watched a knot of workers gather around the trailer steps, sipping from stainless steel thermos cups and holding forth on . . . *what?* she wondered. *What does a group of macho guys talk about at six-thirty in the morning? Probably planning the important stuff they're going to do today, what they need to accomplish.*

"Hey, Packard, there's your tractor buddy coming to life." She leaned down to scratch his ears as the air filled with fumes. "Mmm, don't you love the smell of diesel in the morning? Uh oh, there's Mr. Intensity." Catlin held back as Neil sprinted over, sharply gesturing to the operator to turn the machine off.

"What the hell are you doing, Bill?" he shouted. "You know the regs. Don't start the equipment until seven a.m. You want to get us shut down before we break ground?"

Bill shrugged and held up his wrist. "Sorry, Neil. Forgot my watch this morning."

"Yeah, time seems to be an ongoing problem for you. Cool it until I tell you, okay?"

Bill slid back in his seat. "Sure thing. I'll just enjoy the scenery." He looked down the block, tipping his ball cap at Catlin.

Neil turned and regarded her quietly behind mirrored sunglasses, recognizing the dog before the woman. "Uh huh. Francisco noticed them yesterday. Kind of an interesting dog. Like a huge chocolate lab with long curly fur. Never seen that before. They must live around here. You could have introduced yourself if you'd been here on time."

"Maybe we'll work in her street and I'll show her how good I lay pipe." Bill grinned.

"Yeah, I'll put in a good word for you. I'm sure a pretty woman like that would be real interested in a loader operator who's gonna lose his job if he screws up one more time."

"C'mon Neil, lighten up. All that attitude is bad for your blood pressure."

"Thanks, mom. Hey, look at that. My *watch* says it's seven o'clock. Go for it but don't run over any innocent bystanders."

"I'll be careful, dear." Bill snickered and turned the ignition.

Neil watched their observer effortlessly yank the dog back from an infuriated lunge as the machine passed. *Walking that big guy must be good exercise*, he thought, scanning the slender legs in tight-ass jeans and the hint of abs under the cropped sweatshirt. "And keeping my guys under control in this neighborhood may be an exercise too," he muttered as he watched her walk by the trailer, smile shyly, and waggle her fingers at the crew.

With the unified precision observed in schools of tuna, the group turned while Catlin passed. The general discussion shifted from intellectual highlights of the previous night's basketball game to whether the before or after view was preferable.

"And you guys haven't started working yet because?" Neil snapped, storming up.

"Just appreciating the neighborhood that we're improving, boss." Francisco laughed as they mobilized for a day of noise, dirt, and progress.

"That was kind of fun," Catlin commented when they were safely back home. "Thanks for not doing any business back there. Nothing like picking up dog poop in front of ten hunky guys. And what if Mr. Intensity didn't approve of my clean-up methods?"

All during the drive to work, her mind drifted to what might be happening in her neighborhood. *Okay, Catlin, time to focus*, she told herself as she pulled in the driveway to ESTA, the company that had been her part-time employer for three years. The name stood for Environmental Studies and Technological Applications, but she always liked that it meant "it is" in Spanish. Her fluency in that language had come in handy on archaeological digs in Mexico where she got her field experience after earning a master's degree in anthropology. She enjoyed the flexibility and camaraderie of the small company, which nevertheless did its share of surveys, documents, and construction monitoring for projects throughout the county.

"Good morning, Catlin. How's our little bride-to-be?" Nancy DeWitt greeted her co-worker. "Did you have a lovely engagement anniversary dinner?"

"Dinner?" Catlin looked blank for a minute and then laughed. "There's so much going on in my neighborhood, I completely forgot."

"You forgot a big date with John? He must have been pissed." Nancy's eyes went wide in alarm.

"No, no, he called in the afternoon to cancel. Postpone. Whatever. No, listen, there's a huge excavator down the street, plus all these construction workers. It's a sewer replacement project."

"Men with big equipment, my favorite." Nancy laughed. "Well, try to concentrate for a few days. We need to make progress on the environmental impact report for the county water district's storage tank. They were so pleased with the work you did on their water supply pipeline document, you don't want to disappoint them."

"I won't. Half the EIR is already written. How's your biology work going?"

"Mark and I will do the survey this afternoon. You'll have our part by the end of the week."

"Monday's okay too. Remember I'm not here on Fridays."

"Wooo hooo! Yes!" A sudden shout from the corner office froze the entire staff of fifteen. Nancy and Catlin exchanged startled glances and turned to watch the distinguished company president, Michael Lanyard, dance a jig accompanied by air guitar, then pump his arm and whoop, "We win! We win!"

"This'll be interesting," Nancy said. "I've never seen him dance like that, even after four beers."

Michael waved a letter and gestured for the employees to gather around. "You guys, this is great news! Our EIR for the county water district's pipeline has been selected as Document of the Year!"

Catlin gasped. "You're kidding!"

"Nope, got the letter right here from the Organization of Environmental Professionals. We'll get the award at the annual banquet this summer. Excellent work, everybody. We're barking with the big dogs now!"

Nancy's eyes glistened and she clapped her hands. "How wonderful! This will really help our credibility. Your archaeological work was a big part of this, Catlin. Isn't the Harrison site the biggest prehistoric village site in the county? I still can't believe the water district got permission to put their main supply line through there. Congratulations!" She gave her friend a quick hug. "Now watch, Michael will tell us all to get back to work," she whispered.

"Ahem, I guess that's the news, folks. We'll talk later about who'll attend the banquet. Thanks again for all your hard work. Let's get back to it." Michael nodded to the group and returned to his office, skipping and making one last arm-pump before settling behind his desk.

"Told you," Nancy said.

What an amazing day, Catlin reflected on the drive home. *Our first major award. Wait till I tell Mom. She'll be excited.*

As she turned down her street, she was surprised to see orange No Parking signs littering both sides. The road was scribbled with mysterious lines and letters, like a first grader had gone wild with red, green, blue, and yellow spray paint.

Are they going to work on my street already? she wondered, pulling into her driveway. She got her answer when she flipped through the mail and found a letter from the city, noting the beginning of a sewer replacement project To Benefit Your Neighborhood. "Hey Packard, looks like we're up tomorrow," she said, letting him bound into the house from the backyard.

"And since we're still on our own, tonight's for research. I need to learn more about Old West prostitutes if I'm going to write a good article."

Packard barked.

"Okay, first Frisbee, then research."

He barked again and pawed her leg.

"Okay, okay. First dinner, then Frisbee, then research." She laughed. "How am I going to make my mark as a free-lance writer if all I do is feed you and play Frisbee?"

After Packard got his full complement of retrieving at the dog park, they headed back home. Catlin gazed up at the towering excavator and touched its heavy steel tracks. "They say dinosaurs are extinct. I think they live in machines like this. Where will you be grazing tomorrow, Mr. Diplodocus?" she asked.

Packard pulled out toward home to the full extent of his leash and looked back at her.

"Oh, you're no fun. Where's your imagination?"

At home, seated in front of her computer with Packard settled at her feet, she stared at the blank screen, fingers poised over the keyboard. Books and articles about the Old

West were scattered across her desk. *Such an interesting era,* she thought. Harsh conditions, high passions, sudden death. What if she were a "boarder" of a parlor house, dressing for work in sheers, lace, and naked skin? Could she be so desirable that many men would spend large sums of money for a brief time with her? But how would it feel to be so trapped in love that suicide was the only way out?

She leaned back, closed her eyes, and waited for the muse. Before long, her hand slid off the table, fingertips brushing Packard, and her breath slowed.

Catherine rocked slowly in the ornate front-porch glider, watching the morning sun rise quietly along Holladay Street. She caressed Sampson's ears and whispered, "Yes, I know what you like, don't try to pretend."

She reached up to adjust her organdy garden hat, carefully pulling out a long steel hat pin with a jeweled top and reinserting it through her thick hair. She pulled her Chantilly lace jacket closer around her shoulders. Sampson yipped in protest at the interruption. "Oh, you are so demanding," she cooed to the white ball of fur in her lap. She leaned down to kiss the curly poodle and rubbed her cheek against the top of his head. "This is my favorite time of day, Sampson. Just you and me."

She leaned back against the silk cushions, letting the sun warm her body through the ruffled muslin dress, and tenderly stroked the little dog. "Long night," she murmured as her eyes closed.

Catlin woke with a start when Packard yelped softly and his leg twitched. "Chasing bunnies again, big guy? I had a strange dream too. Maybe I'll write tomorrow. Now it's time for bed."

3

The next morning, Catlin rose early to catch the initial gathering. Packard barked while she lingered at the mirror. "Oh quit it. I'm not primping," she said as she hooked on small gold earrings. "I'm just getting ready for a big day. You could use a little grooming yourself." She reached down and gently brushed the long tendrils of curling fur away from his eyes. "You want to look your best for your new friends."

She took the long way around the neighborhood to avoid the appearance of snooping. As she approached the trailer on the way home, she conducted a mental inventory of the fascinating visitors. There was Bill, whose name had been sounded at full volume, leaning back in the operator's seat of the excavator, black ball cap pulled low, apparently snoozing until zero hour.

The dark-haired worker with the cherubic face who had placed the sign sat on the trailer steps munching a donut. A cluster of men listened attentively as the one Catlin had dubbed Mr. Intensity read from a list attached to his clipboard.

"He's definitely the boss," she whispered.

As if on cue, Neil told the group, "Let's get to it." He looked over at Bill and shook his head. "Hey, Francisco, if you're done with breakfast, go wake up Sleeping Beauty."

"With what? A kiss?"

"I don't care if you use a two by four. Get him rolling. We need to get started on Truman Street as soon as I talk with the residents. The barricades will be up by the time he is, so he can dig right in."

Catlin passed by as Francisco headed to the excavator, muttering "*Pendejo*" under his breath. But his face lit in a broad smile when he saw her.

"Good morning, *amigita*. Back for more construction observation?"

"Hi. I may not have to look far. Truman is my street."

"Then things will be noisy for several days, I'm afraid. The foreman will talk to you and your neighbors this morning. The city was late with their noticing letters."

"*Que lastima.*" Catlin smiled at his look of surprise.

Francisco laughed. "So, I'll have to watch my words around you."

"No problem. I've used worse. See you." She continued down the block.

"Now why can't she be the one I need to wake up?" he sighed as he turned to his assigned task.

"Okay, Packard, no loitering. We need to get home if Mr. Intensity is on his way." Catlin tugged on his leash and quickened her pace. She saw the white truck with Altman Construction emblazoned on the side parked at the end of her block. Neil wrapped up a conversation at the corner house and turned toward her as she reached her front steps. "Sit, Packard," she said, and waited with a polite smile.

"Good morning, Miss. I'm Neil Prescott, foreman on this job." He extended his hand as he walked up.

"Catlin Davis." She reached out for a professional hand-shake. In the corner of her eye, she caught a tiny rainbow refracting through a crystal prism. *This won't be such hard work* flashed in her mind.

Neil's stomach lurched and his eyes widened behind his impenetrable sunglasses when he realized he had almost lifted her hand to his lips for a gentlemanly kiss. *Where the hell did that come from?* "Um, did you get your letter?" he asked.

"Yes, thanks. Will you need access to the backyard? That's where Packard is during the day, so I need to make plans."

"Is he friendly?"

"He can be territorial. Plus he doesn't like your tractor."

Packard woofed.

"Right, you're the one who walks by our staging area. Actually, it's a loader."

"What's a loader?"

"The Cat your dog wants to have for breakfast."

"I'm not sure what you mean. Packard is very good with cats. He just doesn't like your tractor."

Neil lifted his hard hat and pushed his hand up through his hair. "I mean we don't call the machine a 'tractor.' It's a front-end loader, made by Caterpillar. Cat."

"Oh. I see."

"So what kind of dog is he?"

"A Labradoodle."

"Is that a real dog?"

Catlin looked down at Packard then back up at Neil. "Well, of course he's real."

Neil sighed. "I mean, is that an official breed?"

"Sort of. He's a chocolate Lab–standard poodle mix. They're great if you have allergies. He's big for his breed."

"Packard's a good name for him. He's built like a car."

"Tell me. I get to feed him and clean up afterward."

Neil grinned at the thought that they both dealt with loads of crap but decided against commenting out loud. "We may need access next week, after we finish replacing the main line, to check the lateral connection. I'll let you know."

"Okay. Is there anything else? I guess I should get my car out of here before you start tearing up the street."

"That's a good idea. But you can always tell the guys to stop a minute," he told her. *And I'm sure they'll be glad to grant your every wish*, he continued to himself.

Rushing to get dressed for work, Catlin snagged her hose on her engagement ring and cursed. "Gosh darn this thing! I don't know why John insisted on such a monstrosity anyway. It's too ostentatious." She studied her hand, remembering how difficult it had been to agree on a stone and setting. She had always dreamed of how romantic it would be to pick out a ring. But the jeweler he had insisted on using was impatient and dismissive when she hesitated over the displays. Of course, her indecision had embarrassed John, so she yielded readily when he took over the selection process. "Discretion is the better part of valor, right, Packard?" she said. *Or is that peace at any price?* she asked herself. Why did the ring suddenly weigh on her hand and the thought of impending marriage weigh on her mind? *Okay, Catlin, focus on the happy memories. Choosing a ring is a hassle for lots of people.* She took a deep breath and smiled, remembering how they met at a friend's "come-as-you-aren't" Halloween party. She dressed as a French maid with a short skirt, lacy apron, and fishnet stockings and carried a feather duster. John was a proper English magistrate complete with a curly white wig. He told her she was supposed to come as her own fantasy, not everyone else's. Feeling uncharacteristically flirtatious, she replied, "Being everyone else's fantasy is my fantasy," and bopped him on the head with her feather duster. His laughter seemed to surprise him; she remembered feeling happy she had lightened this serious person's mood. His maturity and focus impressed her. While the other males at the party drank themselves silly, John held a meaningful conversation with her about life purpose and goals. He told her he had been unhappy at the first two law firms where he had worked but was confident that the firm he had just joined would promote him as quickly as he deserved. Their dates through the fall and winter were sophisticated and cultured: symphony, opera, and ballet. She felt like a grown-up at his side.

Still smiling at memories, she brought his April marriage proposal to her mind: the candlelit dinner at the fancy French restaurant; his toast, "To a fruitful partnership;" and his glittering smile when she said yes. She could hear the soft piano and violin in the background again. Then he said— what was it?—"This will make five people very happy—you, your parents, and my parents." The music in her head stopped. She had let the comment go, enmeshed in the joy of engagement. Like she ignored so many other negative comments from him. Lots of things bother sensitive people, she knew. But soon they'd be making more choices together— invitations, flowers, dishes. How easy would that be? And that was just the start. Would she always have to surrender to keep the peace?

"Peace is very important," she said aloud. In reply, Packard leaped up and raced to the front windows, barking madly. She followed him down the hall, hopping into shoes and buttoning her blouse as she went. A low rumble made the wine glasses in the dining room cabinet tremble.

"Something's coming, and it's big," she said, kneeling on the window seat and peering out. "Diplodocus," she announced with a dramatic sweep of her arm, as the excavator thundered to the corner and stopped inside the barricades. "I hope they don't finish everything today. I want to watch tomorrow. Meanwhile, it's time for you to go outside and me to get to work." She tempted Packard to the backyard with a treat, locked up, and headed out.

Keys in hand, she stopped on the sidewalk to watch the action. A large gray box with saw blades protruding had been fitted into the front bucket of the tractor—*No, loader*, she corrected herself—and several men were directing the operator to center the machine and lower the box.

"What on earth are they doing?" she said to herself.

"They're going to saw-cut the street before digging with the excavator," Neil said as he walked up behind her. "The Zipper cuts the asphalt and chews it up. We get a cleaner trench line and it's easier to fix the street later."

"Will you finish the whole street today?"

"No, you'll have to put up with us for longer than that, Miss."

"Catlin."

"Right. Catlin. Cat. That should be easy to remember."

She smiled, absurdly pleased at the nickname. "I'll look forward to watching more tomorrow—I work at home on Fridays."

"We'll be here."

She waved good-bye, and he caught the flash from the diamond on her left hand. *There's a depressing sight*, he thought and then turned back to his clipboard with a philosophic shrug.

Hours later, the usual spell of prehistoric artifacts was failing to engage Catlin's interest. Chin in hand, she tapped a pen idly against the stack of paper she was supposedly editing.

"Planet Earth calling," Nancy said, poking her head in the door. "We didn't find much on the storage tank site yesterday. Biology won't be a problem."

"Uh huh. That's good."

"Are you okay? Did you and John have a fight?"

"No. I haven't heard from him. There's just a lot going on in the neighborhood."

"Oh yes, your construction homework. Should I come over for lunch tomorrow? Will I see anything interesting?"

"You'll see a lot of dust and dirt. They've started digging up my street. And I met the foreman this morning," she added casually.

"Yes? Is he attractive?"

Catlin laughed. "I don't know. I didn't look at him that way."

Nancy eyed her friend with a mischievous glance. "Everybody looks."

"I don't. What's the point? I'm engaged."

"There's nothing wrong with staying in touch with the world around you. And who knows? Maybe there's someone else out there, someone who . . ."

"Nancy, stop," she said more sharply than intended. "Look, I know you don't like John. He can be a little aloof, but you need to get to know him better. Anyway, I've got to finish this editing. You'll have your part written soon?"

"Yes. I'll have it for you Monday."

"Thanks." Catlin returned to her stack of papers.

Driving home, her mind was a confusion of disconnected thoughts and feelings. Sad about the tiff with Nancy, angry that she had to defend John, apprehensive about what would be coming next with their relationship. Wondering if all the new male faces in the neighborhood were generating her restless questions and undeniable excitement. She had always been extremely clear about her goals from one educational and career step to the next. She felt John was a good planner too, and his vision for their future together had been a strong attraction. Or what she perceived was his vision. When was the last time they had discussed where they were headed in the long run? The project of the wedding had taken over, and soon the brunt of the work would consume her. Maybe they should rethink the date before the invitations set everything in stone. *Good solution*, she told herself. *John was so busy now, he'd probably welcome a postponement.* She'd bring it up next time they were together, maybe this weekend. Her shoulders relaxed at the thought of more time, and she sang along with the radio the rest of the way home.

She screeched to a stop when she turned the corner to her block. "Whoa—what a mess."

A pile of dirt and cobble ran along the curb in front of her neighbors' at the corner, and a stack of pipe sat across the intersection. Bumpy asphalt scarred the middle of her street partway down the block. Catlin's eyes lit up when she saw the excavator parked in front of her house, neck extended and head buried in the dirt pile as if enjoying a tasty supper. "Hello, Diplodocus," she said. "It'll be fun watching you work tomorrow."

She called out to Packard as she came inside and opened the back door. "Hey, Bumblebutt, look who's guarding the house tonight."

He jumped up to give her a sloppy kiss, raced into the kitchen, and skidded on the linoleum as he ran toward the front windows. He leaped onto the window seat and sat as if awed by the yellow machinery that filled the view.

"Pretty cool, huh? Scoot over." Catlin rubbed his head as she joined him on the cushion. "It's going to be a very interesting day tomorrow. But tonight I'm writing. No excuses." Packard licked her face. "I'm serious," she said, hugging him. "Dinner, a few quick throws in the backyard, and I'm getting to it."

True to her promise, she soon sat at her desk, fishing through a thick history of Old West businesses, legitimate and illegitimate. "Hey, here she is again, Packard! 'Catherine Porter, a tragic figure in the heyday of prostitution in Denver during the late 1800s,'" she read aloud. "What a sad story." *Historical romance might be a good angle*, she thought, and her fingers started tapping on the keyboard. Pausing occasionally to check in her references, she worked steadily for hours, compiling several pages. "Okay. Save again and print." She leaned back and stretched her arms above her head while paper inched out, documenting a productive evening.

"Did she know she was meeting her destiny when she first saw the wealthy rancher? What do you think?" Catlin reached down to scratch Packard's ears. "Did she find him attractive? I guess customers didn't need to be. All cats are gray in the dark, right?"

Packard howled.

"Oh, sorry. Bad cliché." She laughed and slipped the papers into a file folder. "That's enough for one night. Getting started is eighty percent of the battle," she quoted from her father and reminded herself to call her parents soon.

As was her routine when she slipped into bed, she enjoyed a contented perusal of the room, scanning the dark antique wardrobe, softly glowing lamp hung with glass prisms, and curving brass of the fanciful headboard and footboard. She loved the enveloping warmth and unabashedly feminine comfort of the furnishings. She knew that John preferred the sleek, modern style of his beachfront condo outfitted in stark lines with leather and chrome. "Another looming battle," she sighed, then pushed the thought away. "What was Catherine's room like?" she asked Packard. She chuckled when she heard him snoring, curled up on his pillow next to the bed. "Hmm, good idea. I'll join you." She snuggled under the down comforter and fell asleep.

Catherine pulled back the soft blankets on her bed and ran her hand over the smooth linen sheets. She heard the piano playing and the sharp clap of Madam Joey's hands, calling her girls downstairs to meet the company that had gathered in the parlor.

Several pairings had already been made when she floated down the steps in a beribboned gossamer gown. She had chosen blue that evening and knew that the gleaming lamp light would reveal how little she wore under the dress. She smiled shyly as eyes turned toward the staircase, a smile practiced to convey both innocence and secret knowledge. She saw the usual visitors, established political figures and successful businessmen, porcine and self-satisfied. Several would ask for her, and she was intimately familiar with the hunger and insecurities they exposed behind her closed door.

Madam Joey was embroiled in conversation with a stranger in the corner. Catherine stopped on the stairs to study him. He was tall and lean with startlingly light eyes. Dark hair curled around his ears. A black moustache graced thin lips, set now in a quiet, amused smile. Although he was simply dressed, considerable wealth hung in the finely tooled leather holsters on his hips. No wonder her "mother" was upset, Catherine thought. Obvious displays of weaponry, no matter how expensive, were considered low-class, an insult to the cultured atmosphere of the boarding house.

The stranger kept his calm smile while Madam Joey's gestures intensified and James, their fearsome peacekeeper, stalked purposefully toward him. His gaze shifted upward to Catherine and his eyes widened in a momentary disruption of composed demeanor. Returning to the negotiations, he pulled out a roll of bills that Catherine could tell even from a distance amounted to several times the usual fee collected by the maid.

The sight of money had its typical soothing effect on Madam Joey. She signaled subtly for James to return to the shadows while she patted the stranger's arm and gracefully spun around to face the room for a selection.

He indicated his preference with a tilt of his head and a brief whisper. After a slight hesitation, Madam Joey nodded. Catherine knew before she saw the beckoning finger who would be the first to experience her pleasuring that night. And although it was normally an act for business, she felt a thrilling tremble when the stranger focused his complete attention on her while she approached.

"This is Catherine, my most accomplished girl," Madam Joey said, placing a protective arm around her shoulders.

Light refracted through the crystal pendants hanging on the lamp in the corner, catching her eye as she extended her hand.

"Daniel Hayden," the stranger said. He lifted Catherine's fingers to his lips while his blue eyes locked on hers. Without shifting his gaze, he turned her hand over and kissed the open palm, pulling her out of Madam Joey's grasp.

Catherine moved willingly closer, touching his face with her fingertips. A wave of intense heat coursed through her as he ran his other hand around her waist and spanned the small of her back. She inclined her body toward him with a little gasp at her unaccustomed physical response.

"We'll go upstairs now," he murmured, nodding to Madam Joey.

Catherine lowered her eyes and let him guide her through the parlor and up the steps. He seemed to know her room was at the end of the hall, opening the door for her before she reached for the glass knob.

"Beautiful," he said quietly, taking in the brass four-poster bed and overstuffed chairs with a quick glance. "Heartbreakingly beautiful," he sighed, spinning her toward him and cupping his hand under her chin.

Her heart seemed to skip out of time while he held her there, looking through her soul. She stretched up toward him, aching for his lips. "How can I please you tonight?" she whispered, running her hands over his chest and dropping to his heavy gun belt.

"Let me please you." He caressed her cheek and slid his hands into her long, curling hair.

She reached up to his shoulders and welcomed the brand of his mouth on hers with an intensity that weakened her. His arms enveloped her and again she felt the crash of heat. His fingers splayed across her back and she moaned against his lips when his hands moved lower, delicately but firmly over the fragile fabric of her gown.

"I want your skin on mine," he breathed into her ear.

"Yes," was all she could manage to say. She nearly cried out at the loss of contact when he pulled away but remembered her training and smiled sensually as she knelt down to untie the leather stays of his holsters and unbuckle the thick belt.

"They're exquisite," she said, watching him carefully place the pistols on the chair next to the bed.

"And never out of reach."

"You've nothing to fear in this house. Everything you have is safe here."

"Ah, everything but my heart, I think." Daniel smiled and drew her close for another kiss.

Tenderness deepened to passion. Catherine swayed into him, letting her hands slide recklessly over his muscular body. "Take me," she implored. He yanked the ribbons that held her dress and pushed it off her shoulders to the floor. She hurriedly unbuttoned his shirt and trousers. With impatient hands, they brushed the rest of each other's clothing away and collapsed on the bed.

She felt echoes of her heart pounding everywhere he touched her and reveled in the liquid longing she would ordinarily have to create by imagining herself somewhere else. His fingers seared lines of fire over her, inside her. She reached down for him when he rose above her, celebrating her pure desire as he hardened to stone in her hands. She yielded joyfully as their bodies merged, carried away on the music of their quickening breath and racing heartbeats. She was lost in sensations, skin sliding against skin, weight pressing, lips and tongues entwined, craving complete union. Her mind contracted to a single focal point of sweet friction that edged her upward with each movement. Arching toward him, she soared off the precipice and clasped him tighter as he joined her in flight.

Catlin awoke with a jolt of pleasure, her heart pounding and her body sheened in sweat.

"Wow. I haven't had a dream like that since college." She sat up and pushed her hands through her hair. "Maybe I need to rethink what magazine I send this story to." She slid back under the sheet and slept dreamlessly until morning with a satisfied smile on her face.

4

Friday morning was cool and cloudy. Catlin luxuriated in an extra half-hour of sleep but woke up eager to watch the construction. By the time she rounded the block on her walk with Packard, the trailer area was vacant. "Guess we're a little late today, huh, big guy? Oh well, there'll be plenty to watch at home."

The noise reached her before she could see her street. She yanked on Packard's leash. "C'mon, c'mon, every square inch can't be all that interesting. How different can that tree be from yesterday?"

Rounding the corner, she stopped with wide eyes. Barricades were up, closing the street at both ends. The excavator dominated the scene in the middle of the road, chewing a deep trench and dumping loads of dirt and cobble to the side. Several men shoveled around a spot marked with yellow lines while a worker who looked barely old enough to be out of high school cut the sidewalk with a circular saw. A miniature version of the loader zipped back and forth, carrying sandbags and tools.

In the middle of the action, Neil conferred with the crew and effortlessly juggled his clipboard and phone. He glanced up when Catlin and Packard picked their way around pipe and dirt to take refuge by her front steps. He holstered his phone and followed her.

Remembering the sly advice from Nancy, Catlin decided a little objective evaluation wouldn't do any harm as she watched Neil approach without the ubiquitous sunglasses. He was all business in the construction world's version of a three-piece suit: short-sleeved oxford shirt, jeans, and a well-worn orange vest with those snappy day-glo yellow stripes. Not the fashion accessory of her choice, but she decided that on him it looked good. She approved of his intent walk, the bustling aura of determination that reverberated from him. Bossy, no doubt, but she admired people who weren't afraid to take charge. Stocky, muscular, and fit, he gripped the clipboard with long, thick fingers. A neatly trimmed goatee underlined his lips. *I'll just note what color his eyes are*, she thought. *That's not really looking.*

"Good morning," he shouted over the ruckus of the excavator straining against rocks in the trench.

"Hi. Busy day planned?" That was her last coherent thought for several minutes as she looked in his eyes and her brain fused on one synaptic signal: blue. *Wow, so blue. It's not fair for a man to have such beautiful eyes. Have I ever met anyone with eyes that blue before? What color is that, anyway?* Her mind drifted on shades and hues: azure, cerulean, lapis lazuli, mulberry, robin's egg, wisteria. With a perplexed smile still glazing her face, she gradually became aware that he had been explaining something. It was probably something important from his serious look. She hoped he wouldn't ask questions because she didn't have the slightest idea what he'd been saying.

"Does that make sense?" Neil asked. *She looks confused. I probably used too many technical terms.* "Anyway, that's why we may need you to avoid using your water later today. Francisco will let you know when if I'm not here."

"Oh. Sure. Okay." She struggled to re-engage her brain, which was acting like a recalcitrant lawnmower whose cord had been pulled too many times. "It won't bother anyone if I watch from here, will it?"

"No, that's no problem. It won't get any quieter, though."

"I didn't realize the ground was so rocky."

"Yeah, it makes for slow going. Plus the sewer is deep in your street, so we've got a ways to dig."

"There's so much going on at once. How do you keep everybody in the right place? It's hard enough for me to keep track of people working on paper projects."

He shrugged. "It's my job. A lot of it's routine, typical practice, or in the plans and specs."

"It's still amazing to me. Does anyone ever get hurt?"

"One time Bill was thrown out when the bucket snagged and he didn't expect it."

"Oh my god," Catlin gasped.

Neil laughed. "Don't worry; his head is harder than those rocks."

She turned to watch the machine again. "It's so huge."

"It's not that big. I've operated bigger equipment at a gold mine in Oregon. Ever seen a mining truck? The wheels are fifteen feet tall."

"That's hard to imagine."

"Believe it. Now that's huge."

"Uh huh." *Okay, I get that your equipment is bigger than Bill's,* Catlin snickered to herself. *Men are so competitive about size. They should worry more about what's really important, like* . . . her mind went blank. "Wow. Fifteen-foot wheels." She slowly sank down onto the front steps.

Neil nodded, satisfied he had made his point. Which was, well, he wasn't exactly sure. But he liked her rapt attention when he explained things, and her open admiration for his work was a pleasant change from fussy property owners and critical inspectors.

A sudden beeping had his hand flashing down to the phone on his belt. With a lightning draw, he palmed the phone and flipped it open. "Neil," he barked.

"Bobby," came the answering drawl. "Hey, Baby Bear, Papa Bear wants to know where you are and when you'll be getting your ass down here."

"I hate that handle. Who started that anyway? Tell Greg I'm on Truman. He knows Bill needs more supervision than you do."

"Nah. You tell him. I'm just the messenger, man." A deep chuckle resonated through the phone before it clicked off.

Neil grimaced. "I've got to run to another site for a while. Francisco will be around if you have questions," he told her.

"Okay. See you later."

When Neil drove off, Francisco wandered over. "Hello again, *amigita.* Enjoying the show? The noise doesn't seem to bother your dog."

"Not much bothers Packard except being fed late."

"I'm Francisco."

"Catlin. Neil said you're in charge while he's gone."

"That's right. I'm *el Jefe Efe.*"

She laughed. "Okay, Boss F, I have a question. What are the paint lines all over my street?"

"Good question. They mark where other pipes are buried so we don't dig them up accidentally. Yellow is gas—see there?" He pointed to the men with shovels. "Those pipes can be shallow. That's why we're digging by hand. Red is electric. The blue lines show where the water main and connecting house pipes are."

"There's a lot under the street. I had no idea. What's the green?"

"Ah, the green is *muy importante.* It's the sewer pipe we're replacing. That short green line is the lateral to your house."

"Everything makes a lot more sense now. Thanks."

"Any time. Did Neil explain why we may ask you to stop using water later?"

Catlin blushed, remembering her distraction. "Umm, he tried, but it was a little over my head." *Boy, I sure hope it's complicated or I'm going to look like an idiot,* she thought.

"*Claro.* Most people don't understand how the system works. It gets complicated because we're replacing an active pipeline. We say it's live. You know, has flow in it. So when we put in a new piece of pipe, we need to connect the house laterals. It's nicer for everybody if there's no flow in the lateral at the time. Usually, no one's home when we're working, so there's no problem. When someone is home, we ask for their help in keeping our boots dry."

"Oh, okay. I'm learning a lot today. I better take Packard in. Thank you for the explanations. You're a good teacher." She stood and flashed a sunny smile while swatting the dust from the back of her jeans.

"You're welcome. You're a good student." He basked in her warmth, wishing he could help with the clean-up, and allowed himself a brief look as she turned and swayed up the stairs. When he faced the street again, he saw Bill waggling his finger and mouthing "Tsk tsk" from his perch in the excavator cab.

Inside the house, Packard immediately took up residence in the front window seat. "Guess you like watching construction, too," Catlin said, settling down next to him. "It's better where it's a little quieter, though, huh?" She slipped off her tennis shoes and pulled her feet up under her while she followed the rise and fall of the excavator bucket.

The early morning purposeful scurrying of the group slowed as the hours passed. Catlin left Packard to his observations and spread her report over the dining room table, marking edits with a red pen and shaking her head over typos. She returned to the window seat periodically to check on Bill's progress and to see whether Neil had returned.

When the young worker started saw-cutting the sidewalk in front of her house, Francisco came over to supervise. Seeing Catlin in the window, he smiled and waved.

"You stay here, Packard. I'll let you know what else I learn about sewer construction," she said. She traipsed down the stairs in bare feet to greet Francisco on the sidewalk. "What's happening now?"

"Justin's cutting where your lateral is so we don't make too much of a mess when we break up the sidewalk. Your pipe is old, so we'll replace it up to your property line. The city's records say the house was built in the 1920s—do you know if that's right?"

"Sure. It was 1922. It was the first house on the block. My grandma and I did the historical research. She lived here from the '40s, when she got married."

"This was your grandmother's house?"

"Uh huh. Isn't it a great place? I love the Craftsman style—the big porch and wooden shingles."

"It's very nice," Francisco agreed. "Have you lived here long?"

"I've been here the past three years. I moved in to take care of Grandma, and she left the house to me when she died last year." Catlin's eyes misted and she fingered the slender golden band that hung with a tiny cross on a chain around her neck.

"*Lo siento.*" Francisco murmured. "You must miss her."

"Thanks. We had a lot of fun together. But she's always with me. This was her ring—she wanted me to keep it." Her eyes brightened. "She liked to joke that I was her least favorite grandchild."

"That was a joke?"

"Yeah, because I was her only grandchild."

Francisco laughed and shook his head. "*Abuelas.*"

"I know. Grandmas say the darnedest things, don't they?"

Justin finished the last saw-cut with a flourish, spewing thick gray water from the saw blades over Catlin's feet and jeans. "Oops, sorry." He blushed as Francisco scowled at him.

"Keep the saw low until you shut it off, *payaso,*" Francisco chided. "*Lo siento,*" he said to Catlin.

"It's okay. That's what happens when you're in a construction zone, right?"

"When workers aren't as careful as they should be. We'll have a little talk about equipment operation over lunch, hmm?" Francisco thumped Justin's hard hat. "Enjoy the peace and quiet for a while, *amigita.*"

"You, too." Catlin smiled and headed up her stairs.

"Angela!" John called from his office.

"Yes?" She hurried in.

"I have to leave for a few hours," he said, grabbing his keys from his desk drawer. "Put any calls into voice mail and get that research on the Wilson case done before I get back."

"Of course. Where can you be reached if there's an emergency?"

"I don't want to be reached. I need to see Catlin. I haven't heard from her since I called on Tuesday. Usually she calls here if I don't contact her for a few days."

"I thought you didn't like it when she called you at work."

"Angela, you're a good assistant, but when it comes to relationships you're abysmally stupid."

"I suppose."

John searched her face for any hint of sarcasm, but she remained still, eyes downcast like a dog unsure if the next movement would be a pat or a slap. He opted for the former this time. "Sorry to be so gruff, babe. Here's the thing. Catlin needs direction in our relationship, or her mind wanders off. She gets distracted with these dumb ideas for magazine articles that she thinks will get her published. I need her to concentrate on the wedding and then being my wife, or I'll never make it five years with her. So I'll pay her a little surprise visit. I'll pretend I'm interested in the invitations and get the date firmed up. That'll make her happy and give her something productive to do. See? It's all part of planning the work—." He reached out and touched her face.

"And working the plan," Angela finished.

"That's my girl. Look, I'll be back before five. I'll tell Catlin I've got lots to do and can't see her again until Sunday. Why don't you make reservations at *Chez Viande*, say around seven? We'll have a nice dinner and then go back to my place to talk about the Wilson case. We've got a lot to discuss. It might take all night." He nodded at her beaming smile and gave her a quick pat on his way out the door.

Catlin spent lunch pen in hand, editing in between bites of a sandwich, her typical practice at the office.

Packard spent the time curled up in the window seat snoozing, his preferred activity. He jumped, fully awake, and barked when he sensed action outside the window.

"What's going on, big guy? Ah, the boys are back. I'm ready for a break, anyway." Catlin watched Bill confer with Francisco, apparently about how deep to dig the trench, judging by their stooping and pointing. In clean jeans and tennis shoes, she came outside and settled quietly on the front steps.

"Let's get the last few feet dug to the top of the sewer along here today," Francisco told Bill. "You don't have far to go. We'll finish up by hand."

"Sounds good." Bill climbed into the cab and started the excavator, which roared to life with a metallic protest. The deafening rumble that had filled the morning air returned as Bill backed the machine toward the street corner and started digging deeper into the trench. A small cloud encircled the area as the jagged bucket tore through the ground.

Francisco watched the excavator bucket carefully, hand partially raised to signal Bill to stop as soon as he neared the top of the pipe. Two men waited nearby with shovels. Justin steadied a steel plate dangling from the loader, ready to cover the trench at the end of the work day.

Catlin remained mesmerized, arms wrapped around her knees.

A sudden squealing of brakes turned everyone's attention down the street. A black BMW Z4 twisted around the corner, barely missing the barricades and the excavator, and shuddered to a stop by Catlin's house. A patina of dust dulled the flawless surface of the convertible before John shut off the engine and flew out.

"What the hell is going on here, Catlin?" he raged. "Why didn't you tell me your street's a mess? Look at my car! I just had it detailed. I should make you pay for another wax job!"

Catlin jumped to her feet, flushed with embarrassment. "Why would I call? You—you said you couldn't see me until the weekend," she stammered.

"Well excuse me for making an effort," John snapped. "I left a ton of work to come out here, which is always a big hassle. And now this! Some greeting." He crossed his arms and glared at the stunned crew. "Who the hell are all these monkey boys, anyway? And what are you looking at, Manuel?" he demanded.

"That's Francisco," Catlin whispered. "He's in charge, so please be polite. They're replacing the sewer and your car is in the way. Why don't you pull into the driveway, and we can go in the house to talk?" She reached out and touched his arm.

John slapped her hand away. "Don't tell me to be polite. I'm not a child. And I won't waste my energy on street workers. I came here to talk about the invitations and get our wedding date firmed up, but you've spoiled that."

"Oh!" Catlin's eyes widened in surprise. "That's okay, then," she said, blowing out a breath of relief. In spite of the tension, she smiled as John's triumphant smirk faded. "I've been thinking we should postpone for another eight months.

We've both been so busy, it'd give us more time to plan, you know, and make it a beautiful day . . ." Her voice faltered at the fury building in John's eyes.

"You're thinking what?" he hissed, closing in.

"More time . . . for planning . . ." She retreated up toward the house, but John snatched her arm and pulled her back to the sidewalk.

"Thinking is your problem, Catlin. I don't want you to think, I want you to do what needs to be done." John leaned forward and shouted in her face, "What is so fucking hard about that?"

Catlin struggled to escape, cringing as the force of his ranting hit her like physical blows.

Meanwhile, the crew rumbled to life from their initial shock. Bill lowered the excavator bucket to the ground and was getting set to leap from the cab when Francisco signaled him to stay put. The men standing by the trench gripped their shovels with white knuckles and inched toward John. Francisco had pulled out his phone when Justin yelled, "Here comes Neil!"

The white Ford screeched up as John twisted his grip on Catlin and dug his fingers in above her elbow. She gasped in pain and turned into him, pleading, "John, stop it, that hurts."

Neil jumped out of the truck, instantly absorbing Francisco's panic, Catlin's anguish, and his crew's anger, all focused on a furious intruder. He noted the black BMW sporting personalized plates that read JMK ESQ. "An attorney. Crap. How could this day get any worse?" he muttered. "Sir! Sir!" he shouted as he hurried over.

John turned, distracted, and let go of Catlin. "What?" he said coolly.

"Your car's in a bad spot," Neil said. He winced at the sight of Catlin trying to simultaneously wipe her tears and rub her arm, already bruising where John had mangled it. "It could get damaged. That's why we have the no-parking signs up along the street."

"Do I look like I give a rat's ass about no-parking signs?"

"Frankly, no. But if I had a car like that, I wouldn't park it in a construction zone. That's all I'm saying."

John snorted. "This car cost forty-five fucking thousand dollars. So that's what—three years of your salary? I sincerely doubt you'll ever have a car like this."

Neil shrugged and put his hands in his pockets while he envisioned delivering a quick one-two punch that would knock the obnoxious jerk into the next block. "I doubt it too. I'm always doing something where I need a truck," he said cheerfully. "But we need to get your vehicle out of the way. If you've finished your discussion with Catlin, our company could pay for the car to be washed and waxed."

John's eyes narrowed as he turned back to Catlin. "He knows your name?" He rounded on her again as she backed away. "He knows your name, and you want to postpone the wedding. I'm getting the picture now." His slitted gaze whipped back and forth.

Oh man, Neil thought. *An attorney* and *her fiancé. Yep, the day is definitely getting worse.* "Sir, we introduce ourselves to every resident we can. It's company policy, that's all," he said.

"Yeah? And is it company policy to harass property owners?"

"John, that's enough," Catlin protested. "Neil's been a perfect gentleman."

"Oh, has he? I'm glad to hear it," John sneered. "So exactly how gentlemanly have you been with my fiancée?" he said, shoving Neil sharply in the chest.

What a maniac, Neil thought, shifting his weight to keep his balance. *It's going to take a fire hose to cool him down.* He raised his hands, palms up, and caught Bill out of the corner of his eye, nodding as if in agreement with an unstated plan. The hydraulics on the excavator whined and the bucket lifted.

"Now sir, there's no need for this. Calm down, and I'm sure you'll see—"

"I see all I need to. I want you off my fiancée's property before I call the police and have you arrested for trespassing."

Neil sighed and continued in his efforts at reasonableness. "You're an attorney, right? So you understand we're in the public right of way? If you need to see our contract or talk with the city, I can get you in touch with the resident engineer." He reached back for a business card.

Still frustrated at the ineffectiveness of his initial attack, John used the momentary opening to lunge and shove harder. "Don't patronize me, asshole," he snarled. Neil staggered backward, cursing himself for lowering his guard.

Catlin screamed, "Stop it stop it stop it!" and ran toward John, fists raised.

In the same instant, Bill swung the excavator bucket to the side, knocking over the fire hydrant on the corner and shooting a high-pressure arc over the entire scene. Water rained in John's face, flattened Catlin's hair, and splattered the leather upholstery of the open convertible.

"My car!" John shrieked like a hysterical child watching his treasured toy destroyed. He ran, keys out, and vaulted into the driver's seat, shouting "I'll sue!" as he roared off.

"What a great guy," Neil commented when Francisco joined him out of the geyser's range. "Too bad he had to leave in such a hurry." He pulled out a bandana and wiped his face. "Did you call the water department?"

"Yeah, they'll be right here. They had a crew doing maintenance a few blocks over. This may run for a while. They said the hydrant check valve is pretty old. They don't think it'll work, so they're going to start with the valve up the street."

"Uh huh. There'll be a couple blocks out of water tonight, once they shut down the main."

"They also said it's up to us to repair the hydrant. They're swamped."

"Oh, that'll make Greg happy. Guess I know what I'll be doing tomorrow morning on my own time." Neil dragged off his hard hat and ran his hand up through his hair. "Catlin, it's drier over here," he called, noticing that she was still standing in the artificial rain storm Bill had created.

"I am totally humiliated," she moaned, walking slowly out of the spray. "I'm so sorry, you guys. I've never seen John like that before. He's normally a very calm person. I must have picked the wrong time to bring up a change in plans. He's been under a lot of stress lately." She shook her head. "I apologize for the damage. Do you want to charge me to fix the fire hydrant?"

Neil laughed. "No, no, Miss. Bill's always doing that. It wouldn't be a typical job if he didn't break something."

She grinned. "I didn't realize this is what you meant when you said I'd have to stop using water today."

"To be honest, neither did I," Neil replied. He noticed that all the workers were gazing serenely at Catlin's soaked tee shirt. "Look, we're going to wrap it up for now. Why don't you go in and get dry? The water department will be here in a few minutes to shut off the main. We'll come out tomorrow to fix the hydrant and get everybody's water back on." He nudged Francisco with his elbow.

Jarred from his pleasant stupor, Francisco said, "Right, boss. Don't worry, *amigita*. It'll be a quick fix." He waved to the city truck as it turned the corner and walked off to help.

"I'm sorry for all this trouble." Catlin stared in disbelief at her purpled arm. "I'll talk to John next week, after he's had a chance to calm down. He didn't mean it about suing your company."

"It wasn't your fault. And I'm not worried about a lawsuit. He violated city code parking his car here. Are you going to be all right?"

"Sure. I'm fine. Thanks, for everything."

"No problem. Keeping the peace is part of my job."

"You must have been a sheriff in a former life—you stayed so calm while the rest of us got out of control."

"That's me, Sheriff Prescott." He laughed.

"I guess I better get some ice on this arm." Catlin hung her head and then brightened. "Packard will be glad it isn't my Frisbee arm, anyway. See you tomorrow."

"We'll get your water back on first thing."

Bill walked up as Catlin closed her front door. "You're welcome, man," he said.

"Yeah, thanks for arranging a little emergency weekend work. Just what we needed."

"I figured it was a small price to save your weenie ass from getting whipped."

"Hey, I could've taken him, easy. I was trying to defuse the situation, you know, in a professional way."

"Uh huh. For some guys, a two by four works best."

"I'm glad you chose water instead of wood this time."

"Yeah, me too. She might not want to go out with me if I beat her boyfriend to a pulp. Though it'd be worth it to smash his head into the sidewalk. I think it'd sound sort of like a pumpkin—*ker-thock*." Bill smiled dreamily at the thought.

"Women are a mystery," Neil said, shaking his head. "Just when you think they're impossible to please, you run into one who bends over backward making excuses for a total jerk."

"And nice guys like us go home alone. It ain't fair."

"Not at all," Neil agreed. "Not at all."

Packard jumped from the window seat and ran over to Catlin when she came inside. She automatically reached out for him and gasped at the pain in her arm. Mouth set, she blinked back tears and busied herself, pulling out the ice trays from the freezer, breaking cubes into a plastic bag, and wrapping the bag in a towel.

"There! Just what the doctor ordered." She left the ice bag on the counter to change out of her tee shirt, pulling the soggy fabric over her head with a grimace and slipping on a faded sweatshirt. She took the ice bag to the living room and curled up on the couch. Grabbing a pillow to cradle her arm, she carefully arranged the ice bag on top and leaned back. Packard sat near her, waiting for his head to be scratched.

"This day certainly didn't end up as planned. I shouldn't have brought up my idea of postponing the wedding when John was so upset about his car getting dirty. But I can't believe he hurt me . . ." Her voice trailed off into a sob and she covered her mouth, moaning, "I feel sick."

She pushed the ice bag and pillow to the floor and hurried down the hall. In the bathroom, she stared at the clean white porcelain, thinking, *No, I'll be okay* an instant before rage and shock surged out of her.

Closing her eyes, she sank to the floor. She lowered the lid and reached for the handle, then realized there would be no water until the next morning. She laid her right arm on the lid, resting her cheek, and let the tears slide haphazardly over her face. Her thoughts skimmed gingerly over the past hour like fingers on burnt skin, fearful of the damage. *How did I make him so angry why would he hurt me what should I have said could this happen again is he sorry* . . .

Outside, the murmur of deep voices died and the construction clatter faded. She reached blindly for the toilet paper, wiped her face, and dragged herself up. Though it was still light outside, she felt exhausted. *It's midnight in my heart*, she thought and laughed at herself as her mind systematically filed the phrase for future use.

"Sorry, no Frisbee today, Fuzzbucket," she told Packard as he trotted over and nuzzled her knees. She poured kibble into his dish. "Let yourself out when you need to, okay? I'm going to bed now." She unlatched the dog door to the backyard and shuffled into the bedroom. Throwing her clothes in a heap, she retreated under the covers and fell into an uneasy sleep.

5

Catherine dressed slowly in an extravagant gown of flounced buttercup silk with a deeply cut bodice. Green satin ribbons rounded up the overskirt of loosely woven ivory lace at each side. She smoothed the skirt over her waist, still tiny enough to forgo a corset, which she always considered an advantage in her work.

She shook her tawny curls, hoping to dispel the sense of foreboding that had dogged her all afternoon. Perhaps it was remnants of a nightmare. She had not seen Daniel in several weeks and missed the heat that always overwhelmed them both. He warned her he would be gone an extended time but made a surprising promise. She thought back to their last time together. He was more talkative than usual, excited about a new venture. She listened patiently at first, filling her mind with the sight of his blue eyes dancing, strong hands gesturing to emphasize a point. But she wanted his eyes to light on her, his hands to slide over her, his body to take hers where no one else's could. Nodding and murmuring "Umm hmmm," she unbuttoned his shirt and pulled off her lacy chemise. She moved closer to brush against his skin, kissed his neck, and whispered, "You can keep talking if you like."

He laughed and took her hands in his. "I know this business doesn't interest you much, sweetheart. But it will make my fortune. And then I'll be set for life. *We'll* be set for life." He gazed intently into her eyes. "Catherine, I don't want to share you with anyone else. I want you to be with me always. Lover . . . partner . . . wife."

She turned away from his determined look, fighting off wild exhilaration. "Neither of us can change what I am, Daniel. What I do. I could never be accepted in your world. Taking me as your wife would ruin your plans, destroy your social standing."

How she hated saying those words! It was the right thing to do—talk him out of such a foolish idea. She knew the past three years had branded her, set her place as long as she remained in Denver. This man made her feel there could be a different future. But she understood enough of his business to know his success was tied here. She concealed her awareness garnered from hours with the city's most important men. Once they experienced the physical release her body inspired, they sought intellectual release by relating their numerous schemes. Discreet and sympathetic, she earned their trust while absorbing their knowledge. Banking, industry, social intrigue, she incorporated it all. On lazy afternoons in the garden, she and Amy, the sheriff's favorite, exchanged confidences, shaking their heads over the myriad ways sporting gents maimed and killed each other.

Daniel stroked her cheek. "I know who you really are, Catherine. I know your worth. And I know you love me. We can make this work. Please tell me you'll consider it."

He was breaking her heart, holding out a future she wanted so badly but knew was unattainable. So she took refuge in simple honesty, saying, "I'll think of nothing else the entire time you're gone."

His face lit with joy, and she pushed sad reality aside to share it, losing herself in his smile and, finally! his body.

Insistent clapping broke her reverie, and she rushed out of the room. She faltered in her typical smooth glide down the steps when she saw the loathsome Judge Wellingbrook in the parlor, round face glowering, heavy fingers tapping on the polished mahogany sideboard with such ferocity the crystal decanters vibrated. Catherine's stomach churned when Madam Joey looked to the staircase in relief and gestured sharply for her to hurry.

"The Judge has been waiting for you, dear," Madam Joey said as she bustled over and nabbed Catherine's arm before she could retreat up the stairs. "Where have you been?" she hissed. "You know how he gets if he has to wait."

"I don't feel well," Catherine whispered, vainly trying to pull her arm away.

"Pity. But he's asked for you, and it's you he shall have," Madam Joey replied with a grim smile. "And here is Catherine at last, Judge. Knowing you might come tonight, she took special care in her dress. Is she not a vision?"

"Indeed. A vision in yellow, but more appealing in flesh. The dress is lovely on her, but I'd rather see it on the floor." He snorted and pawed at Catherine with stubby, bejeweled hands, smearing her gown with oily sweat. "You have your fee, Madam, though I should be granted extra time for being forced to wait."

"Of course. You shall not be disturbed." Madam Joey nodded at Catherine. "Hurry upstairs, my child, and please our distinguished guest in whatever he desires."

Catherine bowed her head. She felt as though chains were attached to her delicate slippers, dragging her feet as she ascended the steps, the laboring breath of Judge Wellingbrook hot on her neck.

Again she wished the fates had led her down a different path. Yet how cheerfully she had followed Molly to this house and how willingly she had surrendered her soul to the false promise of luxury and ease. It was a game to both of them, interchangeable green-eyed beauties raised together, sharing their deepest selves only with each other as they shared their bodies with an endless stream of men. Catherine quickly became addicted to the silk and satin of the latest fashions, the bright baubles, the leisurely days of reading and gardening. And the nights, she admitted, were rarely a burden. Most of the house visitors adored her charm, warmth, and skill. But some men took evil pleasure in testing her with brutality and perversion. Such a man was pushing her through the bedroom door as these thoughts crossed her mind, and she steeled herself for what would come this night.

The Judge tossed his traveling coat and hat on the chair beside the bed.

"Don't hide from me, my beauty," he said, gripping her chin and forcing her head back. "So lovely, but so pale. I think you need more color." He dropped his hand and then raised it in a vicious slap.

Catherine stifled her gasp and eyed him defiantly.

"Ah, you want my rouge for your other cheek." He whipped the back of his hand across her face, drawing a thin line of blood with his rings.

She caught her breath and withdrew a step.

"I am so sorry, my dear." He pulled a fine linen handkerchief from his trousers and daubed at the cut on her chin. "Now you see how angry you made me having to wait. You mustn't do that again. Agreed?"

He threw the stained cloth on the floor when Catherine remained silent, and seized her arm, twisting to pull her close. "Perhaps disciplining you gently has been a mistake. Some horses require rougher treatment to be tamed," he spat. "What measures should I take to have a long and satisfying ride? The Madam may forbid whips, but a few swipes of my riding crop might curb your resistance." His cold gray eyes bored into hers. "Shall I conclude by your silence that you concur? I know places that would not scar your creamy skin. Or have you forgotten the last time?"

Still grasping her arm, he reached toward the chair with his other hand. Catherine followed his movement and saw a braided leather handle jutting from the outside coat pocket.

He licked his lips as her eyes widened in fear.

She well remembered his last visit and knew he lied. The stripe from one lash had taken a month to heal and left a stark white line high on the back of her thigh. Madam Joey had been horrified and banned the Judge from the house. But she relented when he paid a substantial bribe and promised his legal influence to protect the establishment from community harassment. It was a powerful combination that reinstated his stature in the house, to Catherine's dismay.

"No," she said, bowing her head. "I stand ready to please you."

"If you stand, that does not please me," he replied with a smirk. "First the dress goes to the floor, then the whore." He tore at her gown, gleefully ripping the fine material to pieces. He panted as her body was exposed and lovingly fingered the thin mark from their last encounter. He pushed her head down and forced her to kneel before him in tatters.

"You know what I want first. Get to work." He casually began undressing as if her services were no more interesting than a bootblack polishing his shoes.

"Enough," he said finally, fisting a hunk of her hair and pulling her up. "I feel ready for a spirited ride. Take off my boots," he commanded, sitting on the bed and rebuttoning his trousers.

Catherine leaned forward to grab his foot as he straightened one leg.

"No, no! You're doing it wrong. Turn around." He nudged her thighs apart with the black leather boot, surreptitiously sliding out the riding crop when her back was to him. "Now bend over and pull from the heel. Gently!" he snarled as she tugged.

Catherine grimaced at the stench when his foot was released but obediently took the other boot as he slid the toe between her legs with an evil caress. She knew he was resisting to keep her in this degrading position as long as possible. She distanced her mind, and her hands lagged.

"Pay attention, whore." A sharp whistle and a stinging slice jolted her back to the present.

"No! You promised!" she cried, spinning around.

"I promised nothing. But you were instructed to please me in all my desires, were you not? And your hapless fumbling does not please me. Therefore, I exert my right to punish you. Madam has given me permission as long as there are no permanent scars." He slapped the crop against the sheet.

With eyes narrowed in hatred, she snatched his boot and yanked it off, throwing it at his face. "There! No more fumbling!"

He caught the boot and tossed it aside with a harsh laugh. "It appears my filly is ready to be broken. Excellent." He lunged and pinned her arms to her sides. "You will submit, even if it takes all night." He spoke low and fast, so close she could see flecks of foam at the corners of his mouth.

"Do you understand me, whore?" he shouted.

She turned her head, as spittle pricked her face, and struggled against his grip. But his fingers tightened and her delicate frame was no match for his massive bulk. He threw her on the bed as carelessly as he had flung the boot and followed so quickly she had no time to resist. She gasped for breath as his weight slammed against her. She flailed at his face, which only made him chuckle; he easily caught both of her wrists in one hand. Kneeling over her, he grabbed a strip of ribbon from the scattered remnants of her gown and tied her hands to the center post of the brass bed.

"There! Now you can buck all you like." He leaned back to enjoy her helpless fury as she glared at him.

"Madam Joey will ban you from the house again if you do not release me." She tried to keep her voice even, but a tremor betrayed her doubt.

"Mmm no, I think not," he replied conversationally, grateful for a lull to catch his breath. "We all know your madam's weakness for monetary compensation, and I have paid enough to buy her a new whore for this room if you prove too resistant." He lifted the riding crop and fondled the stock. "You have such beautiful skin," he sighed. "It would be a shame to see you banished to a dark shack because you were disfigured. Marred. Deformed." He intoned each word slowly as he traced the end of the handle over her breasts and across her face.

Catherine winced. She realized he could ruin her forever as eagerly as use her for the night, perhaps more so. With what madness had she deluded herself she was immune from danger? What kind of life was this, at the mercy of such men? When Molly left for a quieter house, she had remained, wanting to maintain her luxuries and thinking Madam Joey would protect her out of love. Foolish! Josephine's true love was for money, and Catherine was at her mercy as well. No wonder some sisters took poison as their only act of control. Her eyes misted at the thought of lost friends. The Judge, misinterpreting her softened countenance as surrender, smiled in triumph.

"I'm delighted you choose to yield without further persuasion. I have plans to visit this house often. Madam has assured me you will be exclusively available. I confess I find you enticing." He slithered out of his trousers and stretched out naked on top of her. "What do you think of being held in reserve for me? A fine, rare vintage, to be tasted only by a true connoisseur." He flicked his tongue.

She closed her eyes for a moment, and then fastened her gaze on the leering face above her. "Nothing would please me more." Her smile was alluring. "But I could please you more if you untied my hands," she whispered silkily. "I promise to be very good."

"Obedient?" His breath quickened.

"Yes. Obedient to you in all things." She licked her lips, mouth wide.

"I ride my horses hard."

"And put them away . . . wet."

Her breathless emphasis on the last word sent his mind spinning into his loins. He shot up to straddle her. Hands shaking with anticipation, he unraveled the satin restraint and freed her.

She lowered her arms with a small sigh. "Now that I am tamed, what is your desire?" she asked sweetly, running her fingers along his thighs, ending with a gentle caress at their juncture.

"I bow to your skill."

"Then perhaps you would like to lie down and allow me to minister to you for a short while."

His eyes lit. "Yes, a little relaxation before our strenuous work of the night. An excellent idea." He rolled over onto his back.

"Ah, it is my turn to ride a magnificent stallion," she said, mounting him with a girlish laugh. She stretched forward to massage his temples, swinging her rose-tipped breasts tantalizingly close.

When he reached up to crudely fondle them, she murmured, "Rest, rest completely for now. I'll need all your strength soon enough."

Blissful in her servility, he dropped his hands and closed his eyes.

She alternated kneading one shoulder then the other. With a barely discernable movement of her right hand, she withdrew her hatpin from the garden hat balanced on the bed post and swiftly hid it under the pillow.

The door to the next room slammed and rhythmic creaking of bedsprings followed. The Judge opened his eyes. "A pleasant interlude," he said, reaching for her. "I feel most invigorated."

With surprising agility, he flipped her over, pinning her beneath his weight. "Are you ready for your horseman, my sweet palomino? I hope you can accommodate me without pain."

She feigned a gasp and buried her face in his shoulder to hide her scorn as he slid his stunted instrument inside.

Resigned to the task at hand, she tightened her well-trained muscles around him. Once she was through this night, she thought, perhaps she could convince Molly to leave Denver. They could start over in another town as teachers or milliners. Molly always loved children, gathering them from neighboring estates for lessons and play when she was only thirteen, whereas Catherine adored fashion. She scoured each new *Harper's Bazaar* religiously and was constantly enhancing her own gowns with ribbons, lace, and flowers. Surely, she could succeed as a dressmaker, reproducing beautiful Parisian apparel for wealthy clients and herself. Newly established, she could be a suitable bride for Daniel. The possibilities filled her heart with hope. She remembered to shout, "My stallion!" occasionally as the Judge continued his lone ride.

"You are a sturdy mare," he grunted approvingly in her ear. "My last whore at Madam Beth's was not as wise or strong. A pretty palomino, but she needed eight stripes of the crop." He pushed harder into her. "She . . . would . . . not . . . stop . . . screaming." He punctuated each word with a deep thrust.

Catherine closed her eyes in empathy for an abused compatriot at the same house as her cousin. "But then she served you?" she said, sensing his wicked pleasure at the memory.

"No. She resisted too long." His strokes sped up. "And now she serves the Lord," he said with a guttural laugh. "She died in the midst of her lesson. Poor, stupid Molly."

Catherine clenched her arms as a white hot rage enveloped her. *Molly!* Her treasured cousin, lost to this beast! The future that had seemed within a night's grasp vanished. She had no hope, only sorrow and anger. She moaned and arched in grief.

"Your passion overwhelms me," he panted. "I fear I cannot last." He pounded toward a crescendo.

Crying, "You will not last!" she scooped the hatpin from under the pillow and jammed it fiercely into his ear.

Eight inches of hardened steel pierced the Judge's brain, instantly stopping his heart.

He stiffened and collapsed.

Catherine fought panic as his dead weight threatened to suffocate her. She pushed with all her strength and slipped out from underneath him. She slowly pulled out the hatpin, wincing at the sickening friction. She picked up the stained handkerchief from the floor and wiped the trickle of blood from his ear, cleaned off the hatpin and slid it back into her hat. She scanned the room, eyeing the detestable crop and bloated body contaminating her bed. Her own life would be over if his death did not appear natural.

Straightening her shoulders, she resolved to finish the night's role-playing and save herself. She inched back under the Judge's body, grimacing in disgust. Then she started screaming, loud and high.

Before long, she heard James's deliberate footsteps and the rapid clacking of Madam Joey's heels down the wooden hallway.

As they burst through the door, Catherine sobbed, "Help! He's collapsed. Get the doctor!"

James lifted the Judge off her and rolled him over.

Madam Joey rushed to the bed after locking the door. She pressed on the Judge's neck, then his wrist, and shook her head. "He's gone. We don't need the doctor. What happened, Catherine? And stop pretending to cry. I know you hated him."

"He was trying too hard, pushing himself." She sat up and gratefully wrapped herself in the blanket James handed her. "His heart failed him at the climax of his ecstasy," she sighed.

Madam Joey exchanged a look with James. "It's ironic that he should die in your arms, Catherine," she said. "Given what happened at Beth's house earlier tonight."

Widening her eyes in what she hoped demonstrated innocent alarm, Catherine murmured, "Why? What has happened?"

Madam Joey hesitated as her gaze swept the room.

Catherine watched, knowing her clever "mother" was plotting strategies. How would she break the news about Molly? What would they do about the Judge? Catherine shivered under the blanket as a wave of fear passed through her. What if she fell under suspicion and the sheriff examined the Judge's body closely?

Madam Joey plucked the stained handkerchief from the edge of the bed and tucked it into her bodice. She nodded to James, who thudded from the room, placing a silent hand on Catherine's shoulder as he left.

"James will bring the sheriff," Madam Joey said briskly, picking up the scattered remnants of Catherine's gown and tossing them into the trunk at the foot of the bed. "Sheriff Wilson is downstairs enjoying dinner, but he'll miss his dessert, I'm afraid. You will be hysterical, in seclusion for fear you may commit suicide. And tomorrow, you will."

"What are you saying?" Catherine gasped, jumping off the bed and backing away.

Madam Joey shook her head sadly. "You are lost to me, my dear. You are no longer an asset. Due to certain unfortunate indiscretions on the Judge's part, which are as yet a secret, you and the house are in danger. You must be removed." She stepped forward.

Catherine stood frozen, blanket clutched to her chin.

"What? Do you fear me? Child, there's no time now to explain. Go to Amy's room and take the passageway to the basement. You'll find traveling clothes in a trunk by the stairs. Get dressed and wait for me. And be patient," Madam Joey added with a sigh. "This is going to be a long night." She hustled Catherine to the door, peered out, and pushed her across the hall. "The door is in the corner next to the armoire, behind the boxes. Hurry, I hear the sheriff and James."

Catherine padded softly into the room and eyed the brocade wall by the mahogany wardrobe. Her fingers found a tiny latch behind a stack of hat boxes. A cleverly arranged Dutch door split open at her touch. She moved the boxes to step through, closed the bottom half, and leaned out the top half to set the boxes back against the concealed door. Clicking the top door into place, she turned to face a suffocating black stillness. She took a deep breath. She hated the dark. A candle was always burning in her room. The men thought it was part of her romantic allure, but the reality was she needed that small light to avoid heart-wrenching panic. *Molly, I avenged your death. Help me now.*

Catherine closed her eyes, then opened them again, straining to find some hint of light in the darkness. It was as if she were blindfolded, she thought, and then remembered a party game with Molly, the blindfold tight, everything black but, safely surrounded by the laughter of friends and the warmth of a summer night, she spun helplessly, laughing so hard that she finally floated to the grass in a cloud of powder-blue silk and taffeta. Molly embraced her and whispered lovingly, "Do you surrender, Cousin?" She removed the blindfold when Catherine stopped giggling long enough to say "Yes," and the group all gathered round to tease her for quitting. It was her fifteenth birthday party and one of her favorite memories of a carefree and innocent time.

"If I'm ever to see another birthday, I have to move forward," she told herself and began her descent into the basement.

Cobwebs caressed her face and laced her hair as she felt her way down the wooden stairs, sliding one bare foot out to the edge of each step, then down to the next, testing gingerly for creaking boards before placing her full weight. The rough banister was caked with dust and grime. She touched it lightly with her fingertips, resisting the urge to grasp it for balance. She labored for breath in the thick, earthen air, focused only on progressing.

Finally, her toe felt cool dirt instead of wood. Inching forward with her hands waving slowly in front, she sought some physical reference point in the space.

"Ow! I found the trunk," she whispered as her toe and shin radiated pain and she nearly tumbled over the curved top. She knelt and slid her hands over the dusty surface until she found the latch.

Stifling coughs, she released the catch and lifted the lid.

"Please please please, Josephine. Did you plan ahead and put some matches in here?" Her fingers fumbled through layers of clothing, homespun wool and cotton, a thick cloak, leather boots. "Oh Blessed Mary," Catherine whimpered as she felt a packet of wooden matches and, next to it, a small oil lantern.

"Bless you, too, Joey," she added. She set the lantern on the floor, struck a match, and celebrated the tiny circle of light. She shrugged the blanket off her shoulders and kneeled, naked before the flame, a confusion of prayers in her mind.

"Holy Father, I know it is wrong to kill, but doesn't such a one with so little regard for the rest of humanity forfeit his right to human consideration? If I must be punished now for my sin, then so be it. I could never have let that monster draw one more breath." Not exactly begging for forgiveness, she decided, but the best she could do at the moment.

Reminding herself that the Lord helps those who help themselves, she pulled out the clothes from the trunk to examine them in the lamp light.

"A far cry from my satin gowns," she mused, holding up a rough cotton shirt and plain wool skirt. But the linen chemise and long drawers were of fine weave, and a flourish of white lace finished the edges. Dressed for the first time in hours, she dug deeper in the trunk and found stockings, then brown boots. Expecting sturdy footwear, she was surprised at the elegant cut and supple leather of the tall, laced boots. She giggled in delight when she found them a comfortable fit.

"Now what? Sit and wait, I suppose." Weary and bruised, she sat on the blanket and leaned against the trunk. She raised her eyes to the invisible ceiling, wondering what was happening on the floors above. Slowly, she lowered her head into her hands as tears washed her begrimed face. Silent sobs racked her body, and grief overtook self-preservation. She surrendered to the power of sorrow, curled on the blanket like a child. Finally, spent, she slept.

6

Catlin tossed from her right side to her left and gasped awake as pain radiated up her arm.

Disoriented in the early morning darkness, she felt her way down the hall to the bathroom, where a small nightlight glowed. She tapped some aspirin into her palm and padded into the kitchen for milk. The refrigerator door light illuminated smooth tanned skin. She opened the cupboard for a small glass, poured milk, and gulped the aspirin with a toss of her head.

The clock on the oven reported a red digital message of 2:15. Catlin turned at the sound of tentative clicking on the linoleum and smiled at Packard's wide yawn.

"Hey, Slumberpuppy, did I wake you up? Sorry about that."

She put the glass in the sink and crouched down to caress Packard at eye level.

"I made such a mess," she sighed. "How am I going to fix it with John? What do you think? Let it go until after the weekend?"

Packard licked her nose.

"I'll take that as a yes," she said, standing up.

More time, she thought wryly. Wanting that is what caused the problem to begin with. Maybe it was inconsiderate to blurt out a long postponement. She certainly wouldn't like it if John said he wanted to put off the wedding almost a year without any explanation, especially if she was already upset about something. She slowly stretched her arm, flexed it, and stretched it again, working out the ache, and wished she could do the same with her heart. Being inconsiderate was one thing; hurting was another. *But physical abuse happened to other women, not someone well educated, financially independent, and emotionally stable.*

"Okay, maybe not the third one so much," she admitted out loud, causing Packard to lift his head from where he had curled by her feet.

Anyway, there was no sense exaggerating a one-time event, she decided. They would talk about it, set it aside, and get back to normal.

"Okay." She nodded her head and nudged Packard gently with her foot. "Let's go back to bed. I've thought enough."

The big dog followed obediently, circling once before flumping onto his cushion. Catlin settled carefully on her right side and focused on breathing in time with a vision of the excavator bucket rising and falling. She caught a glimpse of intense blue eyes on the outside edge of consciousness before slipping into sleep.

Metallic thumping woke Catlin later that morning. She squinted at the light and sat up groggily.

"Whoa—nine! How'd it get so late? Thanks for letting me sleep in," she said as Packard put his front paws on the bed and barked.

"I guess breakfast is long overdue. You've been very patient. Good boy."

At the sound of more pounding outside, she realized getting dressed should be a priority. She pulled on loose shorts and a long-sleeved linen shirt.

"Okay, now I can feed you."

While Packard devoured his kibble, she peeked out the front window.

Unintelligible cursing blended with irritated hammering as Bill repeatedly struck a rusted metal box mounted on a trailer. Catlin scanned the area for Neil or Francisco, but Bill was alone.

For all the noise, it didn't appear that much progress had been made on the repair. The upended hydrant lay on the ground. The excavator sat unattended at the curb.

"Start, you worthless piece of crap!" Bill shouted, swinging a mallet.

Catlin debated her next move. On one hand, she'd like to have the water back on before she approached the bathroom or, at least, ask Bill when to expect that welcome event. *On the other hand*, she thought, *he looks pissed*. "And on the third hand, I wish I hadn't used that word," she commented to Packard as she watched him trot out through the dog door to the backyard. "Because I may have to use your method in a few minutes."

She headed back to the window at the sound of beeping. The white Ford backed up to park at the corner. Neil yelled out the window, "Don't you have the generator started yet, Bill?"

"Man, I've pounded on this mother for an hour—no luck." Bill straightened up and threw the mallet at his feet in disgust.

Neil turned off the engine and jumped out to pull metal fittings from the back of the truck, laying them by the hydrant. Catlin headed out the front door as he sauntered over to Bill, picked up the mallet, and coolly tapped the box twice. A ragged motor coughed to life.

"Shit," Bill said. "How do you do that?"

"It's all in knowing where to tap." Neil grinned and slapped Bill on the shoulder. His smile broadened when he saw Catlin coming down her front stairs. He forced himself to hold the smile while he inwardly flinched at the shadows under her eyes and weary posture. *She looks like something*

"The cat dragged in," Catlin finished.

"What?"

"I said, I know I look like something the cat dragged in," Catlin repeated. "Though Packard hates it when I use metaphors like that."

"You look fine, honey," Bill said gallantly.

Neil nodded, eyes narrowed in suspicion that she could read his mind.

Catlin laughed halfheartedly. "Thank you. I didn't want to get in the middle of the work, but I was wondering when it might be safe, um, you know, to use my bathroom."

"Bill's going to get right to it, now that we have power for our power tools," Neil assured her.

Bill said, "Right," and headed off.

"Is Francisco coming today?" Catlin asked over the rumbling of the motor.

"No. This is a small fix. He volunteered, though. He keeps telling us you were so excited to talk to him yesterday morning, you ran out of the house without any shoes."

"Is that what he's saying? *Que payaso.*"

"What's that mean?"

"Clown."

"I thought that was *pendejo.*"

"Um, no, that means 'dick.'" She giggled. "Does Francisco call you that?"

Neil's face darkened. "That guy's cleaning up after live lateral connections for a month."

"Ewww." Catlin wrinkled her nose.

"Yeah. You better believe it." Neil glanced over to check on Bill. "Okay, I'll call the water department pretty soon to reactivate the main. I'll give a holler when it's back on."

"Thank you." Watching him walk off, she realized she felt happier. *Maybe it's the anticipation of having running water again,* she thought. It wouldn't be right to be attracted to someone else. Although she didn't feel attracted to John right now, they would work things out. She had made a choice and would stand by it. Meanwhile, Frisbee at the park was next. A brisk walk and fresh air sounded good. "Let's head out, Packard," she called, and ran up the steps.

On the way back from the park, she repeated a musical mantra from her favorite Deva Premal CD. "*Om namo bhagavate vasudevaya,*" she sang softly to Packard. "It means 'Om is the name of that inside me, which is aware of the Oneness of all things.' And it's not too late to get to yoga," she said, glancing at her watch.

Focusing on breath and balance would be particularly useful today, she thought. She enjoyed the Saturday yoga class, which was slow and meditative. She quickly learned when she started attending this studio that there are as many kinds of yoga as toothpaste. Kundalini, Iyengar, Astanga, Hatha, Vinyasa, Raja. Although she could handle the intensive classes, she preferred this teacher's emphasis on bringing mind and body, heart and soul together as one. It was hard to not be competitive, since that was her nature. But it seemed whenever she was tempted to stretch beyond her boundaries because the person next to her could fold completely in half, the teacher would remind them that yoga is about being compassionate to yourself and accepting where you are at any given moment.

"Look, Packard, a message," she said as they came up the stairs. She slipped the note from the clip on the mailbox and unfolded it. Butterflies danced inside her as she saw the heavy, looping signature: Neil.

"I am such a goofball. Come on, Catlin, calm down," she said. "It's only a note." She took a breath and read, "Cat—Water is on. We'll be back Monday."

While the logical part of her mind registered a courteous communiqué, the undisciplined part cartwheeled, somersaulted, and back flipped, singing, *He wrote me a note a note a note, this is his handwriting, his signature, gosh it's messy, did he write to anyone else?* She peered down the block for folded notes on mailboxes, white flags signaling she was not unique and this was standard public notification procedure. Seeing none, she smiled and skipped inside the house.

"Cool your jets, big guy. I'm going to change for class." She hummed her way to the bedroom and placed the note carefully on the mahogany nightstand. She untied her tennis shoes and kicked them off. Stepping out of her shorts and panties, she pulled on a thong and black tights, then replaced her shirt with a long sleeved knit yoga top. She grabbed her sandals, yoga mat, and a bottle of water.

"Be a good boy," she told Packard as she put on her sandals and headed out the door. "I'll be back in a few hours."

On the way to class, she focused on breathing and not thinking about anything except driving. She especially tried not to think about how Neil was settling into a region of her brain that was supposed to have a population of one and how the current occupant was moving to a different place. "Watch it, girl," she warned herself. "Don't be an idiot and embarrass someone who's trying to do his job."

Arriving at class, she calmed her mind. She took off her sandals and entered the sunlit room with its warm hardwood floor, quietly unrolling her mat and sitting cross legged. She closed her eyes to the bustle of classmates coming in and securing their space. She let her breath ebb and flow like a wave. She didn't open her eyes when the teacher began speaking, but merged his familiar words with her breath, standing at his instruction, slowly stretching her arms overhead, extending toward the ceiling, bending back then forward, reaching for her toes, inhaling, exhaling, losing herself in the concentrated effort to stay centered and balanced. Upward Facing Dog, Downward Facing Dog, Lunge, Warrior Angle, Five Pointed Star, Tree Pose, Dancing Sheba, Seated Spinal Twist, and, finally, her favorite, Shavasana, Resting Pose. Following the teacher's words, she let all tensions melt away, accepting that nothing was more important than being here in the moment.

"Form the words *Let go* in your mind," he intoned slowly.

Peace. At one with the universe. Silence in her head, except for her breath and *Is that Gary snoring? He should lose some weight. Linda too. I can't believe she wears those hip-hugger yoga pants with high-rise old-lady undies. Did she check in the mirror before she left the house? That's why I like thongs for yoga. I'd hate for the person behind me to see bunchy VPL. Jackie's looking good, I wish I had her skin. It seems like most of the class can touch their toes, but not me. I can balance but I'm not flexible. Who is that woman that keeps coming in late? It's so inconsiderate. Half a row had to shift over in the middle of Sun Salutation to make room for her. I'd like a yoga top like Ruth's, maybe I should go shopping later, no, no, breathe, breathe, breathe.*

"If your mind comes in to judge and evaluate, tell it to hush," the teacher reminded them as a rhythmic mantra played.

Re-centered, Catlin closed her eyes again and managed to focus on her breath the rest of Resting Pose.

"Notice each movement, each sensation as you rise to seated," the teacher awakened them. "Let's end the class with the sound of OM."

"OMMMM," the class replied in unison.

The sound reverberated throughout the room, many voices merging into one.

Then they were released. "Good class, everyone. Have a great weekend."

Catlin gulped her water, rolled up her mat, and left, nodding politely in mellow greeting to similarly subdued classmates.

Yoga soothed her, but it also made her nostalgic. Before her grandmother became bedridden, they would go to the Sunday morning gentle yoga class together and then share a sandwich at the organic market nearby. When Catlin got home, she switched into shorts and dug in the back of the den closet for her remembrance box. She sat on the floor and lifted the lid of the floral-patterned hat box.

Packard came in and sniffed at the musty perfume wafting from the yellowed stationery. She gently pushed his head out of the box.

"There's nothing in here for you, Goofus. Sit while I read a little."

She reached for her favorite packet, the oldest pages in the box, heavy ivory paper tied with a frayed green satin ribbon. The letters were written in a tidy, androgynous hand, addressed only to "C" and signed with an exuberant "J." There were no dates or postmarks. The writer used initials throughout, so no proper names provided clues. Even her grandmother didn't know the origin of the letters. She got them from her mother with strict instructions to preserve them and pass them down to the next daughter.

Catlin smiled, remembering Grandma saying, "I knew what I was supposed to do, but your mother took so long to marry and have you, I had almost given up on there being a next daughter. So I kept these until I could give them to you myself. It's best to cut out the middleman whenever you can. It's good for business, good for life."

Catlin could picture her 21-year-old self, baccalaureate degree still fresh, being handed these ribbon-tied papers that embodied history, mystery, and romance. She and her grandmother read them together and speculated endlessly about the author and the recipient. In the last year, on those particularly bad days when breathing was the only thing Grandma could handle, she would ask Catlin to pick one of the letters and make up a story about it, falling asleep to the rhythm of her granddaughter's voice.

Catlin slipped on thin cotton gloves to protect the papers. She realized she should do more for their preservation but couldn't bear for them to be inaccessible. She gently untied the ribbon and picked up the first note.

"My Dearest C," she read aloud. "You are missed and cannot be replaced. Though the Judge left us no choice, I wish we could have found a way for you to stay. S pines for you, but A has adopted him as her own, so do not fear for his well-being. May the Lord keep you safe in your travels. You are in my heart and my prayers, J."

Catlin prided herself on her powers of deduction and had developed an elaborate theory about this brief letter. C was a man banished for legal misdeeds, leaving behind a young son, S. J loved C and was undoubtedly a female because of the elegant stationery. But if J was C's love, why did A adopt the boy?

"I don't suppose I'll ever know," Catlin sighed. She felt a wave of sadness for these souls, C ripped from his family and forced to journey far, J bereft, S abandoned. She reflected how easily she could lose her own love. How would she feel if John left her? What if the life they were planning evaporated? What would she do without him? She carefully put the note away before any tears could fall on it. She returned the hat box to the closet, grabbed a Kleenex, and reached for the phone.

Afternoon sun marched in uniform lines through white window blinds onto a spotless slate floor. John sat at a glass and chrome table, surrounded by files. He drummed his fingers and glared at his tiny cell phone, which defiantly refused to ring.

"What a pain in the ass she is," he muttered. "She knows how pissed off she made me. She'd better call soon. I'm sick of waiting."

His ring tone of the opening notes to Beethoven's Ninth tolled.

His hand hovered over the phone. "Let her sweat," he said to the dust motes. Then he casually flipped the silver cover. "McKenzie."

"John?"

"Yeah. Who else would it be?" He let "you idiot" hang unspoken.

"Listen, I'm sorry about yesterday." The woman's voice faltered and rushed on. "I—I don't know what happened. Things got out of hand. Your car and everything—it was too much. I couldn't fix it all. I wish I could have. I'm sorry I made you angry."

John heard her stifled sobs and smiled. Another triumph. But he would be gracious in victory.

"I understand, babe. I got impatient, so it's not your fault entirely," he told her. "Look, why don't you come over? We can have lunch on the balcony."

"Really?" A hopeful sniff.

"Sure."

"That'd be great."

"Yeah. So pick up lasagna for me and whatever you want. Be here in twenty."

"Okay, no problem."

She was cheerful again, eager to serve, exactly how he liked her.

"That's my girl. How's your cheek?" he asked, idly glancing at his university ring.

"Oh it's fine. A little Neosporin, a little make-up. It's fine."

"Good. See you in a bit. And Angela—"

"Yes?"

"Make a note to order flowers for Catlin on Monday. I'll write something appropriately apologetic on a card. We've got to keep the future in mind, right?"

"Of course."

He flipped the phone shut with a satisfied nod. "Everything's back on track," he assured himself. "No problem."

Catlin hung up the phone with a happy sniff. Talking with Mom always made her feel better. There was so much to share—the award, the construction, her latest projects. She hinted that she and John had a spat but didn't mention her arm. She wanted her mother to have a good opinion of John, and she definitely didn't want her dad to know John had hurt her. She would see how it went next week. Certainly John would apologize, and she would, too, for springing a postponement on him with no notice. Then everything would be fine again. Maybe she would do some planning, since he seemed to want that. She would go to her favorite bookstore downtown to scope out possibilities for their honeymoon.

The air held the thick smell of old books with a hint of mold. Dust lined the shelves and sat in patches on the wooden banister. Dingy lights illuminated the wooden stairs. *A far cry from the brightly lit bookstores of the valley malls,* Catlin mused. But she loved this place. She grew up visiting Wellingbrook's Books with her mom and grandmother. You never knew what you would find, be it basement, main floor, or attic. Adam Wellingbrook, who had owned the building for nearly sixty years, kept it filled with the rare and unusual, although popular books could be had there too, of course. Catlin enjoyed telling the old man about her ideas, and he could always point her in the right direction to help with her research.

She examined the titles in the travel section. Europe was tempting, but she and John had already discussed that. His schedule would not allow a long trip, and he didn't want to go overseas for only two weeks. "Domestic it is," Catlin said. The northeast had always beckoned. Quaint B & B's, covered bridges, winding country roads, rocky beaches. And a long plane flight. Catlin's smile faded as she remembered their last trip. She had accompanied John to a conference in Chicago, their first flight together. She was shocked at his impatience with the travel experience. He hated the security lines, cutting in front of people moving too slowly for his taste and signaling for her to do the same. Embarrassed, she feigned difficulty with her luggage and stayed back. Of course, she heard all about that once they were seated. He made it clear, between his complaints about the service and food, that she would need to keep up.

Maybe a driving trip would be better. He loved his new car and would be in control of the schedule. Catlin ran her finger along the book spines. Far enough to be exotic, close enough to drive, with some enjoyable stops along the way. She stopped and tapped thoughtfully at Colorado. Boulder seemed like a nice town with its share of quaint hotels. Rocky

Mountain National Park was close. They could go through Sedona and Santa Fe on the way there and come back home through Utah's national parks. Take their time, stay several days in each place. If John would rather stay in Denver, maybe she could squeeze in some research. She knew better than to expect him to drop all work and focus on her for several weeks. While he kept in touch with the office, she could get in touch with her interests.

She flipped through the book, admiring the photos of craggy mountains reflected in still lake waters, stark aspen, golden-crowned bighorn sheep. Even if John nixed this idea for a honeymoon, it would be fun to read more about the area. She tucked the book under her arm and headed up the stairs.

"Did you find what you wanted today, my dear?" Adam Wellingbrook peered at Catlin above his reading glasses as she approached the counter.

She nodded. "I found a great travel book about Colorado. But I'm also interested in the history."

"Ah. What period?"

"Old West times, mid- to late 1800s."

"An excellent choice to study." Adam smiled. "They were wild times. The black sheep of my family is from that period in Denver, as a matter of fact. A judge, my great-grandfather."

"Was he a hanging judge?"

"No, but he caused quite the family scandal, regardless. Isaiah Wellingbrook died of a heart attack in a parlor house, you see. Oh, his wife knew he frequented such places, but to die there . . . well! She never recovered from the shame. She moved home to her parents in Boston with her young son and re-took her maiden name. She never remarried. The Judge's oldest son, by his first wife, stayed in Denver. He was twenty and already in business. That's my line of the family tree. Practical folks. The West was the Wild West, after all. Joshua Wellingbrook wasn't ashamed to carry on the family name. The Judge died in the saddle, as far as he was concerned. But he never saw his stepmother or little half-brother again, although he lived well into his sixties. The McKenzies were a snooty bunch. Disowned our branch, don't you know."

Catlin, who had nearly dozed off, stared wide-eyed. "McKenzie? From Boston?" she choked.

"Oh yes, I'm quite certain. Do you know the name?"

"That's my fiancé's name. His family's from Boston. Could it be the same line?"

"Possibly." The old man's eyes glittered. "It would be an interesting connection."

"I've been researching a Denver prostitute named Catherine Porter who killed herself in the 1870s. I got interested because her story seemed so sad. But I never thought John's family might have some history there."

Adam shrugged. "Prostitutes killed themselves regularly in those days. Accomplished women who made a real mark may be of more interest for you, especially women writers. Look here." He moved spryly toward the attic stairs and climbed, gesturing for her to follow. "Isabella Lucy Bird is very popular," he said, pulling a slim volume from the shelf and handing it to Catlin.

The photo on the book jacket reminded her of the pictures in the travel book: fiery aspens and deep green pines carpeting the foreground, with snow-dusted granite piercing a blue sky in the distance. "*A Lady's Life in the Rocky Mountains*," she read aloud.

"Yes, based on her letters to her sister. She was quite the traveler, starting at age forty-one, no less. Rather tame writing, though parts were sensationalized. Marketing ploy, in my opinion. If you want something less reserved, you should read the letters of Carolyn Parker. Here."

Catlin's fingers trembled as she exchanged books with Adam. The black leather cover was supple as a glove. The red inside papers reminded her of . . . something . . . wallpaper? Where would she have seen brocade wall coverings? She shook her head and turned the page. "*Musings of a Chanteuse*. That's an interesting title," she said, looking up.

"She was an interesting lady, if you believe the letters. Traveled alone. Kept to herself. An inspector found the letters in the basement of a house being renovated in Denver's old red-light district. They were wrapped up in a long-forgotten chest. Probably from the 1870s, based on the style."

"Style of what?"

"The clothing in the chest. The story is in the foreword. The new owners let the inspector keep the letters. Developers have no literary sense," Adam snorted. "But the inspector had an interest in history and a bent for writing. So there you are.

The book is rather rare." He traced his finger along the title page where Catlin held it open, delicately brushing her hand. "Quite valuable," he said slowly.

"Oh." Catlin stood still. There was something about holding the book that made her want it, and she hadn't read one word. Was he hesitating because it was expensive and he didn't think she could afford it? Maybe he'd give her a good deal because she was a long-time customer. Not that it mattered. As the seconds of the banjo clock on the wall ticked, she became convinced she would pay whatever he asked. Like will o' the wisps, smoky thoughts emanated from the pages, entwining her hands. Suddenly impatient to be home with the book, she blurted, "How much?"

"There are so few copies, my dear . . . in some ways, it's priceless. But I know what a serious researcher you are. Not many would appreciate the book the way you would, I'm sure. I suppose I could part with it for, say, one hundred dollars?"

Catlin almost laughed in relief but nodded with a serious researcher smile instead. "It's a fair price," she said.

"Excellent. Let's go downstairs then, shall we? I'll be interested to hear your opinion after you've read her."

Adam chattered about genealogical research as he rang up the sale and deftly wrapped the books in brown paper. "To prove your fiancés' connection to the Wellingbrook line, you know. There are a lot more resources these days. It's not like it was ten years ago, having to view reels of microfilm. I bless the Internet every day."

"Uh huh," Catlin said absently, stuffing her wallet back into her purse and reaching for the package.

"Enjoy Carolyn, my dear. I'm certain you'll get along famously."

His gray eyes held hers momentarily with a flicker of wicked amusement.

"Yes, thank you for your help," she said. The close atmosphere suddenly felt stifling. The trusted old man seemed threatening.

"My pleasure. Do come back soon."

Catlin hugged the books and raced out the door. She inhaled deeply on the way to her car. An evening of quiet reading would be exactly what she needed to escape from her emotional overload.

When she got home, she hurried through weekend chores and a light dinner of leftovers, her eyes lighting on the package she left on the end table in the living room every time she passed by, vacuuming, dusting, and walking out the door with Packard. Routine finally completed, she ripped off the wrapping and snuggled into bed with Carolyn's book. She skipped the foreword and listened to the chanteuse.

7

Chapter 1 Darkness to Light

I suppose I should have felt fear, riding into the night. My horse could have stumbled. We could have lost our way. It certainly would be presumptuous to assume God was on my side, given the circumstances. By dawn the faint lights of town were far behind. Ahead was a future I could not begin to imagine, so set adrift was I from all that I had ever been. The monotonous rocking of my pony's careful tread lulled me into a stupor while we followed starlight. But as the sun crept toward us over the plains, it lit the stage of mountains ahead, and I could not subdue hope for a less than tragic end. I am not bitter, and you know I hold only love in my heart for you. I shall follow your plan to the letter (ah, you see, I still have the capacity for a small joke) for I agree it is the most practical solution to an untenable situation. I miss my comforts and my friends, yet I am ready to assume the mantle of self-reliance. A rough and threadbare cloak, indeed.

Pray do not be like the slow friar in Romeo and Juliet and be sure your explanatory letter reaches my love before the sorrowful news breaks. I am not so far that he cannot find me but far enough for a new start among these frame houses that hope to be transformed as well. We will emerge from frosted night to sun-baked day and grow together out of moral shambles to righteousness.

I must thank you again for being a true protector, providing my means and my escort. I believe he shared my sadness at our parting, reticent though he is. He played his role well, recommending his little sister from the East most sincerely. I trust he is safely returned to you with this letter in hand. The hotel is simple but busy. It appears they are in need of housekeeping assistance and I intend to make myself useful. I will not shy from honest work, will keep my own company, and will pray for God's mercy every day.

Blessings on you, dear Mother.

Yours always,

Carolyn

"More mysterious letters," Catlin said to Packard. "This'll be fun." She yawned and giggled when Packard did the same. "Seems like we both have some sleep to catch up on, huh?" She carefully laid the book on the nightstand and turned out the light.

8

Catlin woke the next morning refreshed from a dreamless night. She stretched contentedly. Sundays were her putter time. She liked to sleep late, eat a simple breakfast of Cheerios, and take a long, meandering walk with Packard. She especially enjoyed chatting with neighbors along the way, although Packard would tug at the leash if she stopped for too long.

But this Sunday, the chanteuse tugged at her. So she jogged with Packard to the park and jogged back after a sufficient round of Frisbee. In the warmth of late morning, she headed to the backyard glider with the book and settled happily into the cushions for a long read.

Chapter 2 Snowy Mountains

You will laugh when you learn my trade now. The proprietress believes me mad to prefer this work. She tells me I should be serving food or charming our visitors at the bar. When sweet Mary comes downstairs, she says, "Carolyn, your beauty could be put to better use. We would attract more customers with you upstairs."

But I have no wish to be seen. And it seems suitable penance that I should work surrounded by snowy mountains yet be unable to view the peaks that beckon to the north. Can you guess my labor?

I am the laundress.

Every day these hands are immersed. I transform soiled piles of bedclothes into clean white stacks higher than my head. I wash the master's shirts and mistress's petticoats, starching and pressing until they stand on their own. Mary tells me no one has put so much energy into this task. Little does she know what these hands have done and that they will never be cleansed of their sins. Still I yearn for forgiveness and for my love. I dare not go to church, so on Sundays I read my Bible in the walled garden behind the hotel. I pray, but then my mind wanders and I think of him. I want him so much, I imagine the breeze is the brush of his fingers, the whisper of his kiss.

Do send me word soon.

Yours always,

Carolyn

Chapter 3 The Funeral

Belated news of the funeral finally reached this outpost. Many voiced surprise that hundreds of townspeople would pay respects to such a lady, though none would say her name. The women whispered their shock that admiring speeches were made by prominent businessmen and that the coffin, draped in black and strewn with flowers, was buried within the consecrated boundaries of the Catholic cemetery. "Good work" in the community was noted as insufficient compensation for daily immorality. That she was truly kind was not enough to earn a place in heaven, since she consciously scorned God's laws.

I am dismayed and amused at the same time by these attitudes. But I keep my own counsel. As a "respectable" woman, I am expected to share in this chatter; however, my lack of enthusiasm for condemnation has branded me self-righteous. A laughable change from previous perceptions, don't you agree?

How I miss our conversations! I did not value your sage advice when it was available as I should have. I received your brief letter a week ago and was overcome with joy to see it. Isn't it strange? When I read the note, I realized that this was your first written correspondence to me. I ran my fingers over the beautiful paper and reflected on your organized hand, so well-formed and precise. We were always immersed in the day to day. I never thought to inquire about your history, though you knew all of ours. Now I regret not asking if you needed a confidant, a shoulder, an advisor. I can hear you chuckle at what sort of counsel such a one as I could give, knowing it would pale in comparison to your life experience.

I am grateful to hear my little one is in gentle hands. He will flourish with my dear friend. I could not have wished for better.

I confess a morbid curiosity for details about the ceremony. Speeches and references to good works were certainly more than we expected. I entreat you to provide whatever particulars you deem prudent.

But how does my love? He is absent from your long-awaited missive. As I toil, my mind is free to dwell on him, to pine for the past and imagine the future. And in my mind I can lose my breath remembering what it was like to reach for him, have his arms around me, feel his skin on mine. How I long to surrender to his heat, open to him, watch his eyes watch mine, lose myself in him, forget about the world, see only his face above me, feel only him, inside, outside, skin, hands, lips, tongues, everything. Suspend time, exist only in the present of giving and taking. Taste the salt of his sweat after we're spent, lick him all over, start all over. I could never have enough of him.

I eagerly await the next letter from you.

Yours always,

Carolyn

"Wow," Catlin said. "Carolyn must have had a pretty open relationship with her mom to write something like that. Now I see what Adam meant by these letters being less reserved." She brushed off a trickle of sweat that had formed between her breasts, considered having a bowl of ice cream for lunch, then decided to keep reading.

Chapter 4 Disbelief

Word of another funeral reached town yesterday and my ears could not believe it. Please reply by the most expedient means possible that these wagging tongues are mistaken. No one can understand how one so young, so handsome, and on the verge of fortune could take his own life. Foul play was immediately suspected, but Mary assured me she heard from the sheriff himself that there was no doubt about the hand responsible. I nearly collapsed in my basement lair, first at the news, and second at the thought that Sheriff W– has been in such proximity.

"It is a tragic story, Carolyn," Mary told me. "The rumor is that Cupid pierced his heart before the bullet, and he had nothing left to live for. Can you imagine a man with such devotion? I think if I died, Edward would hardly notice until he realized the books had not been updated." Then she observed my pallor and put her arm around me. "Oh my dear," she said. "There, there, you are a true romantic to be so affected by the sorrows of a stranger. I will have Suzanne cook extra helpings for you tonight. Would you like to lie down on your cot until dinnertime?" Unable to speak, I nodded and she escorted me to my tiny bedchamber. Penning this has consumed all of my strength.

It cannot be true. You must assure me that my love was informed of our plans and, as with our best laid schemes, the man laid to rest was another.

I desperately cling to hope.

Yours always,

Carolyn

Chapter 5 Despair

Your letter tore my heart and soul asunder. Fortunately, no one could hear my cries when I opened the envelope and fell to my knees at your words. It is midnight, and I have only now lifted myself from the floor.

How could our plans have gone so horribly wrong? Why would my love refuse to be reached? Why would he not come to you first, as the source of truth, before taking such a drastic course? Do not mistake these railings as anger toward you, dear Mother. I shake my fist at the evil one who set these hideous events in motion. I thought I could feel no greater grief and wrath as on that fateful night, but to lose the only one who could have healed my heart—words falter, the pen fails—the pain is too great to bear.

I long to join him but lack his courage to face that ultimate darkness. And I fear my penance is not done. If I left this world now, I would most assuredly be condemned to the flames. It would be worse torture than hellfire to never be reunited with his beautiful soul. So I have decided to travel north. I shall ride alone, hooded in black. My tears will water the trail set by the English authoress. Perhaps I will find a small cabin in which to weather the winter. Snow blowing through unchinked walls could not wrap icier fingers around my heart than this news.

I shall write when I can. Mary has agreed to collect letters for me. I hope to return in spring thaw.

Adieu for now.

Yours always,

Carolyn

"Sad letters, Packard," Catlin said, reaching down to rub his head. "Sad, sad letters."

She closed the book and leaned her head back into the cushions, drowsy in the heat. Two funerals, one for a good-hearted but immoral lady, one for a young man who shot himself for love. *Sounds like Catherine's story*, she thought, *except Carolyn isn't dead, obviously*. But something else seemed familiar; that grief at a plan gone awry struck a chord. What was it? Words she had read a long time ago . . . not in a book . . . The image of careful handwriting came to her mind, ink on ivory paper.

"Oh my god, duh!" Catlin slapped her forehead and jumped out of the glider. She trotted into the den and re-trieved the hat box, pulling out the ribbon-tied packet again. She yanked on her white gloves and flipped carefully through the letters. It was near the bottom—right—she never liked this one because it spoke of failure and helplessness. Her heart pounded with the excitement of being on the brink of discovery as she read the short note.

> *My Dearest C,*
> *It is with a heavy heart and deep regret that I confess my failure. Though if only one could be saved, God granted at least that desire of mine. I know you would have chosen differently.*
>
> *Your stubborn love spurned many entreaties and chose the path we feared. I cannot undo this unfortunate spiral of events; I cannot change the truth you heard.*

Would that my arms could reach you now! Words are cold comfort, and I cannot come to you. Even in death, evil spreads its wings wide. May God protect you.

You are in my heart and prayers,

J

"Look, Packard!" Catlin opened the book to Chapter 4 and placed her letter from J next to it. "C is Carolyn. She's writing to her mother, J. The man she loves shot himself before her mom could tell him something important that would have prevented his suicide." Catlin re-read the first letter in her packet and started talking faster. "See? Carolyn did something illegal . . . that she feels was a sin," she added, checking back to Chapter 2 in the book. "S was Carolyn's son, and A was a dear friend who adopted him. But why didn't her mom take him in? Maybe she was too old. Maybe he was illegitimate. That would have been a sin back then. But why would a judge care?"

Packard barked.

"Oh, all right. I'll read the foreword. Don't you think it's fun to speculate?" Catlin laid the packet aside and turned to the beginning of the book.

Foreword

As an inspector of older homes, I'm used to finding a variety of interesting items: broken dishes, whiskey bottles, and lots of rats, both dead and alive. But these letters are the find of my lifetime.

This rambling home, built when Denver was new, was a flourishing parlor house for many years. The basement had been cleared long ago, or so I thought, descending from the kitchen. Shining my lantern around the space, I saw to my surprise another set of stairs rotting in the opposite corner, extending not from the main floor but from the level above. I shuffled across and held the light high. The staircase was impassable and probably had never been sound enough for frequent use. Pieces of a wooden railing were scattered on the steps that had not yet collapsed. Some of the banister had fallen to the basement floor. Curious as to the type of wood and support structure, I squeezed under the stairs and literally ran into a half-buried trunk. Heart pounding, I dragged it out and set my lantern on the ground. There could be anything in here, I thought, envisioning gold bars and priceless antique jewelry from an untraceable robbery. I was aware that in the next moment my life could change completely. I could become wealthy and renowned. I felt I was ready for the responsibilities of fame: managing vast sums of money, granting interviews, appearing on TV, etc.

Picturing how I would like to be posed for the cover of Time (from the right, studiously regarding the pile of gold), I opened the chest. My first thought was "Oh shit" (with apologies, but I convinced my publisher honesty was important) as my grand visions died. My next thought was "Oh well," as I sifted through the jumble of clothing in the trunk. Men's clothing at that, not very interesting except for the size. "I'd hate to run into this guy in a dark alley," I said, *holding up a massive shirt. That's when a bundle of letters fell out, and my life did change. Not in terms of fame and fortune but focus. Tracking Carolyn became a passion. Literate and lyrical, she also proved elusive. I hoped to verify her story from historical documents, but after a year of fruitless searching, had to give up before my publisher lost interest in the project. Maybe Carolyn wanted the story told only in her words.*

Here is what I could discern from her letters. Carolyn writes to her mother, whose name is unknown. Assuming they lived together in Denver, Carolyn could have ridden to Boulder in a night. The time period was probably early 1870s, when Boulder was little more than a collection of frame houses. Carolyn cites an "English authoress" in Letter 5. This could be Isabella Lucy Bird, who traveled the area in 1873. Following a winter in a secluded valley, Carolyn wanders among unspecified western towns, eventually homesteading on the plains. She pens her last letter when she knew death, likely from pneumonia, was imminent.

I never found a record of her birth or death. I never found a single document that would verify her existence. It is as if she lived only in these letters. But the two funerals Carolyn mentions form tantalizing connections to Denver history. In September 1874, Josephine Muget, a charitable and successful madam who operated the parlor house where the letters were found, died suddenly and was buried with unprecedented fanfare, considering her profession. She left her fortune, including the establishment, to James Seeley, a trusted assistant who ran the house for nearly seven years. He died in 1881 and passed the house to Amy Van Buren, a long-time resident, with the stipulation in his will that she overtake the care of his infant daughter. Amy sold the house later that year when she married the sheriff.

The second funeral of note from this time occurred in October 1874. Daniel Hayden, a young rancher/gunslinger of means committed suicide under well-reported but mysterious circumstances. Professing in a handwritten note to have lost the only love that made life worth living, he shot himself in the heart. Though the newspaper raised questions, the sheriff quashed rumors of foul play and oversaw the burial arrangements personally.

Mysteries abound interpreting Carolyn's letters in terms of these incidents. What was her relationship with Josephine Muget? Was Hayden her love? Did his death spur her travels? If so, she eventually finds contentment, as related in her letters. But enough of my speculation. I leave it to you, esteemed Reader, to find the truth. Do send me word if you unravel the mystery.

Best regards,

Stephen Barnett, 1963

"Nineteen sixty-three!" Catlin exclaimed. "So much for consulting with the editor. He's probably dead by now. Well, Packard, looks like it's up to us to find the connections." She skipped to Chapter 6 and continued reading.

Chapter 6 Shelter

I must thank you again for the means to travel. Mary is kind, but a laundress, even a diligent one, makes little. Through your generosity, I purchased a horse and adequate provisions to live in seclusion through the winter. Iris is a spirited mare, deep chestnut with a black mane that shimmers with iridescence when the breeze lifts it. I outfitted her with a Texas-style saddle, never mind the strange looks. Side saddle is no way to ride long distances, and I have far to go.

I covered my lace-trimmed bloomers with a black skirt and hid my face with a black veil falling from my hat. Perceived as a grieving widow, I am accorded the utmost respect and have encountered only good will and sympathy. The roads I am following are well known but not frequently traveled, particularly this time of year. Snow already dusts the ground, and the aspens wink with golden eyes.

I welcome the solitude. The cold does not deter me and seems to invigorate Iris. My heart is so heavy I can scarce believe she is able to carry the burden. But the search for shelter at the end of each day distracts me from my sorrow. Another benefit of riding here, when only the most determined (or addled) traveler would go, is that habitation conveniently abandoned for the season appears readily.

The first night, I thought God surely had forgiven me, as I found vacant a snug cabin furnished with a cozy bed and a lean-to still stocked with hay. The cabin was perfect except for a hideous odor so strong one could stir it with a spoon. It did not take long to find the source: a dead cat in the wood box by the stove. I held a handkerchief over my face with one hand and carried the cat to a suitable burial site with the other. Ah, well, the truth. I confess I was so tired, in actuality I stood on the porch and swung the animal by its tail, hurling it with all my strength into the forest. The smell soon dispersed and I spent the night in blessed comfort. Unfortunately, the owners of the cabin returned the next day, and I had to move on.

The next night I was punished for my callousness. The only cabin I could find was overrun by cats, most decidedly alive. They maintained pure pandemonium from dusk to dawn, howling, yowling, and scampering in and out the canvas doorway. As they were too numerous to shoo, I covered my head with the blanket and did my best to ignore them. My efforts were unsuccessful and I was a weary traveler indeed the following morning. I resolved to show respect for all God's creatures in the future.

The third night that resolve was tested: my sanctuary was a barn. The ranch house was full of motley males, all swearing, smoking, or spitting. Iris and I chose the company of their horses and three milch cows. I settled into a sweet bed of clean hay in the loft above my animal companions, cocooned by blankets and warmed by a black and tan hound who also sought refuge from the chaos of the house. I slept so soundly that the entire crew, including the dog, left before I woke. After a hearty breakfast, I rode on, my horse and I both much refreshed.

I did not realize before riding in the glory of these mountains how small my world has been. From dry canyon to frothing stream, dense pines to expansive overlooks, the landscape inspires and humbles me. The pure air has cleared my petty thoughts and turned my heart toward God. Though I do not know the path, He guides me. Though the road is perilous, He protects me. Though I ride alone, He accompanies me. As He leads me to shelter, He teaches me life lessons. I am convinced that just as at the end of every day I find myself where I am supposed to be, all my experience—the moments I curse and the moments I bless—have brought me to where I need to be. I still do not know what I shall accomplish. But by placing my faith in God, entrusting there is a purpose that I shall find along this road, my heart is lighter.

With those thoughts I began to sing an old hymn from my childhood. I sang softly at first, my music hushed by a deep copse of evergreen. Leaving the forest at a craggy precipice, my notes soared to heaven in gratitude. For there below me was a secluded valley. Three sturdy cabins sat at discreet distances, each shielded by a clump of aspen and connected by stone pathways to a communal well cheerily rimmed with late-flowering vines. A black and white cow stood at the back of one cabin and a big yellow dog snoozed in the sun at the front. The other two cabins appeared uninhabited. Iris trod carefully down a narrow winding track. I gave her the lead and continued to sing.

When we reached the valley floor, an elderly woman came out the cabin door, stooped to pet the dog, and waited for me with a cautious smile. "I know that hymn," she said. "We sang it many a Sunday at our church in Boston."

"It was popular in the Maryland countryside as well," I replied.

"What brings you to McBride Valley?" she asked as I dismounted.

"A search for shelter through the winter," I told her.

"The Lord always provides," the woman said, and reached out her hand. "I'm Abigail McBride. My son owns this land. Our tenants left to spend the season in town, and Matthew accompanied them to tend to business. He was concerned about leaving me alone but needn't have worried, I see. You are welcome if you are not adverse to work."

I assured her I was not and showed her my calluses as proof. With a nod of her head, she took me in. Thus began my winter of enlightenment.

A phone rang insistently. Catlin looked up in confusion.

"What? Oh." She shook her head to bring herself back to the present and jumped up. "Hello?"

"Hi, Catlin, it's Nancy. Are you okay? You sound a little foggy."

"Hi. I'm fine. I had my head totally in a book. I'm glad you called, though. A lot's been going on."

"I want to hear all about it, but I've got to tell you my news first before I explode—I'm so excited!"

"What's happened?"

"Michael called me and said we won that big bridge project in Hawaii!"

"That's great!"

"I know. But this is the best part. He wants me to go out there for three months to get things set up and make sure the local biologists do a good job with the field work. They're renting an apartment for me in Waikiki. Is that cool or what?"

"That's very cool." Catlin smiled bravely into the phone as Nancy chatted about getting ready and all the shopping she needed to do.

"Oops—there's Michael again," Nancy said when her phone beeped. "Can we talk tomorrow? Thanks!"

Catlin hung up and sat on the floor. "That's a big win for us," she told Packard. "And a great opportunity for Nancy. Hawaii for three months." She rubbed his head, and he licked the tears off her cheek. "I'm not jealous. I'm happy for everyone. Nancy deserves to go. She has more experience than me managing big projects."

She continued to tell Packard how glad she was as the tears fell faster. Who was she going to talk to for three months? Nancy was the only friend who knew her true heart. It was dangerous to share deep secrets with people. Some would hate the burden; others would spread the news all over the city within an hour. Nancy was the only one she trusted. *And now she's going to be busy getting ready, then she'll be gone, and I won't be able to ask her what to do about John or tell her about the letters and Carolyn's book or what's happening with Neil. It's so hard to act like everything is fine when there's nobody who knows the truth.*

"My life is such a mess," she sobbed.

Packard shook himself, starting with his shaggy head and ending with a flourish of his tail.

"Okay, maybe it's not such a big mess," Catlin sniffed. "You'll still listen to me, right?"

She thought about what Nancy would do if she felt sad and lonely. Then she remembered her friend telling her, "Sweetie, the best cure for depression is a new pair of shoes. At least when you're looking down, you're looking at well dressed feet."

Her heart lightened at the thought of wandering through Nordstrom's shoe department.

"You wouldn't understand, Bucko, since you're always barefoot."

She put away the letters and set the book on a chair. She dressed like she was going to work: stockings, a pretty skirt and sweater. Twenty minutes later, tranquilized by the scent of expensive leather, she pondered the age-old questions of closed versus open, stacked versus spiked, patent versus suede. *How would these look with my suits? Do I need another pair of black pumps? Are these bows cute or dorky?* She scanned the expanse for her favorite salesman. (*Sales associate*, she corrected herself.) Ah. There he was. A distinguished older man, on her last visit he cradled her feet like Dresden treasures. He complimented her narrow profile, delicate toes, and high arch. She had left with four boxes and a twinge about the hit to her credit card. It was worth it.

She caught his eye. In a moment, he was at her side, "Delighted, delighted!" she had returned. Spring fashions are perfect for her coloring. What about a navy sandal? Or a taupe pump for work? She must try on the mock crocodile black patent leather; it will send a subtle message of power with unquestionable femininity. Catlin sank into a loveseat with a grateful sigh. She declined the big designer names— too much fashion, too little comfort. The shiny black pumps were an irresistible reminder of her grade-school tap shoes; those were a given. She spent the next hour in blissful indecision on her second pair, finally settling on a navy sling-back with flirty retro bows. Nancy was right, as always. Shoe shopping lasted longer and was way more fun than therapy.

In her dreams that night, she wore lacy bloomers and high heels and galloped on a chestnut mare over a sunny valley with Packard in the saddle behind her. When they jumped off the horse to rest under a tree, Packard turned into a blue-eyed cowboy who said, "Nice shoes," and then pulled her to the grass where they kissed and kissed until the alarm rang.

9

"Don't go," Catlin begged as the scene dissolved. "What weird dreams I've had lately. Did you always want to be a cowboy?"

Packard barked and put his paws on the bed.

She rubbed his head and took the note from Neil off the nightstand to read it one more time before entering workday morning mode.

She considered various wardrobe combinations to feature her new shoes as she walked Packard to the park and back. When the trailer came into view, she watched the group milling around like a litter of golden retrievers, yawning, chewing, and scratching. Which one was sexier, rough-and-tumble Bill, gentle Francisco, or—who was she kidding—of course it was Neil: alpha male pack leader, chivalrous, and confident with a hint of vulnerability she found adorable. Suddenly remembering the blue-eyed cowboy in her dream, she laughed.

Neil flashed a smile in response and ignored an elbow from Bill as he crossed the street to meet her.

"Hey dude," he greeted Packard. "How're you doing?" he said casually to Catlin. "Water working okay?"

"Uh huh, it's fine. Thanks. I'm sorry about all the mess. I hope it didn't ruin your weekend."

"Nah. No problem. Bill has no life anyway." He said the last part louder than necessary, generating an indignant "Hey!" from the middle of the group.

Catlin giggled. "I wouldn't want to interfere with your family time."

"Don't worry, honey," Bill said as he stomped past to the loader. "It'll be a cold day in a hot place before this guy finds somebody willing to put up with his bad habits."

"Hey!" Neil protested. "I don't have any bad habits," he assured her.

"Should I tell her what's in your refrigerator?" Bill shouted as he cranked up the machine.

"No, you should get to work," Neil yelled back. "Sorry," he said to Catlin.

"That's okay. I know you're all busy. Besides, I wouldn't want the conversation to turn to what's in my fridge." They laughed over the din.

"We'll be on your street in a bit."

"I'll try to be out of the way by then."

"You're not going to be our resident engineer today?"

"No, I—" She stopped when Neil's phone rang and he turned away, cupping his hand over his ear and leaning into the phone.

"That's that," she said to Packard and headed home.

She dressed carefully in a blue flowered skirt and twin set, pleased with the feminine look of her new shoes. But the block was still quiet when she left. All thoughts of construction and construction workers vanished when she got to work. The office was abuzz about the big win in Hawaii. Nancy and Michael were ensconced in his office. There was lots of talk, but no one seemed to know any facts. Mark said he was sure he would also be going there for several weeks. Joan sniffed that the focus on work outside of the country wasn't good for their local image, and she didn't understand why Michael went after that project to begin with, unless it was to get vacation on the company. Catlin replied mildly that Hawaii was part of the United States, restraining an itch to slap her for being so snotty about Michael. She reminded Mark he was supposed to have his write-up about the reservoir site to her by the end of the day, and he laughed.

"Nice try, Catlin, but there's not going to be much productive work done today. Everybody's too crazy."

"Somebody should try to get something done."

"Don't be such a miss priss. Relax and enjoy the chaos."

Stung by the moniker, Catlin retreated to her office and shut the door. She put her head in her hands but then stiffened her shoulders and resolved not to cry.

"Fine. At least I'll get some work done today," she said to herself. Firing up her computer and pulling the pages she had edited around her, she threw herself into her project. Immersed, she jumped when Nancy rushed in and collapsed in the guest chair.

"Woosh! Insanity! You would not believe how crazed Michael is."

"Isn't he glad we won?" Catlin asked.

"Oh, sure. But you know what he always says, 'The good news is we won the project; the bad news is now we have to do the project.' He hates having to put money up front, and there'll be a fair amount of outgo before there's income.

Keeping him calmed down plus getting ready to go there and supervise the locals . . . I'm going crazy too. But look at you, working diligently. You're an inspiration to everyone."

"That's me, Miss Inspiration." Catlin laughed and unconsciously pushed up the sleeves on her sweater.

"Oh my god, girl, what did you do to yourself?" Nancy gasped at the bruise on her friend's arm.

"Umm." Catlin hesitated, wondering what she should say with Nancy having so much else on her mind, aching to unburden herself but fearing to voice her concerns. Knowing how Nancy felt about John anyway, she hated to give her another reason to dislike him. The decision was taken away by Michael's appearance at her office door.

"Thought I'd find you here. Sorry, ladies, no time for chit chat. Client's calling in half an hour. Catlin, tell Mark he's in charge of the biologists for the next three months. That'll keep him busy. And would you talk to Joan? She's glaring at me like I just laid off half the staff. Maybe you can explain winning projects is a good thing. God, I hate supervision. Remember when it was easy, Nance? You and me, one computer and a fax machine?"

"Yes, Michael, it was such a lovely time." She batted her lashes up at him and then turned back to Catlin. "Of course, I never knew from month to month if we'd make enough for me to get paid."

"Minor detail." Michael waved his hands. "Just the first year."

Nancy laughed. "I know. But it was a long year," she whispered to Catlin. "We'll chit chat later," she added, standing up. "Okay, what are you allocating for rent, boss? You're not putting me in some roach-infested dump, are you?"

"Would I do that?" Their voices faded as they walked back to Michael's office.

Catlin tugged her sleeves back down and readied herself. "I don't care much for supervision, either," she sighed. "Why can't people do their work without being babied?" Realizing that was a negative attitude, she strode out with her head high, determined to set a good example and do what she could to help.

The rest of the morning flew. She bit her tongue and told Mark and Joan how important they were for the company's success, giving them each some good ideas for actions that they immediately adopted as their own. She shooed the rest of the staff into their cubicles and then settled into her own space, happily productive for several hours.

"Catlin?" a tentative voice interrupted.

"Uh huh." She raised her eyes to a towering bouquet of red roses that filled the doorway.

"Where do you want these?"

Speechless, she pointed toward the credenza.

"This is kinda heavy," the voice said reproachfully.

"Sorry. The desk is fine."

"Whew! Thanks." Their petite receptionist lowered the vase with a clunk and stepped back. "Okay, it's not your birthday, I know. Anniversary?" she asked.

"No, a surprise."

"You're so lucky. I wish I had such a considerate man. Enjoy!"

"Thank you, Gabrielle," Catlin called out. She took the card from its plastic holder, which inexplicably reminded her of a devil's pitchfork, and read the message.

It was a silly argument, babe. Say you forgive me and let's get back on track. LY, John.

"Okay, let's do that," she said, moving the flowers to the credenza behind her and returning to work.

At the end of the day, Nancy stopped in. "Sorry I can't talk more, I—wow, that's some bouquet. Please tell me that's for postponing your engagement anniversary dinner and not because you had a fight." She sat down and faced Catlin.

"Of course it's the dinner. John felt bad about having to reschedule. In fact, he said he wants to set the date and pick out the invitations."

"How nice," Nancy said flatly.

"I know. It didn't seem like he was interested much in the planning, but he is. You're still going to be my maid of honor, right?"

"Of course, sweetie. I'll stand up for you no matter what you decide to do. When are you thinking about having the big day?"

"I was going to wait until next spring, but now I'm thinking October. I want to go to Colorado for our honeymoon, and fall would be beautiful in the Rockies. That will give us time to shop—I need you to help me pick out my dress. Or maybe we'd have time before you leave for Hawaii. When are you flying out?"

"Tomorrow."

Catlin sat back in her chair. "Tomorrow? So soon?"

Nancy leaned on the desk, head in her hands. "I know it's crazy. But the client's worried about us getting all the field work done in the spring season, so they've authorized an advance on the contract to get me out there ASAP. Michael wants to show them we're responsive. He doesn't want them regretting choosing a small firm for this job. But don't worry, I'll be back in June, and that'll be perfect for wedding dress shopping." She touched Catlin's arm lightly. "You'll be okay?"

"Absolutely." Catlin nodded. "I've got tons to do, plus I started some interesting historical research. But you have tons to do too."

Nancy looked at her watch and sighed. "I know. I've got to get home and pack. Listen, you take care of yourself and call me if you need to talk. But remember I'll be two hours earlier than you."

Catlin laughed. "Right—no early morning calls."

"Uh huh." Nancy smiled and shook her finger. "If you wake me up at four in the morning, I won't be your maid of honor."

They hugged good-bye. Catlin said, "Don't worry about me. You take care of yourself. Don't get bit or stung or fall."

"Yes mom, I'll be careful."

They hugged again and Nancy hurried out. Catlin sniffed and slowly stacked her papers, checked the water in the vase, and switched off the light.

She thought the construction activities would be finished when she got home but was surprised to see Neil and another man standing near her front steps. She parked her car and joined them.

"Catlin, this is David Merritt with the city engineering department," Neil said. "We found something strange when we excavated your lateral today, so I called him."

Catlin shook David's hand and turned to Neil.

"What was strange?"

"It wasn't there."

"What wasn't there?"

"Your lateral."

"I thought you said you excavated it."

"We did." Neil pointed to steel plates covering the street. "Bill dug where it should be, but the pipe wasn't there."

Catlin put her hands on her hips. "Where is it, then? I'm sure when I flush my toilet that stuff is going somewhere."

"We think it's going to your neighbor's backyard," David said.

"Oh my god, that's gross!" Catlin's eyes widened in horror.

"No, it's quite common in these older neighborhoods. The sewage is in a pipe," David assured her, unrolling a map. "But your lateral goes out your backyard into your neighbor's yard and then joins his lateral. See? That's your house, that's your neighbor. His pipe goes into the main on this other street."

"Is that a problem?"

"It's not standard design now. We prefer to have one lateral for each house and for laterals to go out to the street in front."

"It sounds expensive to fix." Catlin looked down at her new shoes regretfully.

"Don't worry. The city pays for this kind of thing," Neil said. "We'll put the new pipe in your side yard and bring it to the street here. I'll check your clean-out tomorrow morning to make sure David's right and get everything fixed. No problem."

"The clean-out?"

"Right—you have a metal lid in your backyard by the fence?"

"Oh. That's what the plumber did a few years ago. He said it would make it easier to snake the line."

"Do you have that done a lot, Miss?" asked David.

"Once or twice a year. Whenever I hear that menacing gurgle in the shower drain. The first time, I ignored it and ended up with a huge mess. Yuck." Catlin shuddered at the memory.

"That won't happen again once we're finished," Neil said. "And you won't need your plumber so much either."

"That sounds great."

"We'll send you the city paperwork this week," David said. "But since Altman is on your block now, we'll have them do the work right away."

"Thank you." They shook hands all around and the men left. Catlin went inside to tell Packard about the latest excitement.

"Okay, you'll have to be on your best behavior tomorrow. The boys are working in your territory. And Neil's looking in the clean-out. I hope it's not gross." She frowned. "Maybe I should do some laundry tonight, huh? Sound like a good idea?"

Packard turned toward the kitchen and barked.

"Does dinner sound like a better idea? Okay, first things first."

She fed him and herself and then took a leisurely walk through the neighborhood, letting Packard sniff his favorite spots. She said hello to Ted Graystone, who was sitting on his front steps.

"How are you, young lady?" he said cheerfully. "And how's this fine gentleman?" He scratched Packard's ears.

"We're doing fine, Ted. How are you?"

"Can't complain. Oh, I could, but that'd be a waste of time. You'll see when you get older. Knees, hips, everything goes. But you gotta keep moving."

"That's good advice."

"It's free, and it's worth exactly what it costs you." They laughed. "How's the construction going your way? You enjoying watching those handsome men?" Ted winked.

Catlin blushed and fussed with the leash. "Oh, you know. They're doing a good job," she stammered.

"They're a hard-working bunch. Saw the city car by your place. What's happening?"

"They're going to replace my lateral. Apparently it goes through Scott Lindstrom's backyard and not to Truman Street."

"Huh! Isn't that a kick in the pants. You'll get to watch them close up, then."

"I'll be at work mostly. Though I guess I'll have to come by at lunch to give Packard a break, since he'll be in the house. Otherwise, he'll want to help dig." She pulled on the leash. "See you later, Ted."

"'Bye, young lady. Have fun."

"Why was Ted teasing me about the workers?" she asked Packard when they were home, giving him an after-walk treat. "They're professional, I'm professional. Anyway, it's laundry time. That'll clean out my clean-out."

She gathered a selection of dirty clothes from the hamper and set the washer going on the back porch. She played catch with Packard, until his tennis ball was soggy and disgusting, and left him contentedly gnawing it under the pine tree. Clothes in the dryer, she reached for the book of Carolyn's letters but hesitated, realizing she should call John first. After all, he did send flowers and apologize. Or asked her to forgive him. She thought about his note. Actually, he had told her to forgive him. Was that the same as apologizing? And twisting her arm until it was black and blue wasn't a silly argument to her. Suddenly she missed Nancy and wished she could call her. But Nancy was busy packing, and Catlin already knew what her advice would be.

Maybe it's time I assumed the mantle of self-reliance like Carolyn, she thought. *If I'm going to have a successful marriage, I've got to address problems head on. I'll call John and tell him . . . the flowers are beautiful, and I appreciate him sending them, but if we can't talk without him getting all angry and violent—no, that's no good. How to phrase it with "I" messages? I'm upset he acted like a jerk in front of the crew. That's guaranteed to start another argument. Keep thinking, Catlin. I feel sad when he gets angry. Hmmm, closer. How about I feel worried we won't be able to discuss issues effectively in our relationship because of this incident. Sounds like something in an environmental document. Perfect.* She was ready.

A cell phone on a glass table toned Beethoven's Ninth. In the next room, guttural cries and grunts continued unabated.

Catlin listened to John's voice mail greeting. "John McKenzie here. I'm busy. Leave a message if you want." *Should I leave a message or hang up?* She blurted at the beep, "Hi it's Catlin. Sorry I missed you. The flowers are beautiful, uh, call when you get a chance. 'Bye."

Is it a danger sign if you feel relieved you got your fiancé's voice mail? she wondered. *It's because we haven't talked yet. Everything will be okay after we have a chance to clear the air. He's probably working late. He's probably feeling guilty and will be glad to get my message.* She glanced at the clock. There was time to read another chapter. She got ready for bed and settled in with the book.

10

Chapter 7 Winter

The signs of renewal are everywhere: trees budding in the forest, daffodils emerging by Abigail's cabin. Iris kicks up her heels on our loop around the sheltered valley. Rushing water has replaced the crunch of snow. Soon our isolation will end. Abigail expects her son to return next week if the spring warmth continues. Her eyes brighten when she speaks of him. I smile and nod, but inwardly I am wary. He is a well-traveled man of business and may not be so trusting of a stranger as his mother.

How odd to miss the winter! We did not have much time to prepare, but Abigail was organized and a good teacher. Together we finished the livestock shelter Matthew had started—new calluses for my hands from hammering. The shed was small, but Iris and Sophronia (a melodious name for a cow, don't you agree?) seemed content to share the warmth with the chickens. It was cleverly linked to the main cabin by an enclosed walkway so we could tend to the animals even if snowbound. I told Abigail all the crooked boards were mine.

I learned many new skills this winter, but the greatest lesson was discovering how little I knew before starting this adventure. Abigail welcomed my provisions with a quiet smile that told me I would have starved on my own. The Lord always provides, indeed.

The vegetable garden was burgeoning, and we harvested for weeks, pulling, washing, chopping, and cooking. We rose with the sun and worked until after dark. Every night, Abigail read from the Bible by a sturdy oil lamp. We did not exchange life stories, as women often do, but instead discussed our philosophies of a useful life. Perhaps she sensed I had secrets I did not wish to share. I could only guess at the experiences that had given her such self-reliance and competence. She did not put everyone else first, sacrificing her own needs. But pleasant outcomes for all invariably flowed from her actions. She inspired by example and taught me to be a full partner in our survival.

One clear night when the full moon lit the valley, we heard the howl of a distant wolf.

"The music of the forest," Abigail said. "We should make our own."

"What shall we use for an instrument?" I asked.

"Wait here." She threw on her cloak and walked out to the farthest cabin, returning with a fine guitar.

"How beautiful!" I exclaimed, caressing the glossy wood and ivory insets.

"Do you play?" she asked me.

"Alas, no," I replied.

"Then I shall teach you. Music is a comfort you can always give yourself. And it is a way to express joy when words fail. We'll start with simple chords."

So we passed the winter with chores, the Bible, and sweet, sweet music. I began composing songs from the

*poetry that filled my head whenever my fingers touched the
guitar strings. Romantic drivel, but Abigail encouraged me,
and I shall end this letter with my best effort, in a minor
chord.*

Yours always,
Carolyn

Pilgrim
On a forest road in the early evening
Shadows swirling like gentle sighs
I chanced upon a wandering pilgrim
With such loneliness in his eyes
That it seemed like all feeling had died
His eyes were quiet blue in color
And cloudy like the misty sea
Glancing up as I passed by him
How their sadness beckoned me
And I thought I heard a silent plea
So I stopped him with a smile and let my travels go
Excuse me sir may we talk for a while
I only want to know
Pilgrim where are you going
Can you tell me who you are
I would like to travel with you
I could help you find your star
And your road would not seem so far
Pilgrim my weary pilgrim
It is a heavy load you bear

Why not let me walk beside you
A burden is lighter when you share
When you know someone is there to care
My words surprised me most of all
It was more than I meant to say
Yet I had heard his silent call so I still blocked his way
You have closed your mind to others
I can see the doors shut one by one
Give me the key so I can unlock them
Open them wide and let in the sun
Set your soul free to laugh and run
Pilgrim I could love you
If you would only let me in
But he refused me smiling sadly
He could trust no one but him
And was gone before I could speak again
On a shrouded road in the forest dim
I met a mournful man
Though I reached out to comfort him
He would not take my hand
No he would not even try to take my hand
And I doubt that I will ever understand

"So she really was a chanteuse," Catlin said, leaning over to scratch Packard. "That's a melancholy song. It's hard to be with someone who's emotionally unavailable. I mean, I imagine it would be hard. John's not emotionally unavailable; he's just tough to read sometimes."

Packard leaned his head back and yowled.

"Oh don't be like that. You know how guys are. I need to get more attuned to his feelings. Then he wouldn't get angry. Anyway, it's time to fold clothes. Too bad you can't help; you sure get out of a lot of housework because you don't have opposable thumbs."

She tended to the laundry and, finally satisfied that everything was as neat and clean as possible, went to bed.

11

When the alarm rang the next morning, Catlin woke up breathless, as if she had been running all through the night. But whether it was from something or to something, she couldn't remember.

"It probably means I need to get back into my jogging routine," she told Packard as she fixed his breakfast. "That will be a good thing to do after work today. Yes, after Frisbee for you," she added when Packard stopped mid-crunch to eye her. "You'll need to get out since you'll be cooped up most of the day."

She finished her morning bathroom routine and then went back to her bedroom to get dressed. Standing naked in front of the closet, she faced her daily conundrum of what to wear. The new black pumps, of course. How would a suede jacket look? Male voices floated past her window. She instinctively gasped and pulled a dress on a hanger across her body. She laughed. The curtain was drawn, but knowing Neil was on the other side of the wall made her nervous. *Okay, Catlin, decision time.* She grabbed a straight black skirt, turning to her bureau for hose, bra, and a red top. Earrings, watch, her necklace, and she was done.

"Sorry to skip your morning walk, but I've got an important meeting in the backyard. I'll fill you in later, okay?" She checked her hair in the mirror and slid out the back door.

Neil and Francisco stopped their conversation when she walked up.

"Good timing," Neil greeted her. "We were just getting ready to pop the lid."

"Good morning, *amigita*," Francisco said. "Your little house had a surprise for us, *verdad*?"

Catlin nodded. "I knew this was the oldest house on the block, but I didn't realize that meant the sewer was different."

"Your plumber should have told you what the situation was," Neil said as he pried up the metal lid. "I guess he liked the regular work—look at that! Holy sh—"

Francisco squatted next to Neil and they both tsked and clucked as they peered into the opening.

Catlin stood on tiptoes, straining to see over their backs, dreading the mess they must be looking at. "Is it pretty bad?" she asked.

Neil shook his head. "Man, that's one flat line. It's amazing you get any flow at all."

Francisco stood. "But it's a very clean clean-out. Don't be afraid to look." He moved aside and pointed. "See how the pipe angles off? It probably meets your neighbor's lateral near the corner of his house."

"Oh. But you can fix it, right?"

Neil turned in his lowered position and eyed her side yard like a golfer lining up a difficult putt. "There's not much room between your house and the neighbor's wall," he said, rising.

"But we don't have to dig very deep until the part nearest the street," Francisco added.

They looked at each other, nodded, and said in unison, "Smurf."

Catlin tilted her head. "You're going to dig with a fuzzy blue cartoon character?"

Neil laughed. "Sounds crazy, huh? But it's one of Bill's favorite things, so we use it whenever we can."

"Okaay," Catlin replied, arching an eyebrow at Francisco, who gazed back innocently.

"*Es la verdad*, Bill loves the Smurf," he assured her with mock seriousness. "But it's not a cartoon," he said after Neil sauntered off, whistling, to pace the length of the side yard. "It's a backhoe *pequeño*."

"Why would you call a little backhoe a Smurf?"

"Neil named it that because it's blue and because he likes to tease Bill about riding a Smurf. Not nice, I know. Neil can be cruel sometimes." Francisco shook his head.

"In spite of that, I haven't fired you yet," Neil said, coming up behind him. "You have a lot of work to do, my friend. Greg got the approval from the city on the bid for the extra work. Here's the list of what you need to finish by noon, thank you, and good-bye." Neil handed Francisco a sheet of paper and shooed him away. "I know what that word means now, so don't be calling me that," he said as Francisco walked off muttering.

"Sorry we're keeping you from your day," Neil said, turning back to Catlin.

"No, that's fine, it's all so interesting. What will you do here today?"

"We'll start the trench later this afternoon. We'll need to take this gate off. Is that going to be okay?"

"Sure. I planned to keep Packard in the house anyway."

"He can be out here until afternoon if you can come back at lunchtime. Francisco has to get a lot of equipment from another site."

"Packard will like that. I'll leave him in the yard when I go to work, and I'll come back at twelve."

"Sounds good. See you later." Neil let himself out and clicked the gate shut.

Catlin exhaled. "That went fine, I think," she said, trotting to the back door. "Okay, the coast is clear, Budbutt, you may sniff at will."

Packard rushed into the yard, madly snorted where the men had stood, and pawed at the ground near the clean-out.

"Oh no you don't!" Catlin grabbed his collar before he could roll where the lid had sat. "Go take a break and then you can have a cookie."

Distracted by the c word, Packard complied and enjoyed his reward.

"Be good and I'll be back soon," Catlin told him as she locked up and left for work.

When she arrived, she found the office considerably quieter than the day before. Mark had already developed a chart with assignments for the biologists, who were, predictably, already grumbling about the change of pace.

"I'm going to whip this team into shape," he told Catlin. "Nancy's been way too easy on these guys."

"A balanced approach isn't a bad thing, you know. People can get resistive if you ask too much of them."

"People need to work harder, like me. There's twenty-four hours in a day, and I use them all."

"Except when you're sleeping, I hope."

"Sleeping's overrated. I'll sleep when I'm dead. Right now there's too much to do. I've got big plans." Mark lowered his voice. "I could take this company to the next level if Michael put me in charge of marketing. The job in Hawaii is small potatoes compared to what I could do."

"Isn't marketing Joan's job?"

"Yeah. And look what she's done: absolutely nothing. She hasn't even managed to write a job description for herself, let alone resumes and project descriptions for proposals. Michael had to do everything for the Hawaii job. He should have canned her a long time ago. She's useless."

"I'm sure she does something."

"You don't like her either—admit it."

"She can be abrasive. It's that East Coast attitude, I guess."

"Always the diplomat. So why were you late this morning? You're usually the prompt one."

"There's construction going on at my house. The city's going to have my sewer lateral re-done, and the foreman was looking at my clean-out. I was worried it would be a mess, but I did some laundry last night, so it was okay."

Mark laughed. "Only you would worry about how your clean-out looks, Catlin. Listen, I rearranged Anita's priorities and told her to get your reservoir work done first."

"Thanks! I didn't think she'd be available. She's the best."

"I knew you'd appreciate getting her on your project. So anyway, put in a good word for me with Michael, okay? He trusts you."

"You know how he hates changes, Mark. I don't think it'd make a difference if I said something. It would have to come from Nancy for him to pay attention."

"Perfect. You're brilliant. Start with her, then."

"Umm . . ."

"Hey, I gotta run, but thanks for your help."

Catlin watched him walk away, lips pursed. *There's an assignment I don't need. Everyone has all these agendas besides their work. It's so confusing. I wonder what it would have been like to be here when it was only Michael and Nancy.* She looked at her watch and shook her head. Late late late. She hurried into her office and dove into her document.

Eleven thirty came before she knew it. "I'm going home for lunch, Gabrielle," she called out, and took the back door so she wouldn't have to go past Mark's office. She parked around the corner from her house, which was a wise decision because her driveway was filled with plastic pipe. Sitting in her front yard was the cutest baby blue backhoe; it looked like a toy compared to the excavator.

"Hey," Neil said as she walked closer. "What do you think of our Smurf?"

"It's adorable. I love it."

"You'll have to fight Bill, then. He can't get enough of it."

"Yeah. She's a tight ride," Bill grunted, squeezing into the cab. "Now how does this work? I always forget." He turned on the switch and fiddled with the levers.

"Try to be more careful with the house than you were with the hydrant," Neil warned as the bucket swung sideways.

"Oops. Guess up and down is the other one. Don't worry, honey," Bill assured Catlin. "I promise not to break anything, in the next hour, anyway. Lunchtime, boss?"

Neil checked his watch and nodded. "Looks like your living room window gets a reprieve, Cat. I'm kidding," he added at her concerned look. "It'll be fine."

"Yeah, I'm always a little nervous right before lunch," Bill said. "I'll calm down after my ham sandwich and a smoke. I can't believe my doctor wants to put me on blood pressure pills. I'm way too young for that. Once you start taking that stuff, you never stop."

"Yeah. That's a real mystery," Neil snorted. "Smoking and eating too much have nothing to do with your blood pressure, obviously."

"I could stop smoking any time. I'm just worried I'll lose my girlish figure." Bill patted his expansive stomach fondly. "So where do you stand on the cancer stick question, honey? Think all that medical crap is a hoax to keep people from looking cool?"

"Oh, well, I don't want to tell anyone what to do," Catlin said. "But I wouldn't want people smoking near the house."

She gestured toward the wood siding. "Or in the backyard—Packard thinks anything that falls on the ground is legally his to eat, and cigarette butts wouldn't be very healthy."

"Nicely put," Neil said. "You could work for the U.N. We'll be back at one to get started."

"I'll have Packard in the house then."

"You know some of these plants are gonna go, right? We haven't talked about that. Bill's good, but he won't be able to miss those bushes." Neil swept his hand over the rosemary and then stopped, bemused. "Smells good, reminds me of Thanksgiving."

Bill hopped eagerly out of the backhoe and sniffed. "Mmm, dressing and gravy from scratch, just like Mom's. There goes my diet." He laughed and set off to join the crew.

"Sure, I understand I'll have to replace the landscaping," Catlin said.

"It's part of the deal. You tell me what these are and how many need to be replanted, and we'll do it. Let's see what Bill destroys, and then we'll negotiate. But be gentle with me, okay?" He eyed her slyly.

"Um." Catlin squirmed in her incoherence, torn between a professional or flirtatious response. "Okay," she replied. *That was lame. Why does my brain keep turning to mush? It's so annoying. He must think I'm an idiot.*

"Don't worry about how things look for the next couple days. We'll get it all back to normal." Neil touched his hand to his hard hat in a polite salute. "Lunch break, everybody," he called, and left.

"'Bye," Catlin said quietly, her mind still chastising. *Did I make him feel awkward? I wish I wasn't such a dimwit. Nancy would know how to be cool, why haven't I learned anything from her? I give up, I want some chocolate.* Finally smiling at a positive thought, she went inside.

"Hey, how's your day going?" she greeted Packard. "You didn't roll after I left, did you?" She sniffed cautiously at his neck. "Good boy," she said, detecting no undesirable odors.

Packard returned the sniff, snuffling at her ears and licking her nose.

"Thank you for the kisses, that's nice. Now what's for lunch? How about a cheese sandwich?" She reached into the fridge and laughed as Packard immediately sat by the butcher-block counter to await spillage or a handout. "Yes, of course you'll get a piece."

She checked her answering machine on the way out, feeling that same sense of relief at the absence of messages as she did when John didn't answer her call. *That's okay, we're both busy*, she told herself. *We'll get it straightened out at some point.* "Don't bark at the boys through the windows," she admonished Packard and went back to work.

The roses were already starting to droop; she got a glass and topped off the water in the vase. She touched a blood-red blossom, rising from the cloud of baby's breath like a spring bud through snow, and thought of Carolyn cantering through a secret valley. Why couldn't the book editor find records of Carolyn? Of course, 1963 was a long time ago. It was easier to find people now, living or dead, with the Web. Her mother was enjoying genealogical research much more now that she had a subscription to Ancestry.com. Maybe she should take a drive out to Palm Springs and spend the weekend with her folks. Mom would like to help with a research project. And the wedding planning—her mother had been reminding Catlin more and more that they needed to get that going.

As if on cue, Gabrielle appeared at her office door. "Hi. I'm so glad you're back. John called here while you were gone. I didn't know where you were, and he was upset. He said to call him ASAP."

"I'm sorry. I should have gone to your desk when I left to make sure you knew I was going home for lunch."

"I didn't think of that when you didn't answer the page. I tried to tell him the flowers were beautiful, but he said he expects a receptionist to be more helpful and hung up." Gabrielle sniffed.

"I'm sorry. He didn't mean to hurt your feelings. He's very busy and stressed out right now. It was my fault to not tell you where I was going. I'll call him right away."

"Okay. Thanks."

Catlin fidgeted with her Rolodex, although she knew the number by heart. She'd like to put off the call a while longer, but she promised Gabrielle, so now she was stuck. If John had been more patient . . . "Oh, punch the number," she whispered. One ring, two . . . *maybe he's out now.*

"John McKenzie's office."

"Hi Angela. Is John in?"

"May I ask who's calling?"

"It's Catlin." *Why doesn't she know by now?*

"Let me see if he's available. Please hold."

Classical music surged in the wire, Beethoven, naturally. *I wish John liked other music*, she thought, remembering her early dating years, line dancing at country western bars. He refused to learn the two-step and wouldn't think of wearing boots, saying there was nothing dumber than a cowboy. Not wanting to hear such comments, she dropped that activity. Pieces of herself falling by the wayside in the hopes of pleasing . . . why did she do that?

"I'm busy here."

Catlin nearly dropped the phone as it abruptly came to life. "Hi, I called as soon as I got back from lunch. I had to go home to, uh, check on Packard." She remembered to not mention the construction crew at the last minute.

"I had a window then to return your call. I don't have time to talk now."

"That's okay. Give me a call later whenever works for you."

"Fine. Don't hold your breath."

"What?"

"I was telling Angela don't hold George Smith. I've got to take another call—talk to you later."

"Okay, 'bye," Catlin said to the dial tone.

He's still miffed, but at least we've got that first awkward phone conversation out of the way, she told herself. *Now the ball's in his court and I can get back to work.*

Happier than she thought she should be with the phone still smoking from John's annoyance, she pulled out the traffic study for her reservoir project, losing herself in estimates of truck trips and intersection delays.

She stayed at work longer than she intended, and everything was quiet when she got home. The gate was off its hinges but had been set against the opening securely enough for Packard to be in the backyard. She let him out and then went to the side yard.

"Neil wasn't kidding about the plants," she sighed, looking at the open trench and fragrant jumble of rosemary, wildflowers, and dirt that now constituted her landscaping.

The Smurf sat with bucket downcast, as if ashamed of the damage.

"That's okay, little fellow," she said, patting it affectionately. "You're doing a good deed. It'll be fun to do something different here, anyway."

After tending to Packard, she changed into shorts, stretched, and headed back to the park for a blissful hour.

Running was more than simply exercising to her; it stimulated a Zen state that yoga, with that constant pressure to quiet the mind, couldn't match. Breathing in time with footfalls crunching on the dirt trail that circled the quiet mesa beyond the softball fields, she could think whatever she wanted or not think at all. A red-tailed hawk soared overhead, searching for dinner. The late afternoon off-shore breeze flowed past, cooling her skin as she pushed it uphill, loped down, and let it all out at the end for that rewarding euphoric surge.

As always, she gave a little prayer of thanks to the universe for health and stamina while she stretched, panting and sweating, before walking home. After an early shower and quick dinner, she was ready for another chapter.

Chapter 8 Wanderings

I escaped again in the dead of night, trusting God to guide my steps. I led Iris quietly from her comfortable shed, patting Sophronia in gratitude for her milk that sustained us through the winter. I wished I could have stayed with Abigail. But her son and tenants would return soon, and with them, I feared, would come questions I did not want to answer. I could not bear to lie to her or to see her disappointment in my character if I told the truth. So I packed a few provisions, no greater than I had brought months ago, and whispered good-bye while she slept, tucking a carefully worded note of thanks under the neatly folded quilt on my cot for her to find in the morning.

As you may have guessed, the names of my winter angel, her family, and animal companions are of my own making. They treasure their seclusion, and I would not wish for any other strangers to find their valley. By morning, I planned to be well along the trail to a mining town Abigail had mentioned. It appeared a likely place to obtain supplies and to secure passage for my missives to you.

During the winter of work, prayer, and song, I had set aside my sin and sorrow. But these burdens mounted my soul as soon as I mounted Iris at the top of the narrow track and turned into the forest. Patches of snow gleamed in the moonlight. I leaned close to my horse's warm neck as she trod slowly under the trees, the sodden undergrowth of ferns and pine needles sucking at her hooves. My fingers on her pulse reminded me of quiet moments lying with my love, feeling his steady heartbeat. I cannot claim that I treasured those times cradled in his arms above all else, as every moment was precious, but remembering brought a smile to my lips.

Dawn found us almost through the forest. The trees thinned at a tumble of rocks, and Iris stopped, nostrils flaring, head raised into a breeze that carried an ominous scent. We turned at the sound of thrashing and stared at a patch of vegetation near the outcrop. Round black eyes in a giant head topped by tufted ears stared back. Huge clawed paws carried the head closer, and a hump of golden-tinged fur followed. Finally the entire vision emerged: a hulking grizzly, hungry and angry at unwelcome intruders. The head tilted and exploded into a horror of teeth, the forest echoing with a powerful roar. I had no gun, no defense. The bear would destroy us both with a sudden charge.

He roared again, and I could not resist my instinctive response: I yawned. "Iris, he is sleepy; he just woke up," I whispered. "The breeze is toward us. He does not know he has company." We backed away as the bear sat on its haunches, casually scratching. Once in the clear, I set Iris to a gallop, and we raced into the sunrise.

Ensconced in the valley, I had forgotten the glorious views from these ridges. As the sky lightened, so did my heart, and I reveled in the scenery through the day. Water was plentiful in the snowmelt streams, and newly leafed trees granted shade. Across the expanse I caught a glimpse of wagons, white "sails" aloft, skimming over the high grass. Abigail reported that the farming in the plains was near to paradise, with deep fertile soils and endless water supplies. Her cabin walls were papered with enticements from knowledgeable parties on the independent life for homesteaders. An intriguing proposition. The winter granted seclusion, but soon only a black dress and veil will hide me. Could the sea of prairie be my shelter, where I could toil alone, free of questions? What a relief it would be to not have to escape into darkness again!

I did not hurry my approach to town but slept peacefully that night in a cabin still awaiting the return of its owner. I dreamed of working where I could show my face without fear and awoke determined to join a line of prairie schooners headed to the plains.

A foray into the blighted town that had been my goal set my mind to this plan. My widow's garb generated respect but also unwanted proposals of marriage. The miners apparently have been so bereft of female companionship that they are willing to request the hand of a woman whose face is completely hidden. I dashed their hopes with a bowed head. There would only be one master of my heart, and I shall strive to earn the right to meet him again in the next life.

After obtaining suitable accommodations for Iris, I obtained a tiny room in a respectable house and took a solitary meal there. I decided to return to Mary for a visit, leave these letters for transport to you, and (if I can rely on your beneficence) "emigrate" to a new life.

I left town early the following morning, heading in the direction recommended by my host. Comfortable with supplies, Iris and I enjoyed a meandering ride, descending into gorges and ascending peaks, the glorious mountains always in the distance. I slept on the ground with forest litter for bedding, and stars for my candle. Visits to scattered settlements invariably proved disappointing, such that the appearance of lights as dusk approached was my signal to turn back into the forest. But finally I reconciled to the necessity of returning to civilization. On that last night, I waded into a crystalline stream. In spite of the chill, I sat on a rounded rock, leaned back, and let the gentle current wash weeks of traveling from my limbs and hair. I rubbed myself dry and dressed in the one clean gown I had been saving.

Refreshed, I recalled a long-ago day with my love. A secret horseback ride led us to a hidden pool where we became nature's children, laughing, scampering, and wrestling as if we were the blessed inhabitants of the original Garden. Can it be sin to know such joy as I found in his body? We rolled in fragrant grasses, building heat, and then splashed into the water where he lifted me onto him. Blissfully impaled and entwined, we set the pool to ripples that pulsed outward to our rhythm, creating wavelets on the shore.

With these pleasant thoughts, I readied my primitive bed. Tomorrow I shall relate the welcome this prodigal daughter receives and then bundle my winter letters to you.
Yours always,
Carolyn

"I can't believe what she writes to her mom. I couldn't talk about sex like that," Catlin said. *Not that there'd be all that much to share,* she sighed inwardly. "Anyway, tomorrow I'll look through my packet of letters to see if her mom responded." She yawned. "What would you do if you saw a bear? Would you growl and protect me?"

Packard yawned.

"Oh, would you show him professional courtesy because you look like a bear?" She laughed and ruffled his fur. "Okay, time for bed. We'll get up early tomorrow so you get your walk before the boys start working in the yard."

That night, she dreamed she swam in a clear river. She was content swimming alone, although it was hard work because the current was strong. Then a handsome man joined her, not saying a word, and suddenly the current diminished, the sun shone brighter, and it was easier to make progress. They came to a place where the water was shallow and they could stand. She stretched into the sun, feeling a warm breeze on her shoulders.

The man said, "We can go back the way we came."

Catlin said, "No, I want to keep going forward." So they swam on.

13

The alarm rang at five thirty. She groped in the dark for the button and then switched on the light.

Packard nudged his head under the blanket on his sleeping pad.

"I'm doing this for you. I don't like getting up in the dark any more than you do," she told him.

Once they were in the park, she was glad to witness the sunrise, palm trees on the distant mesa silhouetted against the pastel sky. While Catlin gazed at the rosy horizon, Packard focused on the fuzzy silhouette of a squirrel. When it darted toward a nearby tree, he bolted, yanking the leash from her hand. "Hey!" she shouted. "You knucklehead! When are you going to learn those guys are too fast for you?"

Packard barked up into the tree, front paws braced on the trunk. The squirrel chided him from the safety of a high branch for rudely interrupting his breakfast.

"Okay, that's enough hullabaloo for one morning. Let's go home. I need to get to work early today so I can let you out at lunch."

At the office before anyone else, she kept the front door locked and pushed her own door nearly shut so she wouldn't be distracted by her co-workers. When she heard Michael arrive, she considered talking with him about Mark's idea. But she didn't like Mark any more than she liked Joan. His aggressive approach always made her cringe. He often teased her for being "excruciatingly honest," leaving her to wonder where he drew the line at the truth. Besides, she didn't want to use Nancy to influence Michael. *Why make Mark's agenda my priority?* she asked herself. *I'll tell him he's on his own for any career changes. And hope he doesn't ask until he's finished his work on my project,* she thought, knowing his penchant for revenge against perceived slights.

Hands suspended above the keyboard, she realized that she could hear Michael's phone conversation in the early morning quiet.

"Hey, did I wake you? Sorry. Right, you never were an early bird." He chuckled. "So, settled in? Yeah? Okay place? Uh huh, what'd I tell you? Nothing but the best. Flight went all right? Really? Shoes off too? Brother. That's why I hate to fly any more. They might as well play sexy music and tuck some bills in my pants. Then I always miss a belt loop and feel like an idiot later. Chronic problem, right, thanks." Another low laugh. "Got the meeting set with Jason? Yeah, they've got a good rep. Uh huh. You want me to conference in? Okay, let me know, it's no problem. Oh, he's doing fine. Getting off on being the big boss. No, no, don't worry. He needs the chance to experience the joys of supervision. I'll reel him in if I have to. Ah now. They'll survive. Just think how much more they'll appreciate you when you get back. Okay. You too. 'Bye." He hummed as he bustled around his office.

Catlin sat motionless. *Would Michael be upset if he knew I overheard him? Should I make a noise or go out and pretend to come in? But if I do that, would he think I thought there was anything to be embarrassed about in his conversation? I wouldn't want him to think I think there's anything between him and Nancy that isn't strictly professional. Which I don't, of course. It's just . . . that talk of early birds and belt loops sounded so . . . intimate. Well, they've worked together a long time. That's it. At least I know he's on to Mark. I'll call Nancy later in the week.* She breathed a sigh and relaxed her hands, still frozen above the keyboard, when the front door opened and other staff hustled in.

She made a point of telling Gabrielle she was headed home at lunchtime. Someone new operated the excavator. Bill delicately maneuvered the Smurf in her yard; he barely glanced up when she joined Neil on the sidewalk. "How's it going?" she asked.

Neil shook his head. "Slower than I'd hoped. That hardpan layer is just deep enough to be a problem. Like there weren't enough rocks already."

"That's quite a pile in the street."

"Yeah. Feel free to take all you want. It's weight to haul away for us."

"That's a good idea. Maybe I'll do a rock garden out here when it's all done."

"Don't forget plants are included. We could go to Home Depot in my truck and you can get whatever you like. You point and I'll buy. Within reason." He grinned.

"Plant shopping sounds fun. But I can take an hour to pick out a pair of shoes, so you might want to think twice about your offer."

"That doesn't scare me—crap!—Bill, watch it!" Neil sprinted up the yard at a loud crack and a groan from the Smurf.

"Oh my god," Catlin said. "Is it hurt?"

Bill's concerned face dissolved into laughter. "No, Baby's okay. I just strained the hydraulics. Probably time to give it a rest before we both overheat."

"Good idea." Neil touched the machine and quickly drew back his hand. "But we need to finish up soon or Greg's gonna have our heads. How far will you be by the end of the day?"

"Mostly there. Lemme smoke on it. Can't rush this tight work, boss. You know that." Bill winked and pulled out a pack from his jacket pocket.

"Yeah yeah." Neil signaled the rest of the crew. "Tell Packard he can take a break from supervising," he said to Catlin. "He's been in the window all morning."

"He likes to watch the excavation."

"Maybe he's picking up pointers on digging."

"I hope not. My sprinkler system couldn't stand it." They laughed.

"I've got to head south to check on another job, so catch you later."

"Okay. Thanks for everything you're doing. I really appreciate it."

"No problem. All in a day's work."

Packard barked and scratched at the window.

"Oops, I better let him out. That's his 'hurry up, mom' bark."

"I'll let you go. See you tomorrow."

"Great." She smiled and dared a glance at his eyes, hidden by sunglasses, wondering what he was thinking as she gazed at her reflection.

Packard barked again. Catlin jumped, gave a little wave, and trotted up the stairs.

"Okay okay," she said to Packard. He jumped off the window seat. "Just when we were having a nice conversation. Couldn't you wait a few more minutes?"

Packard answered with a yowl and an emphatic tap at the back door.

"Sorry. I know how that can be." She opened the door and he raced into the backyard to his favorite spot.

"Thank you for waiting. You're a good boy." She came outside to guard the opening to the side yard. "But don't go wandering off. They don't need your help with the trench."

Packard dropped his tennis ball at her feet and backed up.

"That's a good idea. You need to work off some steam." After a few throws, she said, "Let's go in. I've got to have some lunch and head back to work."

She checked with Gabrielle to make sure there were no messages before settling at her desk. As she was getting back into her stride, Joan barged in.

"Look who got roses. Very nice. But you're letting them wilt. You should take better care of them so they'll last. Here's what to do. Write this down, Catlin, you'll never remember it all." She gestured toward a pad of paper and waited until Catlin picked up a pen. "All right. First drain all the water from the vase and then trim a half inch from the bottom of each stem. You have to cut diagonally and use good sharp scissors. Now, this is very important—are you getting it all? Mix a quarter cup of sugar in with enough water to refill the vase. That's the key. Hardly anyone takes the time to care for bouquets. Someone spent a lot of money for those flowers, so you should show how much you appreciate it. Right?"

Catlin nodded and quickly flipped the page over so Joan couldn't review her notes. "Thank you. I think I got it. That's very helpful. Did you need something?"

"Yes, yes. Your flowers distracted me." She lowered her considerable bulk into Catlin's guest chair and leaned forward. "It's Mark," she whispered.

"Mark? Is he sick?"

"Don't be dense. No, he's not sick. I wouldn't care if he was. He's plotting to replace me. He wants my job. Not that he could do it. He has no idea how hard marketing is or the first thing about what to do." Joan's whisper became a hiss. "Oh but he has big plans, big man, so important."

Catlin shifted in her chair. "How do you know? He's pretty busy with the biology group."

"I know what I know. I hear he's talking to people, kissing up. Has he talked to you? I noticed he put Anita on your job.

Barbara's not too happy, by the way. Her Farview Ranch housing project was supposed to be Anita's first priority."

"I didn't ask him to reassign Anita," Catlin protested. "I assume he thought it would be more efficient for her to do the reservoir work first, since it's a smaller area."

"Sure. Such an efficiency expert. When I asked for his help with the award announcements, he couldn't manage to buy the stamps. Didn't he ask for something from you in return for his efficient idea?"

Catlin tapped her pen. Office intrigue always made her nervous. That's why she liked working for a small company. But the backstabbing had increased when these two were hired, and Michael seemed resigned to their battles. More than once, she had heard him comment, "The trouble with offices is that they're full of people."

"Mark never said he would reassign Anita if I did him a favor," she told Joan. "He just said he would have her do the reservoir work first. I can't tell you why he did it. Anyway, it's a tight time schedule, and I should get back to it. There's a lot to do."

Failing to find an opening for argument, Joan lifted herself from the chair. "Fine. But in case the efficiency expert should ask, you can tell him I know what he's up to. I'm not stupid."

"Of course not. Talk to you later." Catlin followed her to the door and closed it to silently mouth a frustrated scream. Thus calmed, she opened the door, took a quick drink of water, and returned to her keyboard.

At the end of the day, she stacked her papers and eyed the roses. *Maybe these things would be better off at home*, she thought, and took them into the ladies room, where she poured out the water from the vase. Returning to her office, she ripped the page of notes on flower care from her pad, crumpled it into a tight ball, and tossed it in the trash. She picked up her purse and shouldered the bouquet.

She was relieved to see the pipe had been moved from her driveway to the yard so she could park the car. She lugged the flowers inside and let Packard out. "How was your day supervising?"

He raced around the yard three times in reply, barked at her, and raced around in the opposite direction. Then he spit the tennis ball at her feet and backed up.

"Right, first things first." Catlin laughed and threw the ball, finally stopping the game with a promise of dinner and Frisbee.

Before heading to the park, she walked Packard in the side yard to check on the construction progress. The trench was completed from sidewalk to clean-out. The Smurf rested its bucket on a pile of dirt, ready to fill the trench back in. The scene in the street was similar with the excavator poised to finish the job.

"Looks like the crew will be done soon. What'll you do for excitement then?" she asked, as much to herself as to the dog. "That's okay, it's time to get back to normal anyway," she said, and tugged him from a thorough sniffing of the Smurf.

With chores finished and Packard curled up in a corner, Catlin retrieved her remembrance box. She shook out her grandmother's tablecloth, recalling the clink of china and Waterford crystal from family meals as the cut lace fabric floated over her oak pedestal dining table. She pulled on her cotton gloves and untied the packet of letters, gently smoothing the green satin ribbon flat. She laid the letters she now considered the first two aside and unfolded another.

My Dearest C,
My heart aches for you. It is as dark as these mournful winter skies. Yet our work continues. I trust you receive the contents of this packet before you embark. I shall pray that God lights your sorrowful path.
You are in my heart and prayers,
J

"This one could be her mom's reply to Chapter 5's letter," Catlin told Packard, who snoozed on. "What, are you going to sleep through the excitement? This is history being discovered." She chuckled. "Never mind. I'll let you know how it all turns out later." She picked up another letter from the stack.

My Dearest C,
How joyful I am to know the angels watched over you through the winter, providing music, work, and sustenance. With the spring comes hope and prosperity. Our hands are busy, as will yours be, though at different labors. The

contents of this packet will attest that support for your plan
is assured. May God continue to guide you toward the light.
    You are in my heart and prayers,
    J

"And this one is next, after her mom got the winter letters. I
bet she sent more money. 'If I can rely on your beneficence.'
What a great line. Why didn't I think of that in college?" She
turned back to the book of Carolyn's letters. "Okay, that takes
us through Chapter 8. Unless she wrote one more about
coming back to the hotel." She flipped to Chapter 9 and
hunched forward eagerly.

Chapter 9 A Prodigal's Return
I timed my arrival for the quiet so as to slip in unnoticed by
all but Mary. The joy that lit her eyes brought tears to mine.
Would that my soul deserved such a welcome. Alas, I fear
that I shall always be unworthy. Not by virtue of the act
itself but by a lack of repentance. Had I resigned to the path
determined by the evil one, would I now be sleeping peace-
fully and my love bearing heartbreak? For I could never
have walked that path any great distance without succumb-
ing to the ultimate despair. One must continue ever forward.
And for this one, forward is down to my basement lair. I
shall spend my days with hands immersed again, awaiting
your reply.
    Yours always,
    Carolyn

"Waiting for money. I can relate. But earning your own living is important. Maybe you should get a paper route." She got up to rub his ears. "What do you say?"

Packard stretched and rolled over for a tummy rub.

"Oh, that's dignified." Catlin laughed. "Okay, maybe you should stick to what you know, being adorable and keeping my blood pressure down. Those are good jobs too."

She continued the massage while she thought about the letters. Did they fit, or was she making them coincide because it would be interesting? If the letters from J to C are to Carolyn, how did her great-grandmother get them? She remembered her mom's frustration in doing genealogical research on the female line. Her great-grandmother was adopted as a baby from an orphanage in the early 1900s, and no one knew her original name. Her mother had given up and had more fun researching the Davis line, tracing ancestors back to Charlemagne and assuring Catlin that someday she'd be interested in her own family history. "If Carolyn is a relative, Mom will be right, as usual. Let's think about this scientifically, Packard."

He twitched his hind leg.

"Did I find your tickle spot? Okay, you can go back to your pre-bedtime nap. I need to make some notes."

She returned to the table. "Hypothesis number one: Carolyn is C, and her mother is J. Number two, they're in my family line. Therefore, my ancestor, Carolyn Parker, wrote the letters that were found in Denver, and my ancestor J wrote letters to Carolyn, which were kept in the family. What else? Carolyn did something terrible that she felt was justified but put her on the run." She shook her head. "Maybe I'm trying too hard to figure everything out before I have all the facts. I should read the rest of the book first. But not tonight." She gathered the letters and stored them away, then called Packard to bed.

Catlin stood naked in the dark at the top of a long flight of stairs. A chill twisted around her body and slithered between her legs. She shivered underneath the thin blanket draped over her shoulders. Each step took her deeper into the unknown. Tears of despair ran down her face. She stepped onto a narrow landing where the staircase split in two. A voice said, "Choose." She moaned. An unseen force pushed her, and she fell into the blackness.

She jerked awake to Packard's face inches from hers, his paws on her arm. He licked her cheek.

"Thanks. That was a scary dream. I'm lucky to have a nightmare guardian." She rubbed his head and they both settled back to sleep.

14

She smacked the snooze button twice before dragging herself out of bed the next morning. "These weird dreams are wearing me out. Maybe we need a change of scenery. Would you like to take a drive to the desert this weekend?"

Packard barked.

"Good. I'll call Mom and see if they can entertain guests. We'll leave tomorrow afternoon if the boys are done." Happy to have a positive focus, she greeted the crew with a smile when she passed the trailer on the way back from the park.

"Morning," Neil said. "Did you see that Bill managed to dig the whole trench without hitting your house?"

"I did. Thank you, Bill."

"It's all in the wrist," Bill said.

"Yeah, but don't thank him too soon," Neil said. "He still has to fill in the hole."

"It looks like you'll be finished with everything soon."

"Yep. They'll lay the pipe and make the connections today. Probably have time to backfill too, right?"

"You bet, boss," Bill replied. "Laying pipe is what we do best." He hitched his jeans and waggled his eyebrows at Catlin.

"Bill's the fastest at it, and he has the smallest machine," Neil said.

"Guess I walked into that one. Think I'll go start up my little machine." Bill walked off with an irritated snort.

"Sorry, Cat. Sometimes the guys get out of line with residents."

"Oh no, everyone's been wonderful. Are you really going to finish up today?"

"If all goes well. We start on Blair Street tomorrow."

"Then you'll still be here?"

"Yeah, we'll keep the trailer here for the duration. It's a good staging area. You won't be rid of us for a while."

"That's great." Catlin smiled.

"Glad you think so. Maybe we'll put this big guy to work filling in trenches. What do you say, buddy? Need a job?" Neil scratched Packard and laughed when the dog leaped up to lick his face.

"Hey, no jumping!" Catlin pulled back on the leash. "I'm sorry. He usually doesn't do that."

"No problem. Maybe he wanted to know what I had for breakfast."

Catlin giggled. An image of handing him a plate of eggs in a sunny kitchen flashed through her mind. The roar of the loader jarred her from the pleasant domestic scene. "I should let you get to work."

"Yeah. Hey, can I get your work phone in case we have any trouble with the connection today? Just to be on the safe side."

"Sure." She recited the numbers, feeling her heart race as she watched him write them down. *It's been a long time since someone's taken my number. Of course, it's not the same.*

This is a professional thing. It's not like he's going to ask me out.

"Thanks. And let me know if you want to go get some plants when we're done. Like I said, we'll be here a while. You can take your time deciding what you want."

"That's so nice. Thank you."

"You bet." Neil's phone beeped, and he waved good-bye as he turned away to answer it.

Catlin walked home, commenting to Packard that it looked like it would be a good day after all.

Her contented mood spread through the office, even to Mark, who shrugged and said, "That's cool," when Catlin told him she hadn't had a chance to call Nancy yet. No one was around when she returned home at noon to give Packard a break, but she didn't worry, knowing that the early morning greetings would continue. She enjoyed a quick lunch and returned to work. She would remember later that it was about three o'clock when she heard Gabrielle's page while walking back from the ladies room.

"Catlin, you have a call on line two. Catlin, line two."

Anticipating round two with John, she hurried into her office, stomach tight with dread. She took a deep breath and picked up the receiver. "This is Catlin."

"Hey, Cat, it's Neil with Altman."

"Hi!" She couldn't keep the relief from her voice.

"I wanted to let you know everything's wrapping up fine." He continued as she listened, leaning into the sound of his voice as if into a caress.

"Uh huh. Okay. You are?" She burst out laughing. "That's so funny. All right. Thanks so much." She giggled again. "See you tomorrow."

The smile from their conversation stayed on her face until she pulled into the driveway that evening and saw a black BMW parked out front.

John was on his cell phone, standing on the sidewalk and gesturing impatiently. He flipped the phone shut when she walked up, and kissed her cheek.

"Hi, babe. Sorry I couldn't talk longer before. Clients, you know. The office has been a madhouse. Thought I'd come out here so we can talk without interruptions."

She smiled tentatively. "That's . . ."

"Wait a second, it's George again, I've got to take this one." He cupped his hand over the phone, but not before she caught the letter "A" and his office number illuminated. "McKenzie. Yes, yes of course I can. It's important to us also. That's no problem. My executive assistant will arrange it right away. Yes, she's very capable. Right. I'll speak with you again soon. Certainly. Good-bye." He pocketed the phone and turned back to Catlin. "Everybody wants a piece of me," he sighed. "Look, babe, I know things have been strained, but my work isn't getting any easier, and I need you to understand that. Making partner is critical to the life we want to have. Your work isn't demanding, so you'll have to pick up the slack."

"Pick up the slack?"

"Right. Plan the kind of wedding you want. I'm totally fine with that. Tell me where and when and I'll be there. Let's not have any more foolish talk about long delays, though, all right? A wedding's just a social event. It's not complicated. Angela plans big dinners for the company all the time. I'd have her help, but she has more important duties. Figure out a date and place and make the arrangements. Your family's paying anyway, so I don't care. Run the date by Angela so it doesn't conflict with any trials. Can you do that?"

"I think we have some things to talk about and decide together."

"Catlin, are you listening to me? Don't make me angry again. It's not asking too much of you to handle this. Look, this weekend is shot; I'll be in the office Saturday and Sunday. I'll call you Tuesday and you can tell me what you've done."

Heat flushed her face. "This isn't a work project, John. I'm not your staff."

"That's for sure. This lack of progress would be unacceptable at work." He looked at his watch. "I have to get back to the office for a strategy meeting. What are you doing this weekend?"

"I'm going to my parents."

"Perfect." He nodded approvingly. "Find a place in Palm Springs. Go shopping for a dress with your mother. Pick out the invitations and flowers. See? It's easy. I don't know why you're making such a big deal out of this."

She stood speechless.

"Great. I'm glad we got all that settled. Pick the month with your parents and we'll fix the date on Tuesday. Talk to you then." He kissed her cheek as his phone rang, and headed to his car.

She watched him drive away, rooted to the sidewalk. Why wasn't she happy he wanted to set the date? She used to fear his indifference; suddenly he seemed more eager to get married than she was. Although eager wasn't quite the right word. Determined was more like it. Before she could process the scene further, Packard barked and scratched at the window. She hustled inside.

On their evening walk, she noted the changes from one day of construction. The gate was back on its hinges. The Smurf sat at the curb, its work in her yard completed. The big excavator seemed similarly satisfied, having filled the deep trench in the road. Sometimes she measured her progress by how much paper was in the recycle bin at the end of a day. Would building something be more satisfying? Installing a new sewer sounded more appealing than planning her wedding. That certainly wasn't how she imagined it would be.

"Attitude is everything," she told Packard on the way to the park. "Maybe John's right—it shouldn't be that complicated." *Palm Springs would be a beautiful place for our wedding*, she thought. One of the classic old resorts would be perfect. She could even have a historical theme. It seemed that she had John's permission to do whatever she liked, so why not? She would drive around with her mother on the weekend and collect brochures. Mom knew all the best spots.

They could pick a time period for the theme and look for a florist. That should be acceptable progress.

"It's always good to have a plan," she said as Packard trotted up with the Frisbee for the tenth time. "Now we can relax." She threw the disc until he finally settled in the grass, one paw on top of the Frisbee. She sat down next to him. They watched other dogs play until dusk and then headed home.

After dinner, she called her parents. "Everything's set," she said, hanging up.

Packard tilted his head and yowled.

"Yes, Mom will have Snausages for you. Just don't jump on her and knock the bag out of her hand like you did the last time we visited."

He barked and wagged his tail.

"Uh huh, that worked great . . . treats all over the floor. But remember we ran out of them later," she said, shaking her finger at him. "And Dad's not going to race to the store for you, even if you are his favorite grandson. Lucky for you you're their only grandchild."

Packard danced around her.

"I know, I'm excited too. Mom can't wait. She said she was afraid I'd never ask her. And Dad's pleased he won't have to drive far for the wedding. Everybody's happy."

Mom will help me get excited about the wedding again, she thought while packing. She was always happiest when part of a team. With Nancy gone and John abandoning involvement, she had been feeling bereft.

"This weekend will be what we need to recharge. We can swim in the pool, and maybe I'll finish reading Carolyn's book. You know how early Mom and Dad like to go to bed. We'll leave tomorrow morning. After your walk, of course. You have to say hello to Neil and make sure he had a good breakfast. You like him, don't you? How come you've never been so friendly to John? He'd appreciate some affection from you."

Packard sat and scratched his ear.

"Don't pretend you didn't hear me," she said as he licked his feet. "You always find a way to avoid the tough questions. Come on, let's get ready for bed. I sure hope I don't dream about cold dark staircases. That was creepy."

Her subconscious complied, and in her dreams she cheerfully walked across a broad plain. Her initial gratitude for warmth waned as the sun bore down. Tall grass gradually closed in the open path. She focused her attention on two narrow dirt ruts at her feet as if they held the secret to her future. "Follow the track, one foot in front of the other," she repeated to herself. Suddenly the grass disappeared and she gazed in joy at a rolling expanse of hillocks cut by a meandering stream. Two words formed in her mind: "home" and "salvation." She turned to share this vision with her companions and realized she was alone. "It's up to me," she said, and strode onward.

15

"What do all these dreams mean?" she asked the next morning. "I feel like I should see a therapist. Or go shopping at Nordstrom again."

Better than psychology or shoes, she had to admit as she and Packard returned from their stroll in the park, was seeing the crew in the morning.

"So what do you think? Not exactly back to normal, but close," Neil said as she approached.

"It looks great."

"The best part is that the line will drain a lot better. No more backing up into your shower."

"That's such a relief. It was so awful when that happened, you can't imagine."

"Trust me, I can. Nothing like standing in a trench when there's unexpected flow."

"That would be terrible. What do you do?"

"You learn to jump fast if you want to save your boots."

They laughed. Catlin slackened the leash while they continued to chat.

Packard edged closer and snuffled at Neil's shoes.

"Whoa!" Neil jumped just in time to avoid a well-aimed stream.

"Packard!" Catlin exclaimed in horror. "What are you doing? Bad dog!"

Bill laughed. "Looks like you can still move fast when you have to, boss."

"I'm so embarrassed," Catlin said. "I don't know why he did that."

"Don't worry about it. These boots have seen a lot worse."

Bill said, "Maybe he caught a whiff of your feet and was trying to improve the smell."

"Shouldn't you get over to Blair Street?" Neil asked him.

"I dunno, it's still kind of early."

"I'm sure by the time you get situated it will be past starting time."

"Whatever you say." Bill patted Packard on the head as he left. "Good doggie. Thanks for getting my day going with a laugh."

"I'm sorry," Catlin said.

"Hey, forget it. I had a yellow Lab once that was notorious. My mom called him Sir Marks A Lot. Anyway, let me know if you have problems with the line. We'll be a block over. You know where to find us." He raised his voice to a shout as Bill roared past in the loader.

She nodded in response and waved good-bye.

"I cannot believe what you did, you knucklehead," she lectured Packard when they got home. "What were you thinking? After all Neil's done for us, too."

He scratched her leg for a treat.

She sighed and reached into his cookie jar. "This is routine, not a reward. Just so we're clear."

He sat and offered her a paw.

"Okay, you're forgiven. I guess if Neil doesn't hold a grudge, I shouldn't." She gave him the Milkbone. "Let's hit the road. The sooner we start, the sooner we get there, as Dad says."

Once past the crush of freeway commuters, she relaxed into the drive. Her father's daughter, if it weren't for Packard needing regular breaks, she'd power through without a stop. But he reminded her with a bark from the back seat when his favorite places came into view, so they enjoyed a leisurely ride. Before she knew it, the wind farm appeared on the horizon, and she turned onto Highway 111, her favorite approach into Palm Springs.

She loved the main drag—*Is it politically correct to call it that?* she wondered—the shops and restaurants streaming mist, the pedestrian bridge built to shield crossing nudists, the celebrity stars in the sidewalk. She was surprised when her parents moved here, to the Hacienda, as they called it, a rambling ranch house that encircled a blue-tiled pool. But they loved the year-round warmth. Her mother swam every day and never complained about being a golf widow, although her father complained plenty about his game.

Three blocks toward the rock-strewn hills, she drove through an elaborate wrought iron gate already opened in anticipation of her arrival.

"Remember what I told you about jumping," she said as Packard bounded out of the car to greet her parents.

"How's my buddy?" her father said. "What's your name again? Chevy? Studebaker? It's been so long since I've seen you, I've forgotten."

"Oh Dad, we were just here at Christmas," Catlin said, stepping into his bear hug. They rubbed noses with a silly Eskimo kiss, saying, "Woogie woogie woogie," while Packard pranced around them.

Her mother laughed. "Don't I get a hug? Come here and let me look at you. Have you lost weight? We'll have dinner at the Kaiser Grill tonight. That will put some meat back on your bones."

"Sounds good, Mom. How are you?"

"As well as can be expected with my daughter wanting her wedding planned from scratch in seven months instead of a year."

"We'll make it simple."

"My dear, Luther and Amanda Davis's only child will not be married in a simple ceremony. Your grandmother would never forgive us."

"Okay, Mom. But I have some historical research I want to show you too."

Catlin pulled her bag from the trunk.

"Let me take that, honey," her father said.

"Thanks, Dad."

"Come on, Buster Brown," he said to Packard. "We'll let the women gab. Have I told you about my new putter?"

Packard woofed and trotted into the house.

Catlin arched an eyebrow at her mother. "Another putter?" she whispered.

"I don't question it. Golf is not my expertise. Apparently the technology changes rapidly. Lunch?"

Technology and conversation topics both change fast in this household, Catlin reflected, following her mother. But lunch was pleasant. Her parents listened attentively to Catlin's project updates, particularly the new Hawaii work.

"Remember our first trip to the Islands, dear?" Amanda said. "You loved driving that Mustang all around Kauai."

"You bet. Nothing like the fairways at Princeville. Wide open. Plenty of room to slice. And whoo boy, did I need it back then."

No wonder they call it a round of golf, Catlin thought. *The conversation always comes back around to it.*

While she and her mother cleared the table, her father retired to his La-Z-Boy for a siesta. "They know what they're doing in Spain," he liked to say. "The whole country shuts down between noon and two. Good planning."

Amanda washed the dishes, and Catlin grabbed a towel to dry. When she mentioned her idea of a historical theme for the wedding, Amanda clapped her hands in delight, sending explosions of soap bubbles into the air.

"How fun! What kind of bride do you want to be, darling? Elegant thirties in sleek satin? Fabulous fifties with yards of tulle? Please don't say you want to be married in a hippie granny dress, though. I never liked that style."

"I'm not sure. I want to look pretty. And fancy, definitely. I'd want Grandma to approve if she were still here."

"Let's look around the antique shops and see what inspires us. You can't go wrong with a touch of Old Hollywood, whatever decade you pick. Your grandmother loved the classic movies. That was a big deal when she was growing up. But what does John want?"

Catlin dropped the spoon she was drying. "Oops. Sorry," she said, handing it back to be washed again. "He's willing to do whatever I want. He wants me to be happy."

"That's a good quality in a groom." Amanda smiled tightly. "We'll see what we find tomorrow. Would you like to relax by the pool for awhile? I put out fresh towels on the chaise under the cabana."

"That sounds great. Thanks, Mom."

"I'll join you later for a swim. Go ahead. I'll finish up in the kitchen."

"Okay." Catlin kissed her mother on the cheek and went to the guest bedroom to change. Packard had already crashed on the tile floor; she didn't disturb him.

Her parents kept the pool warm even in the summer. "Life's too short to swim in cold water," her mother insisted. Catlin agreed. Sliding into the still water felt like slipping into a silken sheath. She stayed under for half the length of the pool, then surfaced and swam ten laps, rested in the Jacuzzi for a few minutes, and repeated the cycle. She dried off and pulled on her cover-up, leaned back on the chaise and closed her eyes.

Her mother joined her twenty minutes later. "You're welcome to visit more often," Amanda said, laying a towel on the adjacent lounge chair.

"I know. Work gets crazy, and the weekends are gone so fast."

"We're all proud of you for working, darling. It made your grandmother very happy. But she had other hopes for you, too."

"I know, Mom."

"Does John?"

Catlin sat up and jammed on her sunglasses. "Let's please not have the pre-nup conversation today. That's not what I came here for."

"It's just an agreement, Catlin. John's an attorney. I'm sure he would understand the need for clarity. Have you mentioned it to him yet?"

"No."

"If he had an inheritance pending, I imagine he would be talking with you about a clear agreement."

Catlin shrugged.

"He has a high potential income. Perhaps if you worded it in terms of protecting his own interests he'd be open to the idea."

"Okay, Mom. I promise I'll bring it up with him. Let's talk about the wedding, all right? Where do you think would be a good place for the ceremony and reception?"

She felt her heart rate come back to normal as Amanda listed the places they could visit and the pros and cons of each. When Amanda dove into the pool, Catlin flipped over and drifted off to the sound of her mother's slow, methodical laps.

After a dinner that included a relaxing prickly pear margarita, Catlin showed Carolyn's book to her mother.

"I think the letters are linked to Grandma's letters."

"Really?" Amanda eyed the book appraisingly. "It's beautiful. I never knew much about those letters. Your grandmother held onto them pretty tightly. That was something she shared with you but not with me."

"I haven't finished it yet. I could be all wrong." Sensing resentment in her mother's tone, Catlin set the book aside and changed the subject. "If we did a fifties theme, could I wear a tiara?"

"Absolutely. If you can't be a princess on your wedding day, when can you? I saw a gorgeous picture of Grace Kelly in a magazine the other day. Now where did I put that? I tore it out just in case you might want to see it. I think I put it in my desk. Hang on. I'll go get it."

Watching her mother hustle from the room, Catlin considered the mysteries of maternal relationships. There was a formality between her mother and grandmother that spoke of issues unaddressed and never settled, even when they both knew Grandma would die soon. It always seemed sad to Catlin, but then she reminded herself that repression has its place, and it worked for them. She smiled when her mother returned, waving the magazine picture.

"I had a feeling you would be interested in this. Look how beautiful she is. We could have something made for you to seem vintage. What do you think?"

"I love the skirt. How would it look in all white?"

So the evening passed with talk of fabric, fashion, and accessories, staples of feminine bonding.

"Thanks for your help, Mom," Catlin said when they hugged goodnight.

"I'm happy you asked me, darling. Sleep tight. Don't forget to lock up after you take Packard out."

"I won't."

Her father kissed her and rubbed Packard's ears. "Good night, you two. Don't stay up too late. Buster Brown needs his beauty sleep."

"Okay, Dad. Goodnight."

It wasn't long before she curled up in bed with the book.

16

Chapter 10 A New Life
I had nearly relinquished my plan and accepted a less adventurous future when your packet arrived. I am deeply grateful to you and eager to begin anew. Even so, for many days I hesitated, praying for a sign from God.

It came wrapped in tragedy.

A wagon fully supplied, including a clutch of chickens, arrived yesterday. The owner was a stately woman, genteel though browned by the sun. She had come from San Francisco for the independence of the plains, but an incessant cough caused her to end her travels here.

Mary told me the woman hoped a like-minded adventuress would purchase all she had acquired, complete the trek to her land, and live her dream. The price was merely what she would need for comfortable subsistence the rest of her days.

"Bless her dear soul," Mary said, "It will be a small sum, judging from the blood in her dainty handkerchief. I cannot see how she will last a week. Will you visit her and read from the Bible?"

I said that I would.

Within the hour, following prayers, tears, and gentle negotiations, I placed a mutually satisfactory bankroll in the woman's weak hands and took possession of what she had intended to be her life.

All doubts were eased when I stepped into the compact wagon that would soon be my home and found a worn guitar carefully placed amid the tins, bundles, and crates of provisions. Tomorrow I shall tether Iris to the wagon, hitch a hearty pair of oxen, and join a caravan headed eastward. I am promised by my soon-to-be-companions that the difficult parts of the journey are done. Within the month, we shall reach our respective homesteads and begin our new lives.

My heart races with anticipation!
Yours always,
Carolyn

Chapter 11 Homesteading
While we traversed the plains, we laughed at the sight of prairie dogs running and barking as we neared and disappearing into their underground houses until we passed. Little did I realize how soon I too would have an underground home.

My angel from San Francisco (for indeed, we received word not long into our journey that Mary's prediction was correct) had chosen a fine location with low hills and a stream close by. There was more than enough time for instruction on prairie living as we made our way across the plains. Several women of the wagons and many of the men took turns relating the tasks to be done, walking next to me as I guided my oxen. Building shelter, preparing the soil, planting a garden, and storing food all presented chal-

lenges, and everyone had their opinions on the best approach. I felt well informed and ready to begin work when I waved good-bye to my traveling companions.

My wagon held all manner of tools. The first to be used was the shovel to dig into the hillside and to cut sod bricks for walls. Next was the saw for tree limbs to form my roof rafters. The trees along the creek bed are small but adequate for the task. I am fortunate there are a few willow trees for boughs to layer on the roof that is topped with sod. One blessedly tall trunk supports the ridgepole in the middle, keeping the whole from collapsing, so I have some confidence I will not be buried alive. I put the hoe to good use for a vegetable garden, planting the seeds my angel packed for this purpose.

How clean your house and my basement lair seem now in comparison! Dirt constantly rains from the ceiling and constitutes the floor. The bugs that share my home are numerous and varied. They creep, crawl, and fly at me night and day. I most appreciate the ones that are large enough to see but small enough to swat. Last week, a rattlesnake greeted me as I emerged into the morning, and I was forced to slice its head off with the hoe. My general philosophy is live and let live; however, such brutality is occasionally necessary.

The water that I took for granted in all my previous lives is scarce and wearying to collect. I must not waste it bathing, but when vanity triumphs I indulge in a gentle splash of creek water carefully poured into my washbowl from a bucket left standing to settle out the mud.

I need not have worried that I would miss the bustle of "civilized" life. I toil alone in the sun, building blisters on calluses, with my chickens and Iris for company. I let my companions who had farther to travel take the oxen. In trade, I received a new sewing machine complete with rich wooden cabinet. What a marvelous invention! At night when I am not too tired, I practice my favorite craft— transforming flat cloth into functional beauty. My San Franciscan angel thoughtfully included many bolts of fabric, lovely and practical, some heartbreakingly intended for an infant. She had confided in me during our sad negotiation that she also hoped to find love and found a family. Alas, a hope that I will not be able to fulfill for her. But I will labor to prove her claim and justify her faith in me.

Another comfort for the evenings is her guitar. Even in the dark my fingers can find the strings, and I take refuge in rhythm and rhyme. Yesterday when I stood on the highest hill and looked into the sunrise, I saw a cloud of dust that may well be a westward caravan, which would be a means for my words to reach you. So I will end with my latest effort, which is, as ever, about my lost love.

Yours always,
Carolyn

Evening Dreams
The sun is going down in a bright blaze of red

As I sit in my doorway the thoughts in my head
Like soft silver clouds that slowly float through the sky
Drift gently by
It is late in the evening and my work is all through
I lean back, close my eyes, and my thoughts turn to you
Days are not easy but at night it is too hard to hide
My desolation inside
I think of your hands and I long for your touch
Warming and tender that I loved so much
The peace I received when I reached out to find you there
Cannot be compared
I remember the night I first learned your name
Your eyes gently watching while I played social games
Did you know as I did when I first felt your hand touch mine
I would be yours for all time
Did you realize that one single kiss
Could be the start of a love strong as this
A passion and a meaning that would fill us body and soul
And make us both whole
But I am alone in the present and the evening is gone
The sun has disappeared, cold night is coming on
All I can do to ease my pain is to sing
And lie back and dream

Chapter 12 Death and Transformation
Days and seasons merge. How can it be so many years since
we corresponded? I have worked steadily and moved above
ground from my first primitive home. But there has been an

even more profound shift in my life this winter that I must relate.

The snow was coming. Robert said it would be the worst storm in years. A good-hearted neighbor, he worked frantically to help all of us get ready. Once the blizzard started, he said, we may not see each other for weeks. So we laid in buffalo chips for burning, dried plums, molasses, salt, cornmeal: the essentials. We plastered cracks around the door frame with clay, and I prayed the wind would not break my precious glass window in front. Since Robert was the only one with a sturdy barn, he took in livestock from homesteads for miles around. I knew my milk cow, chickens, and beloved Iris would be safe with him.

It started mid-day with gentle powdery flakes. Soft, innocent, pure. I admired the crystalline patterns on my window shimmering in the sun. But then the wind rose, darkness fell, and the world disappeared into the blizzard.

I worked a rag rug by candlelight, sitting on the footstool next to the stove, until a chilly breeze blew out the candle. The stove would not stay lit because the clever wind found its way through the smallest cracks. Bitter cold filled my house. I dragged clothing from my trunk and layered petticoat upon petticoat, wool skirt over calico dress, shawl over cloak, and huddled in bed under all my blankets. I closed my eyes against the chortling wind. I recited every prayer and psalm, sang every hymn, named every book from Genesis to Revelation.

"Come daylight," I said, "the storm will be gone. I will light the stove, warm up coffee, and cook cornbread. I will brush my hair and sweep the floor." I calmed my mind by listing the routine tasks that had comforted me for these lonely years on the prairie. I rubbed my calloused hands, and recalled days of leisure when these hands caressed my love and committed the ultimate sin. I slept heavily and awoke expecting to see the sun. But there was no relief from the darkness or the wind. It seemed that daylight would never come. I felt a chilling weight settle on my feet. Snow was creeping through the roof, swirling around the stove, clinging to the blankets.

"So I shall freeze to death," I said. And then I realized my damnation would not be writhing in flames with multitudes of other unfortunate souls, but shivering alone in fearsome, dark cold. For me, there could be no worse punishment.

If that was how I would spend eternity, I resolved that my last thoughts would be of my love. I conjured his face. I transformed the weight of the invading snow into his body pressing down on mine, the confining blankets into his arms wrapped around me. I remembered how he loved to watch me dress, fascinated by each garment. He studied the mechanism of the bustle and laughed in wonder that women would wear such a contraption. He often returned from his travels with an exquisite gift of silk or lace and admired my own creations. How I wish I had accepted his proposal! I sobbed at the thought of all I had lost in one fateful moment. Suddenly my sorrowful mind registered a change. The night was still. The wind had ceased. In the bleak silence the cold grew deeper, and snow continued to drift through the roof. Curiously, I stopped shivering and a peaceful calm enveloped me. Finally I can rest, I thought, and fell asleep with his name on my lips.

In a joyful dream, he stood in a doorway that opened to brilliant sunlight. His face was weathered and bearded, but I knew his eyes. He called my true name and I ran to him, toward the beautiful light. Other angels stood behind him, crying, "Carolyn!" and I wondered if God had been fooled and would reject me when He learned the truth. But I would have one more moment in my love's arms, and that would sustain me for an eternity in icy purgatory.

I cast off the weight of regret and fear. Light and warmth surrounded me. A host of angels sang, "Praise God!" and "Thank the Lord!"

In the lead was my love, lifting me up, cradling me to him, covering my face with grateful tears. "Thank God you're alive," he whispered.

How I hated to awaken from this dream! I moaned, "I love you so," and slowly opened my eyes.

At first I thought I had indeed died. A crystalline white light filled the room. My love held me tenderly, while other voices clamored around us.

"Am I in heaven?" I asked.

"No, sweetheart, you're on the plains." He chuckled.

"You've been snowbound for two days," Robert said, stepping into view. "Your house was buried up to the eaves.

Canyon Jack here helped us dig you out. He wanted to bust in your window when he looked in an' saw you in a heap under all the snow. But I told him 'Miss Carolyn would have our heads if we broke that glass she waited three months for!' So we dug out the door. Listen t' me jaw! Let's get that stove a'goin' and warm you up. Beatrice, put those dry blankets around her. Who brought coffee?"

Robert directed my angelic neighbors so efficiently I was soon thawed inside and out. The snow was swept from the house and the stove glowed with comforting heat. Everyone took their leave with handshakes and blessings, last of all Robert.

"I take it ya know this stranger, Miss Carolyn? An' you'll be safe?" he asked.

"Yes, Robert, we are old friends. Thank you for everything," I said.

With a nod of his head, he stooped under the frame and closed the door.

Finally alone, we looked deeply in each other's eyes, and burst out, "I thought you were dead!" Tears flowed as we clasped hands.

"Where have you been, my love?" I asked.

"When I heard you had taken poison, I blamed myself," he said. "I intended to end my life, but a friend stayed my hand and convinced me to disappear into the mountains instead, while he spread the story of my suicide. I've been wandering ever since. I spent a season hunting buffalo but couldn't stomach the mayhem. I lived off the land for years,

and then started leading wagon trains through the mountain passes. Some old codger told me over glasses of whiskey about the homesteaders this way, including a green-eyed beauty who built a sod house by herself. I thought it might be Molly, so I rode here to see her and reminisce. Got caught in this god-awful storm and your neighbor Robert took me in. He was worried when the blizzard blew out and he hadn't seen you. He said something was wrong because you hadn't come for your animals. We rode out and picked up other folks along the way. I figured Molly would be the schoolmarm, but Robert said no, Miss Carolyn was a seamstress. Kept to herself but was the one the womenfolk went to for fancy things like christening gowns and wedding dresses. Then I dared hope you were still alive. When we saw your house buried up to the roof, I nearly went crazy thinking I found you too late. It's a lucky thing you have good neighbors."

"God brings us the people we need at the right time," I said. "Although I wish He had brought you to me sooner. Why didn't you talk to my mother? She was supposed to explain everything to you," I said.

"I returned to town too late," he told me with a shrug. "And I never trusted your house guardian. But enough of that. Tell me your story, sweet Carolyn."

"Miss Carolyn Parker," I said formally.

"I'm charmed to meet you, Miss Parker," he said, drawing my hand to his lips. "I'm Jack Rayburn. Known to

wagon trains as Canyon Jack for my skill at negotiating the countryside."

"It's a pleasure to make your acquaintance," I said, and we laughed. He grew serious as I told him of that horrible night, my sin, escape, despair, and enlightenment. I hope you will forgive me for not mentioning everything you have done for me since then. He had accomplished so much on his own, I wanted him to perceive me as likewise self-sufficient.

We talked through the day, over supper, and into the night. Finally I asked him, "So, Mr. Rayburn, do you intend to stay on the plains?"

He pulled me close, and said, "Yes, Miss Parker, there's a choice homestead I want to help farm. A beautiful, strong-willed woman is already working the land, but I hope to make her my wife and be her partner." He brushed my tears gently, and said, "Carolyn, will you marry me?"

It gives me great joy to report that there will be another simple wedding on the plains. Though I know you cannot come, please be here in spirit and grant me your blessing. With utmost gratitude for all you have provided, I am

Yours always,
Carolyn

Catlin grabbed a tissue. "What a beautiful story." She blew her nose and continued reading.

Chapter 13 Dreams Fulfilled

Our harvest has been blessedly rich. The rains have been plentiful and our crops have been spared the monstrous clouds of grasshoppers that devoured others' less fortunate. Sharing a life with my love has yielded so much more joy than I ever imagined. We left our pasts behind us completely and never speak of the time before we reunited here. The single secret I keep from Jack is the occasional correspondence to you, dear Mother, when the news is of sufficient import.

The news I relay in this brief letter is that I am the mother of a beautiful baby girl! How happy my San Franciscan angel must be that her hope to find love and found a family is fulfilled at last. I never would have believed it possible that God would bestow such forgiveness and grant my deepest desire. But she is here in a cradle Jack carved for her, sleeping so sweetly, our dear Samantha Lynn.

No reply is needed from you. I know you share my happiness. All my wishes for your continued prosperity, and gratitude for your contributions to mine are enclosed.

Yours always,

Carolyn

Chapter 14 A Final Request

I did not expect to write again so soon, or for the joy of our lives to reverse so quickly to bleak sorrow. I can only remind myself that not long ago I wrote that I would be content to have one additional moment in my love's arms. I am blessed to have had a full circle of seasons with him and to still look into the innocent eyes of his legacy.

Death, like my rebirth, came in a covered wagon. A desperate family, traveling late in the season, steered toward our lights and begged shelter. We could not refuse them, in spite of the signs of dangerous sickness. Jack tended to the father, whose ailment was too terrible to describe, cleansed his body and respectfully buried him when he passed into the Kingdom the next day. The mother and two children left soon after. She said that she would only become weaker with her persistent cough, so needed to continue onward, but would always be grateful for our kindness.

Within two days Jack was stricken with the same awful affliction as the father. Our neighbors wanted to help, but I refused to let them near. I shall have no more lives on my head. I cooled his fever and prayed for an end to his suffering. Late that night, God took him home. In those last moments, we pledged eternal love in our true names and vowed to renounce pride if God would be so merciful as to grant our souls another opportunity to serve Him on earth.

In his delirium, Jack told me stories from our separate years that I cannot write in this letter but must tell you in person. For now, although you have given me so much, I have a final request. I would not ask for myself with death all around. But there is one life that must be saved, or everything will be for naught. I cannot explain this conviction, which extends beyond a mother's devotion. There is a connection of souls through time that must continue unbroken. We are at that juncture. Please come. Please hurry. This husk that was once your best girl may soon be blown apart by wracking coughs. Mother or brother, you have been my savior and I must prevail on your love once more.

Yours always,
Carolyn

Epilogue
On this sad note we leave Carolyn. One additional letter was found in the chest. As can be seen from the photograph of the letter at right, in contrast to the photograph of Carolyn's letter in Chapter 2, this additional letter is not in Carolyn's handwriting. Because it was most likely meant for her, I include it below, although as with so much of historical information, it generates more questions than it answers.

Editor

My Dearest C
One last letter, never sent, for your angel and the angel you bore, to say that I loved you both from the moment of first sight to the final image of each, everlastingly on my eyes, at your last breath and near mine. You say you were ruined at the end, a specter already by the time I arrived. I say your beauty transcended beauty—your skin transparent to your soul, your eyes ethereal windows to Heaven.

If I vowed I had never loved you so much as at that moment, it would be a lie, for my love is constant still. Would that it had made a difference! I wish that I could

carry out your request to find the half-seed sown by your
beloved. But alas, that duty I must bequeath to another.
Time was ever fleeting and never lasting. What endures?
Perhaps only our words. But with God's grace, the angel you
and your beloved created will carry a living message of
hope forward, and heal all our wounds.

You are in my heart and prayers

J

The picture of the letter didn't register at first. Catlin wiped her eyes and re-read the romantic ending of Chapter 12. Blinking away fresh tears, she turned to the last pages of the book. Then she stared at the letter with its familiar handwriting. She jerked her head back as if she'd been slapped.

"Oh my god it's true! They're connected!" she whispered to Packard. "I wish I could tell Mom. But that look on her face when I mentioned the letters . . ." Catlin shook her head. "Can't go there. I can still ask her to help me with searching for Catherine Porter, anyway. That'll be fun. Carolyn will have to be my own project."

Packard yipped.

"What, are you sleepy? Sorry to keep you up so late. Do you and Dad have an early tee time?" She set the book on the nightstand and switched out the light.

That night, she dreamed that she and John sat in front of a television. John held the remote, as always, clicking through channels impatiently while Catlin watched the scenes flash past. A giggling teenager in full skirts the color of the sky twirled in front of a mirror. Two young women with long hair embraced in a dusty street. A fat man snapped a leather riding crop and shouted fiercely. A yellow dog howled while a beautiful woman strummed a guitar and an old woman laughed. A woman in a filthy dress wiped sweat from her face and continued to stack blocks made of clay and grass. A couple gazed lovingly at a baby in a wooden cradle. A woman wept over the still body of a dark haired man lying in a brass bed. The same woman, gaunt and coughing, folded a packet of letters into a finely sewn christening gown as the giant shadow of a man fell across her open doorway.

"This is boring," John said in disgust. He punched the power button and stalked from the room.

Catlin picked up the remote and held it gingerly. She aimed it at the TV and pushed the button. Her mother's face appeared, saying, "Catlin, it's time for breakfast. Wake up, darling."

Packard bounded onto the screen, barking insistently. The sounds finally registered as reality and she opened her eyes.

"Catlin?" Her mother knocked again.

"Morning, Mom. I'm up, thanks."

"Waffles will be ready in a few minutes. It sounds like Packard is ready for breakfast too."

"We'll be right there."

Over breakfast, Amanda laid out the plans for the day, the shops and resorts they would visit, where they would have lunch, and their afternoon spa appointments.

"Your father's already off for eighteen holes, and we'll leave the AC on for Packard. He'll be fine."

Catlin nodded, mouth full of waffle. It felt good to surrender to the force that was her mother.

17

"All in all, it was an excellent visit," she told Packard on the drive home the next day. "Even if I didn't find a dress. The Ingleside Inn will be great for the ceremony and reception. Mom's got the florist and photographer lined up already. I can do the invitations. And our nails look great." She tapped her fingers on the steering wheel and smiled at her French manicure. Confirmed researcher that she was, she had most enjoyed looking at early census sheets with her mother Saturday evening.

"Let's see if we can find your soiled dove the easy way first," Amanda told her, bringing up Ancestry.com on the computer. But a search for Catherine Porter yielded no matches in Colorado. "All right, let's look at 1870 Arapahoe County in Colorado Territory for early Denver residents. It's the slow way, but maybe something will pop up."

They laughed at the column labeled "Whether deaf and dumb, blind, insane, or idiotic."

"It's amazing the data the government decided to collect in the census," Amanda commented. "In the 1930s, it was if there was a radio in the house." She scrolled down the sheets. "Here's an interesting household. Looks like Nugat? First initial J, occupation boarding house keeper, with James a musician, and a slew of females with various jobs. There's Amy a domestic cook, Catherine a seamstress, Molly a teacher, Emma a bookkeeper, and Laura a washerwoman. All of them age nineteen to twenty-five."

Catlin squinted at the computer screen, trying to read the handwriting with its elaborate flourishes. "All the boarders kept busy, I guess."

"Oh, yes, I'm sure they were busy girls," Amanda replied with an arched brow.

"What?"

"These are legitimate jobs, darling, but sometimes they're euphemisms for the occupation your Catherine had. Mr. Nugat may have been running a parlor house, and the other members of the household would have been his workers. Houses often had a piano player to provide background music and protection; that would be James. It's too bad there are no addresses listed here. Early records are scant but fascinating."

"So there's no way to confirm if that's Catherine Porter."

"Not from this census, I'm afraid. If you do go to Denver on your honeymoon, set aside some time to check out early city directories. Maybe there would be a more complete listing and you'll find her there."

"She's mentioned in a couple of books. They must have based their research on something."

"That's right. Look at their references. That would be a good place to start. I'll keep going through the census records and I'll let you know what I find."

Catlin sighed happily at the memory. Her mother loved research too. Their relationship was at its best when they had a project to do together.

The wedding project was also off to a good start, which she hoped would please John. As home approached, she considered how to tell him her progress. She had accomplished almost everything he'd mentioned, but she still felt nervous.

"Should I wait for a sign from God, like Carolyn?" She flicked a glance to the fuzzy head that filled her rearview mirror.

Packard gazed back steadily but silently.

"What, you won't offer advice on spiritual matters? Isn't dog God spelled backward? I figured you'd be an authority on the subject."

Packard turned toward the side window and barked.

Catlin looked over. In the next lane, a semi towed a loader on a flat bed trailer. "No, no, that's not a sign. Neil is not the answer. Third parties just complicate things. John and I will straighten it all out, you'll see. He'll be happy with everything Mom and I did this weekend. Instead of calling, maybe I should e-mail him. That'd be painless, I mean efficient."

Packard huffed and lay down on the back seat.

The more she thought about e-mailing instead of calling John, the better she liked the idea. She could scan the brochure for the Ingleside Inn and attach the file so he could see how nice it would be. And she could explain how they were fully committed in October but had several November weekends available. She knew e-mail lacked emotional content, but the way things were going lately, that would be good. She could send him information without appearing anxious, and that would keep him from getting angry. With a few weeks of low-stress communication, they would transition back to normal relations.

Enthused about the plan, she composed an informative and cheerful message as soon as she unpacked and was rewarded that evening with a hearty reply: "Excellent work. Second Saturday in November should be fine. Angela will confirm. LY, John."

Over the next month, she kept in touch through John's secretary, who provided cordial e-mail updates on his schedule. She learned more from Angela that she ever had from John, whose response to any questions about work was invariably, "It's fine." She and Angela found common interest in the Old West, one of Angela's ancestors having come from the East Coast to be a teacher but getting lost as a soiled dove instead.

With the wedding under control and her fiancé in the background, Catlin enjoyed greeting the crew in the morning. She confessed to "stealing" rocks from the dirt piles that moved from street to street, which made Neil laugh. Casual conversations became brief hellos, and then distant waves as the crew moved farther from her street.

One weekend, she arranged the rocks in a meandering stream pattern and bought new plants at the nursery. "I'm channeling Carolyn," she told Packard, pointing out her freshly planted rosemary, garlic, and lavender. "And don't you go watering these plants; they don't need your help."

She hoped to show Neil her handiwork, but that Monday when she walked by the staging area, she pulled Packard up short. The trailer and crew were gone.

"He left without saying good-bye! I can't believe it. I guess I didn't mean much to him after all."

Packard sat, tilted his head to the sky and howled.

"You didn't mean anything to him, either. See, I told you Neil wasn't the answer."

She peered at the street where the trailer supports had left deep impressions in the asphalt. *Like in my heart*, she thought, tears in her eyes. Not that the relationship was ever going anywhere, but the sudden vacancy made her realize how much of a space Neil and the other men had filled.

"Time to move on," she sighed.

For the rest of the week, every morning they walked by the spot she felt the loss anew. Eventually, she forgot to look, and finally she forgot to think about them. Angela kept her alerted to John's busy times, so Catlin knew when to let him be, and their relationship improved. He took her to the fancy French restaurant he loved for their delayed engagement anniversary dinner. Although afterward was basic brass tacks and he couldn't stay the night, it was enough for Catlin to feel like they were still a couple. June came before she knew it, Nancy returned from Hawaii, and the office returned to balance.

Michael had to leave town for a client meeting the same date as the Organization of Environmental Professionals banquet, and he surprised Catlin with a pair of tickets so she could accept the award for the company. He filled her in on the project construction and gave her his acceptance speech notes. He gave Nancy his ticket with an admonishment to behave herself.

"I can only promise to behave like myself," she told him. "But I'll do my best to keep your reputation in mind, Mister Boss of Me."

Michael just laughed.

18

On banquet night, Catlin greeted Nancy at the ballroom entrance. "Isn't this exciting?" I still can't believe ESTA is getting the Document of the Year Award for our pipeline EIR. It's such a thrill."

"And fun for you since Michael is letting you accept it. Well, you deserve it. Documenting all that information about the village site was tough. I hear the contractor is getting an award for applying new construction equipment."

"That's right. They used these new rubber-tracked excavators to dig the water-line trenches and protect artifacts near the ground surface from being crushed. They didn't have to grade any access roads. And you'll like this part: the equipment just rolled over the plants, and the ground pressure of the vehicles was so low the vegetation sprang right back up. Michael said it was amazing to watch. I wish I could have been there."

"Uh huh. You've become quite the construction junky. Personally, I don't get the appeal. By the way, nice dress. That midnight blue is a great color for you. So where's your dear fiancé? Why isn't John here to see your triumph and dance the night away with you?"

Catlin winced and shifted her beaded gold purse to her other shoulder. "Oh, you know." She waved her hand airily. "Meetings, briefs, trial preparation. They've got a big case coming up and he needs to be there 100 percent to make partner soon enough to suit him. He's very ambitious."

"I don't get that appeal either. He should be here for you."

"It'll be different once we're married. Then we'll be living together and he'll come home to me, not to his empty condo at the beach. Anyway. We should find our table. Charlie's coming up to the microphone to tell us to sit down."

Nancy pulled out her ticket. "And the lucky table that gets me is . . . sixteen. Where are you?"

Catlin glanced at her ticket and scanned the room. "Eighteen. Probably toward the back." They meandered through the room, dodging elbows and half-full glasses of wine. Catlin exchanged congratulatory hugs and handshakes along the way, glowing in the rush networking always gave her and the heady satisfaction of a job well done being publicly acknowledged. She continued through the room after Nancy said, "This is me" and sat down at her table.

My lucky table is . . . right there, she thought, and stopped in her tracks as a pair of piercingly familiar blue eyes regarded her over a bottle of Corona. *Oh boy, lucky night or total disaster*, she mused while confusion, excitement, and fear flashed over her face. *Okay, Catlin, you're a professional, you can do this*, she chided, and plastered on a courteous smile as she strolled to an empty chair. "Is anyone sitting here?" she asked the trio already seated.

"Neil was saving that chair for the girl of his dreams but now that you're here we can all relax." The husky, curly-haired man in the middle laughed and slapped his friend on the back, looking up at Catlin with an appreciative gaze.

"Pushing, Bobby, pushing," Neil muttered around his beer as he took a strengthening slug and gestured to her with a welcoming tilt of the bottle. "Hi. You clean up nice."

"Good line, man. Great start," Bobby snorted. "Let me show you how it's done, junior." He stood up at his chair and extended a burly hand. "Hello. I'm Bobby Anderson, this is Neil Prescott, and that's Greg McFadden, our office manager. He's a suit, so he's a little dull; you don't have to bother talking to him." The elegantly dressed man with graying temples smiled tolerantly and nodded at her over a glass of merlot. "We're with Altman Construction, or the A Team, as we like to say. We built the county water district's pipeline. In case you hadn't heard, we're getting an award tonight for being very sensitive guys." He cocked a knowing eyebrow at her as she watched her hand being engulfed by his.

God help me, did I just giggle? she asked herself when her hand reappeared. "Catlin Davis. I'm an archaeologist with ESTA. I did the cultural resources work on the Harrison site for the pipeline project you built. I'm getting an award too." She raised her eyebrow and Bobby chuckled. "It's nice to meet you." She nodded to Greg and sat next to Neil, straightening her dress as she smoothly crossed her legs. "And it's nice to see you again, Mr. Foreman. Maybe we can have a real conversation tonight and not just shout at each other over machinery. Your company also replaced the sewer in my street," she explained to Bobby. She folded her hands primly on the table and forced herself to breath normally.

"That's your cue, son," Bobby whispered. "Start talking." He looked up at Catlin. "He's kind of dim, though we let him boss the crew around in the field. I'll help as much as I can here. Umm, how about this? It was Neil's idea to use the rubber-tracked Caterpillar equipment through the site. Saved us a bundle on access, *and* showed we care about the environment. Right, man?"

"Yes. Thanks for making me feel like a total idiot." Neil brushed his hand up through his hair and hoped the sweat he felt wasn't dripping off his face. "So, you're an archaeologist? I guess I didn't realize we both dig ditches for a living." He glared at Bobby, who gave a cheerful shrug and mercifully turned toward Greg.

"And I didn't realize you were the hero who protected my artifacts." *I hope that didn't sound lame. Am I flirting? I'm engaged, for crying out loud.*

Neil reached for the wine bottle to distract the back of his brain, which kept asking questions like *Are you wearing anything under that dress?* and *Are you still engaged to that asshole attorney?* "Can I pour you some?" He hoped that was the only question he asked out loud.

"Maybe later. I have to walk to the stage after dinner and not fall down. I'm kind of a lightweight with alcohol."

"Oh. That's good." *Get a grip Neil,* he told himself as Catlin sat back, startled. "Uh, do you like archaeological digs?"

She thought a minute. "I started out loving it. When you're in the field, the sun on your back, sitting in your own dusty grid with your tiny brushes, tweezers, and picks, painstakingly exposing shards of pottery that could give you important clues about previous cultures, it's just . . . oh, I don't know . . ."

"Fulfilling? Exciting?"

"Mind-numbing, actually. That's why I went into doing analysis and document prep. I think I should have a bumper sticker that says, 'I'd rather be writing.' Except my dad would never forgive me if I put a bumper sticker on my car."

"Good man. Cars aren't billboards. You always do what your dad tells you?"

"Pretty much. I kept a detailed log of mileage, gas, cost, all that. Until I moved out. Then I threw it away. I still feel a little guilty when I fill up and don't record anything."

"Catholic guilt?"

"More like military guilt. I'm a well-trained Navy brat."

"No kidding? Me too." Neil slid his arm along the back of her chair and leaned closer. "So how many schools were you in during elementary?"

"Umm, let's see. Four up to third grade."

"Ouch. I hated being the new kid in class all the time."

"Yeah. But then he retired and we moved here so it wasn't so bad. How many for you?"

"We moved every two years until I was in high school. It was great to finally settle down."

"You know, I kind of thought you were Navy stock." She bent forward with a conspirator's smile and whispered, "Because my dad's the only one I know who uses the word 'skivvies' for underwear. Remember you phoned me when you hooked up my lateral? You said you tested the connection by using the washer on the laundry porch, and you were all running around my backyard in your skivvies. That was funny."

"I'm surprised you remember that."

"It's an image that's tough to forget. My boss laughed and laughed when I told him. I think it stayed in his mind because a week later he suggested I call you to get the 'skivvey' on the rest of the construction work. I told him the word was 'skinny' and if he wanted to know if you wore boxers or briefs, he'd have to call you himself."

Neil snickered and picked up the beer bottle. "Boxers," he murmured before taking a sip.

Catlin blushed. "Thank you for sharing," she managed. "I wasn't curious."

"No?"

"No. Contrary to popular male belief, women are not interested in . . . that topic." She pushed her hand through her hair and slid her eyes away.

Amused he'd broken through her professional veneer, he said, "I guess we're all just projecting our own interests. How about you sharing?" He lightly tapped her arm.

"I am so not telling you." She laughed and shook her head.

"Ah c'mon."

"No way." She pursed her lips smugly. "It's for me to know and you to find—wait, that's not right." She stopped in confusion. "Thank God, dinner's here! I mean, I'm really hungry," she said as Bobby and Greg turned toward her in surprise. With an effort, she realized the table had filled and switched back to networking mode. Introductions flowed and business cards were dealt. Rolls and salad dressing passed hands and the general chaos of a banquet ensued.

"I haven't been to many of these things," Neil commented when dessert was served. "What happens next?"

"There's going to be some boring announcements pretty soon while we're still eating our . . . chocolate mousse, yum, thank you," Catlin beamed up at the waiter and started scooping with an eager spoon. "Then comes the awards—our big moment—and a speech from the president. Then talking will be like when you were on my street before, because the band will start."

"So if I have any more questions, I better ask them now, huh?" *That ring on your finger tells me all I need to know, unfortunately.*

"So there's gonna be dancing? You eating your dessert, man?" Bobby tapped on Neil's dish. "Thanks."

Nancy waltzed over and laid a casual hand on the back of Catlin's chair. "Hi, I just wanted to check in before all the excitement starts. Are you making friends and influencing people?" She locked her gaze on Bobby as she leaned down and whispered in Catlin's ear, "Be nice and introduce me to the hunky bear in the middle, and I'll let you keep Mr. Blue Eyes here."

Catlin sputtered with shocked laughter. "Sorry, um, girl talk," she said to the men. "This is Nancy DeWitt, Senior Biologist with ESTA. Neil, Bobby, Greg with Altman Construction." She pointed in turn. "Nancy, these guys built the pipeline through the Harrison site."

"Really? There was a lot of sensitive vegetation in the area. I was glad to learn you were so gentle with it." Her voice was smooth, dark chocolate.

"It takes a lot of skill, even with the right equipment, to treat those sensitive areas just right," Bobby told her. "I can tell you more about it later if you're interested."

"Oh yes," Nancy purred. "As a dedicated biologist, I'm always interested in new techniques to protect delicate resources. Oops, got to get back," she said as the microphone on stage whined. "Later."

"You want a cigarette after all that?" Neil muttered to Bobby.

"Mmmm, I'll save it for 'later.'"

Neil snorted. "Sorry, guy talk," he said to Catlin.

Then those dreaded words, "May I have your attention please," echoed through the speakers, the general clatter diminished, and focus shifted to the podium.

"Good job walking to the stage and not falling down," Neil told Catlin when she came back to the table, flushed and trembling slightly as she laid the wooden plaque in front of her.

"Thank you," she said, tracing over the laminated words of praise on the award. "It's a big deal for our office. And of course it's wonderful that the project was so successful, thanks to you."

She flashed a smile that made him think of brilliant sunlight shafting through storm clouds, the warmth of spring after a long winter, and *I am totally losing my mind* Neil told himself. *What is it about this woman? I want to protect her from the world one minute and nail her the next.*

"Yours is nice too," Catlin was saying, nodding toward the plaque Greg had laid to the side.

"Yeah, the suits love that kind of stuff. I was just doing my job, ma'am." He tipped an imaginary hat and let her laughter wash over him like a sparkling stream bouncing over polished rocks *Not again, where does this crap come from?* Neil heard applause and realized with a start that the speeches were finished.

"Thank God that's over," Bobby said. "I've gotta take the dog for a walk, if you know what I mean. If your friend comes over, tell her to save the first dance for me." He pushed away from the table and lumbered off.

"That reminds me, how's Packard?"

"He's fine. Well, I am a little worried about him. He only wanted to catch the Frisbee about thirty times last Sunday."

"*Only* thirty? Still sounds like a lot of retrieving."

"Yeah, but this is a guy who'd spend all day on the dog field if I let him. He seems, I don't know, lethargic."

"If you're worried, take him for a checkup. Maybe it's just the hot weather."

"I think I will take him in. My fiancé hates it when I spend money on the vet, but he's been so busy lately he'll never know." Catlin brightened as the band revved up. "Here comes Nancy, right on cue."

"And there's Bobby. This will be fun to see." Neil stretched back in his chair and crossed his feet.

"You don't dance?"

"Not fast stuff. I was never comfortable looking stupid."

"Bobby doesn't seem to have that problem," Catlin said wryly after watching a while. "I hope nobody gets hurt."

"I think your friend can take care of herself. Anyway, he's a real considerate guy. Don't let all his hot talk fool you. And he's a master with the excavator. I've seen him dig a trench with only inches of clearance on either side."

"So he's got a light touch on the controls?" She sent him a coy smile.

"Yeah, he knows how to get in and get out." They both burst out laughing. "Bobby talks trash a lot better than me," Neil admitted.

"That's okay. You're still the boss. You must have other skills."

"Yes I do. And finally there's a slow song so I can show you. C'mon."

"Yes, boss," she murmured as they rose from the table.

The glow from the light contact of his fingertips on her back radiated through her body when he clasped one hand

and circled her waist. She slid her hand up his arm and tried not to linger over his bicep as she took a proper dance position resting her palm on his shoulder. She relaxed into his slow, easy pattern and closed her eyes when she heard him quietly humming the tune in her ear. *It's like being wrapped up in a warm blanket*, she thought, *to be this close, feel this happy.*

"I'll be damned. Nancy, look. Your friend got Neil out on the dance floor," Bobby whispered, turning so she could see the swaying couple. "That's gotta be a first."

"That's nice. I'd hate to be the only one having a good time." Nancy moved her hand up to the back of his neck and shifted closer as he tightened his grip in response.

"Yeah, me too." He chuckled softly.

They all returned to the table when the band started playing a fast jitterbug.

"Catlin, do you swing?" Greg asked her.

"As a matter of fact, I was home-schooled by one of the best," she replied, tossing her head. "My dad could cut a rug all night in his prime."

"Then may I have the pleasure?" He held out his arm gallantly and whisked her away.

"You better look out," Bobby warned. "Women go nuts for those polished older men."

"She's already taken, you moron," Neil told him. "Didn't you see her ring?"

"Yeah, yeah. I noticed the ring. I've broken bucket teeth on smaller rocks."

"Unfortunately the man that comes along with it is just as cold and hard," Nancy said. "And not in a good way," she added as she caught Bobby's eye.

"I ran into him while we were working her street. He's kind of a jerk," Neil said.

"If that's what you think, I can assure you you're wrong." Nancy crossed her arms. "He's a first class, A-number-one asshole. He treats Catlin like dirt, and I'm pretty sure he's cheating on her. It's so scary to think they're getting married in November."

"You're her friend, right? Why don't you talk to her?"

Nancy raised her eyebrows at the intensity in Neil's voice. "You're apparently interested in her. Why don't you talk to her? She thinks we all misunderstand him. And of course he's an expert at maintaining that 'poor me' façade. He gives her just enough to keep her roped in. He tries to isolate her as much as he can, but he's so busy he never has time for the things she wants to do."

"Sort of like being in a restaurant with bad food and small portions too?" joked Bobby.

"This is serious, man," Neil snapped. "I don't understand how guys like that get women like her. She's obviously bright, sweet, strong. What's the appeal?"

Nancy shrugged. "I don't know, but maybe you can find out. Here they come, so let's change the subject, okay?"

"How about another dance while Neil investigates?" Bobby grasped Nancy's hand and led her through the crowd to the floor.

"Whew! That was wonderful," Catlin gushed as she and Greg came back. "Bobby was wrong—your office manager is very exciting." She sent a dazzling smile across the table, and Greg raised his glass in a toast.

"To your quick feet and excellent training. You better take lessons if you want to keep up with this one, Neil."

"Great. Another assignment," he muttered.

When the band packed up, Catlin said, "What an excellent banquet. I had such a good time."

"May I walk you to your car?" Neil asked.

"No no. That's okay. Nancy and I are leaving together. Oh." Catlin frowned as her friend waved from across the room before walking out the door arm-in-arm with Bobby.

"Lose your escort?"

"Apparently."

"Then, shall we?" He offered her his arm.

On the way to the hotel garage, she said, "Please don't interpret this like Nancy was saying it, but I'm really interested in your equipment."

"You need to be more specific before I get all excited."

"I mean the special excavators and bulldozers you used for the pipeline project. My company's done construction monitoring, and it's never occurred to anyone to use machines like that. How did you know they existed?"

Neil fought the urge to swagger while he basked in her admiration. "I just keep up with that stuff," he replied casually, as if it hadn't involved hours of his own time searching the Web, talking to manufacturers, and negotiating with suppliers.

"It could avoid a lot of damage if everybody did that."

"Maybe everybody needs to hire our company to build their pipelines."

"I guess that'd work too." Catlin laughed. Then her smile faded and she announced sadly, "There's my car."

"I'm sorry you found such a good parking space. I wouldn't mind a longer walk."

"Me either." She took her time searching for her keys in the tiny gold purse while she frantically searched her mind for first date etiquette and wondered how she could consider the night a first date anyway when she was engaged and it was her fiancé's busy schedule that put her in the garage next to this disarming, charming, intriguing man with those incredible blue eyes that bored right into her soul and made her want to melt melt melt into him . . .

"Lose something?" Neil tilted his head and cocked an eyebrow at her fumbling in the metallic pocket that didn't look big enough to hold a comb.

"Um, no, I found them." She drew out her keys and studied them as if she had forgotten what they were for. "Thank you for . . . tonight. I didn't expect to be so glad I came alone." She felt a sudden heaviness as she realized she would never see him again, and commandeered a bright smile to compensate.

"I had a great time, too. You're a lot more fun to be with than Bobby."

"It seems like Nancy would disagree, but I'll deal with her at work next week."

"Hey, maybe we'll see each other at their wedding, you think?"

Catlin had to laugh at the thought of watching Bobby dance again. "The world is full of surprises," she said. "I should get going. Packard gets worried if I'm out too late. I don't want to lose any shoes."

Neil reached back for his wallet and pulled out a business card. "Look, I hope this doesn't sound strange, but call me if there's anything wrong with him, okay?"

"Sure. And I don't think that sounds strange, it's nice that you care. About him, I mean." *Keep it up, Catlin, make him sorry you ever sat at his table*, she berated herself as she carefully put the card in her purse.

"He's a cool dog. Special." *Like his owner, would that be so hard to say? C'mon Neil. Maybe deep down she has reservations about getting married to that guy, maybe there's time, maybe you've got a shot.*

And maybe not, he amended, as Catlin held out a polite hand, and said, "Thanks again, I've got to go."

"Sure. Take care." He imprinted her smooth hand, luminous green eyes, and gleaming smile in the instant before she turned away, then stepped aside while she backed up and drove out of the garage and out of his life.

"If Bobby is prancing around on Monday bragging about getting lucky I swear I'll firebomb his car," Neil grumbled as he walked to his truck.

19

"So, Missy, did you have a good weekend?" Catlin greeted Nancy the following Monday, hands on hips with feigned disapproval.

Nancy laughed. "Now, now, mom, calm down. Nothing happened Friday night, I swear."

"Then why are you blushing?"

"Because I know what you're thinking. Honestly, we just went out for coffee after the banquet."

"And?" Catlin prodded.

"And talked."

"Uh huh, just talked?"

"Sure. Don't you know men love to talk?"

"About what?"

"About whatever they think will get them in your bed," Nancy whispered, giggling. "Ha! Made you blush."

Catlin shook her head. "Oh, we are so having lunch today. You're not telling me everything, I know it. I can't believe nothing happened between you two."

Nancy grinned. "I didn't say nothing happened, just that nothing happened Friday night. Mercy, it's after eight o'clock! We better get to work before Michael lectures us on productivity again." Her grin broadened as Catlin pointed at her and mouthed "Lunch."

At noon, they picked up chicken pita sandwiches and lemonade at the counter of their favorite European deli and settled at an outdoor table.

"Okay, girlfriend, spill it," Catlin insisted.

"No way. This dress is dry clean."

"You're merciless! Tell me what happened, please, please, please."

"And why are you being so nosy? Are you hiding something? Maybe we should start with what happened between you and Mr. Blue Eyes."

Catlin laughed. "That's easy. Nothing happened, Friday, Saturday or Sunday. He walked me to my car, we shook hands goodnight, and I'll never see him again. End of story. Your turn."

"Wait, I'm still wiping my tears from your sad tale. He left you with no way to contact him?"

Catlin couldn't resist a smug smile. "He gave me his card, and wanted me to let him know about Packard. But I don't plan to call him."

"Why would he want to know about Packard?"

"He's lethargic."

"He didn't seem lethargic Friday night. He danced every dance he could with you."

"No, no. Packard's lethargic. I'm taking him to the vet tomorrow."

"Oh. I'm sorry to hear it. I hope he's not sick."

"I'm sure he's fine. It gets hot for him under all that fur. You're distracting me. Time to confess. What's up with Bobby?"

Nancy pretended to take a bite of her sandwich, but stopped when Catlin sent her a warning glare. "All right. I've kept you in suspense long enough. It's true what I said. We did only talk Friday night. But, oh, Saturday morning!"

"You got back together the next day?"

"Umm, I guess 'back together' wouldn't be the correct wording, exactly."

"I'm confused."

Nancy sipped her lemonade. "I mean technically, Saturday morning starts at midnight."

"Oh my god. You took a big chance being with someone you hardly know. Remember the girl who thought she'd have a nice time with that famous basketball player and it turned into a total disaster?"

Nancy snorted. "Her first mistake was thinking a famous basketball player would be fun in bed. Men like that are notoriously crappy lovers. They can't get out of their own heads long enough to consider satisfying a woman."

"Okay. I'm assuming Bobby's different?"

Nancy bit her sandwich and chewed thoughtfully.

Catlin watched her friend and tried to interpret the emotion in her eyes. Contented? Plaintive? Worried beneath the bravado that she had given herself too soon?

"I wouldn't have invited him home if I didn't trust him, Catlin."

"So how did you know you could?"

"I think it was because we have compatible bumper stickers."

"Uh huh. So what goes with "You Say I'm a Bitch Like It's a Bad Thing?"

"Let Go of My Ears I Know What I'm Doing," Nancy recited, deadpan.

Catlin tilted her head quizzically, and then laughed. "Okay, he has a good sense of humor. What else?"

"He was very sweet, very considerate, and very..." Nancy trailed off with a complacent smile.

"Very?"

"Very *very*."

"Wow. Not that it matters, of course."

"No, of course not."

They both snickered and chomped voraciously into their sandwiches.

"So will you see him again?"

Nancy nodded. "He wants to go hiking next weekend. He said he's never done that with someone who knows the names of the trees."

"You sound like you could get serious about him."

Nancy waved her hands in protest. "I've made that mistake way too often. I'm just going to enjoy his company and everything that comes with it. I'm in no big rush for commitment."

"You're so together. I wish I could be that sure of myself."

"It's a long road. Sometimes the lessons come the hard way. I could tell you some real sad tales. But not today," Nancy added, looking at her watch. "We've both got lots to do."

"I'm glad I'm in the loop," Catlin said, slurping the last of her lemonade. "Lunch with you is always interesting."

"Men make for an interesting topic, good or bad."

"Do you suppose they talk about us the way we talk about them?"

Nancy laughed. "Only if sports talk is code for emotions. I think they prefer to figure things out for themselves."

"I'd be pretty clueless if I tried that."

"My point. But you still need to leave them alone when they retreat. It's their way of dealing and you've got to respect that. The best ones ask questions and aren't afraid to hear the answers."

The sly smile on Nancy's face made Catlin more curious. "What did Bobby ask you?"

Nancy picked up her purse. "That's for another lunch. I've confessed enough today."

20

"I know this isn't your favorite thing to do, but we need to find out why you're slowing down so much," Catlin soothed as she opened the car door. "In. Good boy." Packard immediately settled down on the back seat. Catlin got in, adjusted the seat, checked the mirrors, and fiddled with the radio before buckling her seatbelt. She turned to the back and patted him on the head. "I guess I'm not any more eager for this vet appointment than you are," she said.

In the vet's waiting room, Packard demonstrated his usual stoicism while Catlin fussed with his leash and stroked his ears. "Our turn," she said, when his name was called, and followed him into the examine room. He headed right to the scale and sat patiently for the vet's assistant to take his weight.

"He's so well trained."

"Yeah, he knows the drill, don't you, big guy?"

"Dr. Berger will be right with you."

"Okay, thanks."

Waiting again, she looked in his quiet eyes and said, "I don't know why I'm so nervous if you're not. I could take some lessons in peace of mind from you, huh, boy?"

"How's my favorite dogmobile?" hailed the vet. "What seems to be the trouble with the Packard? Do we need to check under the hood?"

"He seems to be tired a lot lately, walking slower, and it's like he's having trouble breathing sometimes," Catlin told him.

"Okay, let's have a look. And we can do a chest x-ray today while you're here, to rule out any obstructions."

"Sounds good."

At the end of the visit, the vet explained that they'd have a radiologist examine the x-rays and then he'd call her with the results. "He seems to be eating fine," Dr. Berger commented, watching Packard inhale a large Milkbone.

"Eating's never been a problem for this chow hound." Catlin laughed.

On the way home, she told him, "You were such a good boy. Everything went fine. We'll just take it easy on those hot days, right?"

The vet called back the next morning. "Catlin. I wanted to catch you before you left for work. The news isn't good."

Her breath caught in her throat. "What do you mean?"

"The x-rays indicate a tumor in Packard's chest. It's pressing on his right lung, and that's what's causing the shortness of breath."

"Can you take it out?"

"This kind of thing is beyond general veterinary practice, Catlin. I can recommend a good oncologist and send the x-rays on. Tell him Packard's my patient when you call. He may want to do more tests to characterize the growth better." He gave her the name and phone number. "It does appear to be localized, and that's good news. Let me know when you make the appointment, and I'll coordinate with the oncologist. Okay?"

"Okay." Catlin choked back sobs and hung up the phone. "Oh my god, oh my god. Packard, what are we going to do?" She sat on the couch and covered her face with her hands, letting the tears flow through her fingers. Packard nudged his head between her knees and she wrapped her arms around him. She buried her face in his neck and wept. He stood quietly while her shoulders shook and she clung to him, drenching his soft fur. "I can't lose you, I can't lose you," she wailed.

Finally, she sat up and took a steadying breath. "We're not giving up, okay big guy?" She swiped at her face with her palms. "There's a lot more options now, you're strong, and we're going to do whatever it takes to make you well. If you've got a chance, and the treatment doesn't make you miserable, we're going for it. What do you say? Sound like a plan?" Packard licked her face, barked sharply, and pawed at her knee. "As long as you still want breakfast, we're okay." Catlin smiled wanly and sniffed. "First food, then I start phoning."

"God damn it!" John pounded his desk with his fist.

"What is it, what happened?" Angela rushed in and locked the door behind her.

"Catlin's dog has cancer."

"Oh. Is it curable?"

"The canine oncologist isn't sure. A canine oncologist, can you believe there's such a thing? Whatever happened to a quick injection and the dog's gone, problem solved? The doctor told her he thinks surgery for the tumor and radiation may work."

"Is there a chance?"

"Who knows? All I know is that she's already spent thousands on tests, MRIs, you name it, every money-wasting idea there is. And she's taking an extended leave from work to be with the stupid dog full time, so she'll be living off her savings."

"For how long?"

"She says as long as it takes. She's not worried about the money. She says she'll pay herself back with the trust fund next year. It's what her grandmother would have wanted her to do." John rolled his eyes toward the ceiling, and then buried his face in his hands. "God, why do I have such an idiot for a fiancée? All that money she's going to inherit, she might as well flush it down the toilet."

"Do you think the dog will die anyway?"

"Probably. Just not soon enough."

The room was quiet for several minutes. "I hear chocolate's bad for dogs," Angela volunteered.

"Right. I slip him a few Hershey bars and my troubles are over? Give me a break. If you're not going to help, just leave."

"What about antifreeze? I've read about dogs licking that off garage floors and dying."

"Hmm. Not bad, but she's never put him in the garage, and sure won't start that now. She's letting him sleep on her bed at night and he's got full run of the house with her during the day. I need something I can slip in his food, something neither of them would notice."

"Warfarin."

"What-farin?"

"Warfarin. It's a rat poison. Colorless, odorless, tasteless. It causes internal bleeding."

"Angela, you are devious and evil. Come here, you scheming bitch. I could take you right here on the desk." John bared his teeth in a glittering smile and coiled her in his arms. "Get me a bag of that stuff," he hissed against her throat.

"All right," she breathed and clawed to draw him closer.

"In a while," he grunted, and shoved her back onto the leather couch in the corner.

Catlin's focus narrowed to the evolving world of canine cancer treatment. When John volunteered to watch over Packard before the surgery to give her a break, she thanked him for being so supportive, but told him she'd be out of touch for a while and didn't give a second thought to his exasperated protest.

After she dropped Packard off at the vet hospital, she sat in her car and cried. She stayed at the complex the whole day, not trusting herself to drive home, and re-entered the lobby at three o'clock.

"Hello Ms. Davis," the assistant greeted her. "The operation went very well. Dr. Oberbauer said he was pleased with the appearance of the tumor. He'll be available in a bit to talk with you. Packard needs a little more time, and then you can take him home."

Catlin nodded and sat quietly.

The vet came out and explained postoperative care and procedures. "Marilyn will give you paperwork that describes everything," he said. "Don't worry about trying to remember it all. I'll go check on your dog now."

Catlin watched the hallway, took a deep breath when she heard slow tapping of nails on linoleum, and exhaled in tears as Packard stumbled into view. Chest bandaged, eyes groggy, he looked like a war victim. But he managed a weak wag when he saw her and leaned into her arms as she knelt to hold him.

"Don't worry, Ms. Davis, they always look worst right afterwards," Marilyn assured her. "He'll be pretty much out of it for a few days, between the stress of the operation and the pain pills. But then he'll perk up, you'll see. Can I help you put him in the car?"

When they got home, Packard went straight to his bed. Catlin read the vet's instructions and boiled potatoes and eggs for his bland diet. Nancy called to ask how it went and told her not to worry about her projects.

Though it seemed like forever, a few days later, Packard woke up barking for breakfast. At the follow-up visit, Dr. Oberbauer announced the incision was healing on schedule, but the pathology wasn't as favorable as he would like, so he recommended a course of radiation. "Then we'll see where we are," he said.

Catlin kept writing checks, following instructions, and praying. John continued to offer caregiving, but she put him off, recognizing that at some point she'd have to deal with his anger. Finally, she felt that Packard could be alone for a few hours and accepted Nancy's invitation to a cozy Italian restaurant near home.

"This is nice." Catlin smiled across the table.

"I know. We haven't had lunch together in ages," Nancy agreed.

"It's not just the food. Though this pasta is good." Catlin stopped to take another bite. "It's so relaxing to talk with you. Every conversation with John has been such a hassle lately. Everything I say and do bothers him. It's like we're on opposing teams or something. He's really been unpleasant."

"You need to speak up. Tell him the way he's acting is unacceptable. When a guy's being a jerk, I tell him."

"You tell him? You mean . . . you tell him? What do you say?"

"I say 'you're being a jerk.' What else would I say?" Nancy took another forkful of salad.

"I don't know. That doesn't sound very nice. I never wanted to get them mad or hurt their feelings. Men have pretty fragile egos, don't you think?"

"No. If he's not man enough to treat me with respect, then he's a wuss and I'm not interested. Catlin. If I weren't nice to you and we didn't get along, would you be friends with me? Would we be having lunch together right now?"

"No, probably not."

"Then why would you accept less from a guy? Especially in a close relationship?"

Catlin shrugged. "I guess I'm afraid of being alone."

"Are you? How do you feel when you're in your house by yourself?"

"Oh, it's great." She smiled and leaned back in her chair. "I love it. I'm in my comfort zone with Packard, doing research, writing, just putzing around."

"And when John's there?"

"Well, he doesn't like the house, you know, or how I furnished it, so there's a lot of tension. It's stuff we need to work out. Doesn't everybody have that?" She sipped her iced tea.

Nancy sighed. "No, not everybody. But that kind of pain is all too common, I think. It's up to you, but don't fool yourself about him changing after you're married. If he doesn't like your stuff now, he won't later. If you're fighting about money, furniture, sex, whatever, now, it's going to get worse after you say 'I do'."

"How do you know?" Catlin challenged. "You're still single."

Nancy waved her empty fork. "Let's just say I lived it long enough to know I had to get out."

"You were married?"

"I was young and stupid." Nancy's mouth twisted and she gazed up at the ceiling for a minute. "I was so starry-eyed and lost in him, eager to be part of his family. I ignored all the negative stuff and just concentrated on the isolated positive moments. I didn't ask myself the tough questions."

"Which are what?"

"Oh, I don't know. Am I happy when I'm with this person? Am I at peace or am I anxious something's going to piss him off at a moment's notice? Am I comfortable with myself, confident that he believes in me? Do we have similar values? How does he treat other people? Is he nice to his mother, the waitress, my dog? Does he say positive things, or is he always negative, expecting me to cheer him up? Does he make our relationship a priority, or do a zillion other things come first?"

"That's quite a list." Catlin pushed the ravioli around on her plate. "How would you have answered those questions?"

"You mean, if I had the courage to be truly honest with myself? I would have admitted that I was unhappy lots of the time, that I was always walking on egg shells, trying to say the right thing that would make him happy, make him appreciate me. I would have opened my eyes to the distain he had for his mom, how curt and dismissive he was with service people. And on and on. Denial is more than a river in Egypt, my dear friend."

"You think I'm in denial about John, don't you?"

Nancy shrugged. "It's what you think that matters. I just want you to be honest with yourself. If you think a wedding is a lot of work, try getting divorced. It's no fun, whether you're the leaver or the leavee."

"For crying out loud, we haven't mailed wedding invitations yet and you're seeing us in court?" Catlin slapped down her fork.

"I understand why you're angry with me, but this is important. Otherwise I wouldn't press it. My marriage only lasted three years, but it was long enough to get complicated financially and make us both bitter. I don't want to see you make the same mistakes I did. I care about you." Nancy reached across the table and touched her friend's hand. "I want you to see that real men are kind."

"It's that simple?"

"It's that simple. And it's consistent. Not that 'sometimes he can be so sweet' crap. If he knows how to treat you right sometimes, then the rest of the time he's choosing not to. Doesn't that bother you? Would you treat Packard that way?"

Catlin leaned forward eagerly, back on firmer ground. "Random reward is a very effective training method. I don't do it myself, but experiments show that animals work harder when the payoff is unpredictable . . ." Her voice trailed off and she looked away. Then she met Nancy's patient gaze. "What are you saying? That John's been training me like a dog?"

"Do you come when called? Do you sit and stay on his command? Do you go down when he says to?" Nancy broke off at Catlin's horrified look. "Sorry, that was nasty. Anyway, yes, that's what I'm saying. For a guy who doesn't like dogs, he uses the techniques pretty well."

"Yeah, I guess he's proved he doesn't like dogs. He told me last week he's not going to watch me waste much more money on Packard's treatments."

"What does that mean?" Nancy's eyes narrowed.

"I don't know, exactly. Just more of his ranting, I figured. He's very conservative about money."

Nancy snorted. "Uh huh. *Your* money. I notice he didn't skimp when he bought his new car."

"You are on a roll about him today, aren't you? You want to just slap me and get it over with?"

"Would that help you open your eyes? As opposed as I am to physical violence, if I thought it would do some good, I might be tempted." Nancy raised her hand, pretending to take aim, and they both laughed.

"You know, I got a little nervous when John said that about Packard," Catlin confessed. "He sounded serious, like he had a plan. I told him the radiation was working, and the vet expects a full recovery."

"Is that true? That's great!"

Catlin stared down at the table. "I hope it's true. It's what I want more than anything."

Nancy tilted her head in confusion. "But is it what the vet said?"

"No. He said it's too soon to tell. I just wanted to head off the argument. John was totally furious, like that time in front of the house when the construction was going on." She rubbed her arm and winced with the memory. "That was so scary, Nancy. He was like a different person. Even though he apologized, I still can't forget it. He was hurting me. I don't know what would have happened if the Altman guys hadn't been there."

"It must have been awful."

"Yeah. Kind of funny too, when Bill knocked over the fire hydrant and everybody got wet." Catlin giggled but her eyes remained downcast. Then she glanced up. "What would people think if I broke off the engagement? Would they think I'm an idiot?"

"First of all, why do you care what anyone else thinks? It's your life, and you have to look out for yourself, not make a bad choice because you think that's what other people want you to do. The truth is most people are too busy thinking about themselves to worry about anybody else."

"I guess."

"But second, and I hope you don't get mad at me for being honest, the people who care about you don't like how John treats you. If you said the wedding's off, we'd probably throw you a big un-engagement party. We could have a band and invite some old friends."

Catlin's eyes lightened. "Like Bobby, your hunky bear? Whatever happened to him?"

"Mmmmm, we had some nice times together." Nancy smiled mistily and leaned her head on her hand. "He got assigned to a big project in Phoenix and I haven't heard from him for weeks. That happens." She shook her hair back. "But we digress. What about you? What are you going to do?"

Catlin slumped with the weight of indecision and fear. "I think I know what I want to do. I know I know what I should do."

Nancy crossed her eyes and Catlin laughed.

"Okay, I'm babbling. I'm a little afraid of him now. He wants things a certain way and he gets totally pissed off if I do something that isn't in his plans. Except I'm not sure what his plans are, anymore."

Nancy tapped her fork against her plate thoughtfully. "We can be fairly certain his plans don't include you spending your inheritance the way you want. And I don't think Packard's in his long-range plans either. Have you ever wondered why he's so hot to marry you?"

"Thank you very much. You're being such a good friend today."

"Sweetie, you know I think you're quite a catch. And I'm not the only one."

"What? Who?"

"No, it's who, what, where, when, why. Didn't you learn anything in high school English?"

"Stop teasing and 'fess up. Who thinks I'm a good catch?"

"Oh, c'mon, Catlin, are you that dense? Who was your hero when John was all pissed off? Who spent the whole banquet glued to your side?"

"Oh, c'mon, Nancy," Catlin mocked. "What other choice did Neil have? You were monopolizing his friend the whole night."

Nancy laughed. "Uh huh, and you wanted to spend the evening chatting with me. But we're digressing again."

"Yeah, thinking about those boys tends to make us do that, doesn't it? The thing is, John got so angry when I talked about postponing the wedding, I don't know how he'd react if I said it's off completely."

"I understand. But we should explore why he gets so angry. If he loved you, don't you think he'd be sad? What does he want from the marriage?"

"Not sex—with me anyway," Catlin whispered ruefully.

Nancy opened her mouth and then closed it again. "Okay. We'll eliminate lust from the list. What else? Shared interests? Children?"

"No and no."

"Property? Oh, never mind. You already said he doesn't like your house."

"Right. You know, this is getting depressing." Catlin frowned and sipped her tea.

"Better realistic and depressed than in denial."

"Are you sure? I think I'm going to need something stronger if we keep at this much longer."

"Stay focused. How about earnings?"

"He makes a ton more than I do, or ever will, unless I write the next great American novel. Besides, when I inherit my grandma's trust fund next year, I may drop my hours back more so I can concentrate on my writing."

Nancy raised her eyebrows. "Is the inheritance that much?"

Catlin shrugged. "Sure. I haven't checked with the managers lately, but I think it's about five million."

"Oh my god, really?"

"Yeah. Grandma picked great stocks early and stuck with them. She wanted me to be free to write. That's why she set up the trust. Isn't that incredible? I've missed her and her faith in me so much since she died."

"I know, but Catlin, think. Does John know how much is in the trust fund?"

"Uh huh. I told him after we had been dating about six months because he asked what my future plans were."

Nancy swirled the ice in her glass with her straw. "And how long after that did he propose?"

"Umm, it was the next week . . . oh shit." Catlin stared at Nancy while disconnected bits of conversations and actions over the last two years clunked into place. The weight of time wasted in a fog of negativity, confusion, and heartache settled in her stomach. "The whole time it's been about money?" She buried her face in her hands. "I have been such a total moron," she groaned. "No wonder he didn't want to postpone the wedding. He wants us married before I inherit. Stupid, stupid, stupid."

"Hey, hey, don't beat yourself up," Nancy soothed. "He's the bad guy in this drama. He's using you because you're so trusting. Now that you realize what he is, you can get out before it's too late."

"How can I get out? I don't know if I can confront him."

"So . . . you'll go through with the wedding because you're afraid to break it off?" Nancy sighed. "Do you have a spine or what?"

Catlin reached back. "I think there's something there," she said, feeling up and down. "Look, I'm not saying I won't tell him we're done. I need a plan, that's all."

"I agree. And I need dessert. Whew! Trying to save your ass from disaster is tough work."

"Great. My life's a total wreck and you want ice cream."

"No, your life is finally getting back on track, and I want cheesecake." Nancy smiled. "Look, you can do this. You have lots of friends and we're all here for you, okay?"

"Okay. But I'm going to insist on one thing," Catlin said firmly, sitting up straight.

"What's that?"

"Ice cream."

When Catlin's spoon clattered against her empty bowl, Nancy chuckled. "It's a sin how you can eat so much of that stuff and not gain an ounce. I should hate you, you know."

"It's just metabolism. When I turn forty I'll probably explode and have to eat lettuce for dessert. Besides, everyone should be allowed one sin. Though it's kind of pathetic that mine's ice cream."

"Hmmm, that is sad, especially considering you're engaged. So what's the deal? How come your hot shot attorney fiancé isn't so hot?"

Catlin shrugged. "There was never enough time, is what I used to think. Sometimes I wonder why I bother to take the Pill. It's been annoying. I get frustrated, then short-tempered and tense. Now I can't be with him at all, so it'll get worse."

Nancy pointed with her fork. "The problem is that you're not being self-reliant. You need to take matters into your own hands . . . as it were," she added.

"My own hands!" Catlin shook her head and laughed. "That's certainly interesting advice."

"And why not take care of yourself? Love with a wonderful partner is great, but sometimes you just need to, umm, relax, without the complications. Knowing you can satisfy yourself is powerful. Plus you'll be a lot nicer to be around." Nancy leaned forward and whispered slyly, "C'mon, do it for your co-workers."

"I . . . I'll . . . I'll take it under advisement. Oh god, I sound like my mother."

"And if she were at the table, I bet she'd agree with my advice."

"No she wouldn't! She'd be shocked."

Nancy snickered. "You forget, I've met your mom. She's a very practical lady. Didn't she always tell you to be independent and not rely on a man for anything? You think she was just talking about finances?"

"Okay, okay." Catlin looked down at her watch. "You need to get back to work. Besides, my head's spinning."

"I know. You had a lot of revelations with your ravioli."

"Seasoned with some spicy advice. You're always full of surprises. But thank you. I know you care, and I appreciate it." Catlin sniffed as she scooted her chair back.

"Hey, now. No getting mushy. I'm just trying to avoid buying a wedding gift. You never know, I might need the money for plane fare to Phoenix."

"Uh huh. And what happened to self-reliance?"

"It's important, but I've got to admit, there's nothing like a nice construction worker with the right equipment."

"Who knows how to use it in those delicate areas?"

Nancy laughed. "Now I'm shocked. Wait until I tell your mother what you said!"

21

That afternoon, future plans also were being discussed over lunch in a locked office downtown.

"Your brilliant warfarin idea isn't working. Catlin won't let me come over. I can't get access."

"I'm sorry, John. I thought she'd welcome your offer to help."

"Yeah, well . . . shit! Are there onions on this? Why didn't you tell them to leave off the onions?" He pushed his sandwich across the desk to Angela.

"I'm sorry. I'll scrape them off."

"Never mind, give me yours. You eat that one."

"Of course. My fault."

"Of course," he mimicked in falsetto. "Anyway, I have a better idea. The way she's acting with the dog being sick, I'd prefer it if he didn't die before the wedding. She'd probably postpone to grieve." He emphasized the last word with an elongated sneer. "But I've figured out how to commute my five-year marriage sentence to one year."

"How?"

"Time off for bad behavior. We take a first anniversary trip that will have a tragic end."

"What do you mean?"

"You know how Catlin loves hiking?"

"Right, which you hate."

"Exactly. Fucking waste of time. Walking in circles, stumbling over rocks, accomplishing nothing. But the point is, she thinks it's great and will jump at the chance to convert me. So I'll propose we go to her favorite place—Zion."

"Why there?"

John pulled out a brochure. "Because this place has exactly what I need: trails with precipitous drop-offs. Look, it says Angels Landing is on a narrow ridge with a drop-off of fifteen hundred feet."

"You're going up Angels Landing Trail?"

"Nah, too popular. This is the best one." He stabbed at a short description and read aloud. "Hidden Canyon Trail. Steep climb up eight hundred and fifty feet. Hikers may continue but there is no maintained trail. Warning! Steep cliffs. Not for anyone fearful of heights." He paused and smiled. "It's perfect."

"For what?"

"For a tragic accident. You're being especially dense today. I'll go hiking a newlywed and come home a widower."

"You're pushing Catlin off a cliff?"

"Of course not. That would be crude. We'll go on this challenging trail and I'll be game but will stubbornly refuse hiking poles, which she swears by. Except at some suitably steep and isolated part of the trail, I'll panic and beg for one of her poles. In the transfer, she'll lose her footing and fall to her death. I'm sure there'll be questions, but it happens all the time. Books are full of stories about death in national parks. I figure with the money I save killing her off after just a year instead of divorcing her after five, I don't care how long the dog lives. Her parents can have him as a consolation prize. See how much better my plan is?" He ate cheerfully, nodding at the brightly colored brochure as if in appreciation for solving a vexing problem.

Angela sat silent, eyes downcast and food untouched. She clasped and unclasped her hands in her lap.

"Told you, onions ruin a sandwich. Maybe you'll remember to keep them off mine next time."

"Yes, I will." She rewrapped the sandwich and stood to take it away. "Do you want me to get rid of the rat poison for you, since you don't need it?"

"No, I'll keep it. Never know when something like that could come in handy." His smile was all teeth.

"I understand."

"Do you?"

"Yes, John. It's our future and I'm totally here for you."

"Okay. There are signs of intelligent life after all. But I'll still keep the poison." He crumpled the empty wrapper and tossed it into the trash. "Good lunch. Got that Wilson research done yet?"

"No, I . . ."

"Guess you've got some work to do, then."

Angela pursed her lips, turned, and left.

The next time Nancy called, Catlin reported there was no change.

"I'm sorry," Nancy said. "Isn't the radiation helping?"

"No. Doctor Oberbauer didn't like Packard's progress, so we're trying chemo."

"How's he doing with that?"

"Not good. Both vets are confused. They say he should be cancer free and feeling better by now. The only bright spot is that John's supportive. He said we have to try everything possible for Packard because he knows how important he is to me."

"That's an interesting about-face."

"Now that it doesn't matter. It makes me wonder what he's up to. I can't believe I was ever in love with him."

"Have you mentioned anything about calling off the wedding?"

"No. I can't handle that right now."

"Of course not. You need to focus on Packard. I sure hope he recovers."

"Thanks. I'll let you know how it goes."

When she hung up the phone, she checked on Packard, who was sleeping fitfully. She soothed him until his breathing evened out and left the bedroom quietly.

As a distraction, she had bought her own subscription to Ancestry.com, and she logged on to pass the time. She had searched Carolyn Parker, but there were no hits in the 1800s. Remembering one of the real names from Carolyn's book, she entered Josephine Muget and clicked a search of the 1870 census. To her surprise, the result in Colorado was the same as her mother had noted as J. Nugat. Catlin magnified the name.

"I guess that could be Muget. If the book editor was right, and Josephine Muget was a successful madam, then these would be her girls, like Mom said. And if her house is where Carolyn's letters ended up, then could Carolyn have been writing to Josephine?"

Catlin folded her hands on top of her head and leaned back. J could be Josephine, but Carolyn's letters and the responses spanned many years after 1874, the year Josephine died. Catlin scrolled through the list of other house occupants: Molly, Emma, Laura, Amy, the intriguing seamstress Catherine, and James. Another J. No Carolyn, but the census was only once every ten years. A new girl could have come the next week and wouldn't appear on the list. Besides, Carolyn wasn't her real name; the chanteuse had written as much in Chapter 12. And Jack Rayburn wasn't her lover's real name either. No wonder the editor got frustrated.

She read the foreword again. The letters were found wrapped in a man's shirt, and James was in the house a long time, owning and operating it after Josephine died. Carolyn thought she was writing to her mother, but what if the letters were going to James, and he was the one sending money? Maybe Carolyn didn't know until her last letter, when she asked "mother or brother" to come and get her baby. Would that be the infant daughter James willed to Amy's care?

"So many questions. Maybe I need to go to Denver anyway, though I won't be there on a honeymoon."

She checked her watch. Time for Packard's meds. She roused him, and he followed her slowly into the kitchen. She wrapped up the pill in a gob of peanut butter and held it in front of him.

Packard sat heavily, but refused to open his mouth.

"If you won't eat, I can't give you your pain meds. Come on, you love peanut butter," she pleaded.

He stretched out on the kitchen floor.

"Okay, we'll try later," she said, and rubbed his ears.

He closed his eyes. His breathing was shallow, each exhale ending on a whimper.

"Oh Packard, this isn't working, is it? Did we do our best? Do you want to go?" She kneeled next to him and stroked the soft fur on his neck, tears streaming.

He opened his eyes, rose slowly, and tottered outside to the laundry porch. She followed and sat down next to him, watching him gaze into the backyard.

Dr. Berger had told her, "Dogs aren't like people. They can't distract themselves, read a book, watch TV, hope for a cure. All they know is that they hurt and they want the pain to end. So you have to help them when they let you know they're ready. If it comes to that, call me, and I'll bring what I need so Packard doesn't have to leave home."

She went inside and called the vet.

"Okay, Fuzzbucket, Dr. Berger is on his way. I have to do what's right for you."

Packard licked her hand. His ears pricked at a rustling in the yard, and his body stiffened.

As if knowing the end was near, a squirrel scampered down the pine tree and hunkered over a pile of bird seed that had fallen from the feeder.

Packard launched himself off the porch and raced after the squirrel, barking in a fury before collapsing under the pine tree.

Laughing and crying at the same time, Catlin joined him under the tree. "You are such a numbskull. I love you so much, how am I going to live without you?" She soothed him as he panted and shuddered. When the doorbell rang, she hurried to answer it.

Dr. Berger came with her into the backyard. "I'm so sorry, Catlin. Sometimes even if we get all the cancer, the stress of treatment is too much. If he won't eat, he's letting you know the only way he can that he's ready."

"I understand. I can't let him suffer any more like this."

"Okay." The vet waited while Catlin said good-bye.

She knelt, caressed Packard's ears and ran her hands over him from head to tail. "I'll see you later, big guy. Be good and wait for me, okay? Watch out for me down here, if you can, I'll need all the help I can get." She wrapped her arms around him, and nodded to Dr. Berger, her eyes blurry with tears.

The vet knelt next to Catlin and laid his hand on Packard's head, studying the dog intently. He turned to her, and said, "You know, it's not unheard of for animals to recover from an apparently terminal condition after they've had extended relief from pain."

"What are you saying?"

"Packard can't see any way to escape from the pain, so he doesn't want to live. But if we can give his body a rest, maybe he could heal." Dr. Berger stood. "It could work. I've seen it before. It's rare, but it could work."

"What should we do?" Catlin asked.

"I'll give him a shot that will be enough to let him sleep. Keep him warm here tonight. I'll come tomorrow morning with another shot to keep him under one more day. Then let's see if he wants to eat so you can give him his meds. What do you say?"

"He could be all right? He might not die?" Joy shone in her eyes.

"It's possible. It's worth a try."

"Definitely. Oh my god, definitely!" She jumped up and hugged the vet. "Thank you, thank you!"

"Ahem, let's just hope for the best, okay? I can't promise. This may only be a reprieve." He pulled what he needed from his bag and administered the shot.

Catlin patted Packard while he drifted to sleep. She skipped as she escorted the vet out and danced as she collected Packard's blanket. "It's like a campout," she told him, tucking him in. "I'll join you too, how's that?"

She gathered her sleeping bag from the closet and a pillow from her bed. When night fell, she curled up next to him, listening to his steady breathing, letting hope fill her heart and dreams.

22

That same evening, another mind plotted death, certain and untraceable. While Catlin was settling next to Packard for his second night of rest, John set the plan in motion when he called Angela into his office.

"Listen, I know there's a lot of stress on both of us. What do you say we take a long drive tonight? Put the top down and put everything behind us at a million miles an hour. We can have dinner at that podunk place in the hills with the piano bar."

Angela smiled the grateful, eager smile he most enjoyed, and said, "That'd be perfect. I'll get my jacket."

"Meet me in the parking garage. I'll be down in a minute."

"Sure."

He tapped on his phone, debating whether to call Catlin since he hadn't heard from her for several days. "Stupid dog'll probably die and fuck everything up. Shit. Whatever. I'll get an update tomorrow." He left paperwork scattered over his desk and slammed off the light.

In the garage, he nodded to Angela as he got in the car. He unlocked the passenger door after he sat down behind the wheel.

She settled in quickly and silently.

"Hey, it's a great night for a drive, isn't it?" he said when he accelerated onto the freeway.

"It's lovely," Angela agreed.

"Too bad about all these shit-for-brains commuters, but we'll be past them in no time." He wove in and out, finding the smallest openings to whichever lane appeared to be moving the fastest. Finally east of homebound traffic, he sped toward the mountains.

"Man I love this car."

"It's wonderful to go so fast."

"Yeah? Want me to crank it up?"

"Yes, crank it up!" Angela laughed with a freedom in her voice he'd never heard before.

He floorboarded it past ninety and turned toward her.

She gazed at him with joy. "I have a surprise for you," she shouted over the wind.

He glanced back to the road—some tricky curves were coming up—then looked over.

"Yeah? Something good?"

"Oh yes. I'm pregnant!" She laughed in that new unrestrained way he already hated.

"You're what?" His foot involuntarily hit the accelerator and the car surged forward, pushing 120. "You're shitting me! You said you couldn't get pregnant!"

"The doctor must have said shouldn't. But I am and it's yours."

"I don't want a fucking baby!" he screamed. "Abort it!"

"No! It's our child and I want it." She stared resolutely into his purple face, the eye to the hurricane of his fury.

"Abort it, damn it!"

"No! I won't!"

"Then I will, you stupid bitch!" He released his seatbelt and swung a hard left hook into her belly.

Angela moaned and doubled over.

He slapped her head back and punched her again.

Freed of control, the BMW exhibited its solid engineering by speeding straight where the road bent abruptly to preserve a massive oak. The car broke the guardrail like pretzel sticks, plowed into the tree and spewed its unrestrained occupant through the windshield.

John's last word sounded like a distant "Fuuuu . . ." to Angela as metal crumpled and air bags inflated around her.

In the instant before death, John's Catholic upbringing flashed one final thought: *I hope there's no hell.* Then his skull shattered against pavement, and his brains exploded into a slime of unrecognizable road kill.

For hours, the scene belonged to the night. The moon rose and crickets chirped. A coyote howled. A passing car caught the broken guardrail in its headlights, slowed, and pulled over to the shoulder. Half an hour later, emergency vehicles swarmed onto the site. Trained hands pulled Angela from the ruins of the BMW and rushed her to the hospital.

A sheriff's deputy threw a plastic tarp over John, sighing, "Another idiot not wearing a seatbelt. When will people learn?"

Catlin woke in the morning to the squawk of a mockingbird. Packard's blanket lay empty. She sat up in alarm. Packard stood near the house. He turned to face her, bowed, and circled around to greet her with a hearty woof and a wet slurp.

"Packard! You're better!" she cried. "Aren't you?" She grasped his ears and looked into his eyes.

He barked and licked her again.

"How about breakfast? I still have potatoes."

He nudged her arm.

"Okay!" She jumped out of her sleeping bag and followed him into the kitchen.

"I can't wait to call Doctor Berger to tell him how awesome he is," she said, watching Packard lap up mashed potatoes and baby food.

Her parents, the vets, and Nancy were overjoyed to hear the news. Thinking to at least give John the courtesy of a call, since he had been so concerned about Packard, she reached for the phone, but it rang before she lifted the receiver.

"Hello?"

"Hello, Ms. Davis?"

"Yes."

"This is Diane Williams, HR Director for Linscott, Jackson, and Krieger."

"Oh, sure, how are you?" she responded politely, wondering why John's firm would be calling. *Maybe he made partner; that'll distract him from the bad news that he won't be living off my inheritance.*

"We've received the terrible news, Ms. Davis, and I wanted to make sure you knew how sorry we are about your loss."

"That's very kind of you, Diane. But actually, it's a happy day."

"You're so brave. You mean because Angela survived?"

"Angela? No, I mean because he's alive."

"Oh no, I'm sorry, but you've been misinformed."

"I'm not misinformed. I just fed him breakfast and he's sniffing around the backyard as we speak."

"I don't know who's in your backyard, Ms. Davis, but it's John who was killed in the traffic accident, and Angela is at Grossmont Hospital in critical condition."

"What?"

"Didn't you know? Your fiancé crashed into a tree last night and was ejected from the car. Apparently he wasn't wearing a seatbelt. His secretary was a passenger. She's severely injured but is expected to live."

"Oh." Catlin didn't know what else to say. "I was this close to calling off the wedding and I'm happy because my dog is okay" didn't seem appropriate. "Where were they going?"

"I don't know. Possibly a late meeting. You can come to the office anytime and collect John's personal effects. We've set them aside for you. I deeply regret your receiving this news from me. I thought you had already been notified."

"That's okay. I'm just stunned. I can come by tomorrow for John's things."

"That's fine. Our deepest apologies. You can ask for Brad Gipson, John's co-worker, when you come."

"Sure. Thank you."

"Good-bye. Good luck to you."

That was unexpected, she thought. A few weeks ago, she would have collapsed in tears, but all she felt was relief. And a morbid curiosity. Where were they going? Why was Angela with him, and why did he crash the car? John was an assured, although aggressive driver, and it wasn't like him to be unbuckled. She walked outside to check on Packard. He had dragged his blanket to a sunny spot and was busy bunching it into a suitable nest. He flopped down with a sigh.

"Will you be okay for a couple of hours, Bucko? I need to visit a sick friend in the hospital."

He rolled onto his back, tongue out.

She scratched his belly. "Good answer. See you in a bit."

She called to confirm Angela could have visitors and bought a pretty potted orchid on the way. She entered the hospital room quietly. A doctor held Angela's chart.

"So all in all, you're a very lucky young lady. With rigorous physical therapy we expect a full recovery. Because of the pelvic injuries, I'd normally advise a woman of your age to plan on Cesarean delivery for any pregnancy, but I see that you had a hysterectomy five years ago, correct?"

Angela nodded slowly. She smiled in spite of the bruises on her face.

"Sometimes that's the best solution for uncontrollable periods. You can always adopt when you're ready for children."

She nodded again.

The doctor looked up from the chart and noticed Catlin. "You have a visitor. That's all for now. The nurses will set you up for physical therapy. I'll check on you later."

"Thank you," she croaked.

When the doctor left, Catlin placed the plant on the shelf opposite the bed and sat next to Angela. "Hi. Umm. Sorry about the accident."

Angela shrugged and winced.

"Did they tell you about John?"

"Yes. He's dead," she said flatly.

"Right. Terrible. But it looks like you'll be okay."

"Unexpected."

"I'm glad for you, though. I wouldn't want you to think I resent you surviving or anything." Catlin fumbled on as Angela stared at the ceiling, her face a blank mask. "You helped get us through a rough patch this summer and I wanted to thank you for that."

"You're welcome."

"I have to ask what happened. I mean, John's a pretty good driver. Was. Well, you know."

Angela nodded. "Speeding. Curve. Dropped cell."

"He dropped his cell phone? Is that why his seatbelt wasn't fastened? He was trying to reach his phone?"

"Yes." Anger flashed across her face. "Stupid man." She paused. "Tired."

"Sure. I'll let you rest. Look, I'm sorry to bother you, I just needed to know. Thanks for telling me. Obviously, it's painful for you."

"And you."

It sounded like a question, so Catlin replied, "I guess I'm kind of numb."

"Numb," Angela repeated. "Numb is good." She tilted her head slightly toward the IV and choked a harsh laugh.

Catlin realized with surprise that was a joke. She stood. "Take care, and thanks."

"Least I could do." Angela looked at Catlin as if she wanted to say something else but then shifted against the pillow and closed her eyes.

"Good-bye," Catlin whispered, and tiptoed out.

With more information in hand, she called her parents again.

Her mother said, "Darling, that's such a shame," and told her father, "John's been killed in a car accident."

"Halleluiah," Catlin thought she heard him say.

"What did Dad say?"

"He said how are you."

"Oh. I'm okay. We hadn't been getting along too well lately." It was as close to the truth as she was willing to share at the moment.

"Cold feet?"

"Something like that."

"Don't worry, darling. It's sad, but it wasn't meant to be. When it's right, you'll know it. Meanwhile, you should concentrate on your purpose. That's what your grandmother wanted and what we want for you. Will there be a service?"

"Uh, I don't know. I haven't heard from his parents. Guess I should call them."

"They may be on their way here from Boston. I would imagine the authorities contacted them last night."

"I'll let you know."

"All right. Call again soon."

"Thanks, Mom."

Mrs. McKenzie called late that afternoon to inform Catlin that John would be cremated and taken home to Boston where he belonged. If Catlin's "people" wanted a local memorial service, it was up to her. She could take the personal effects he had at "that firm," but a professional estate settlement company would handle his condo and contents. "They'll be sure to notify you of any items that belong to you," Mrs. McKenzie said stiffly, and hung up.

"Looks like I dodged a mother-in-law bullet," Catlin told Packard and then immediately felt guilty. What could be more stressful for a mother than dealing with a child's death? Being on opposite coasts, they had never interacted much, and now they would have no reason to attempt a relationship.

"Want to take a walk around the block? I need to clear my head, and you've got a lot of p-mail to read."

Packard barked.

That night she called Nancy, whose response was considerably less restrained than her mother's.

"Wow, the universe has been good to you this week! You should play the lottery."

"Nancy! Someone important in my life has died."

"And have you cried?"

"No, but everyone grieves in their own way. I'm still in shock."

"Okay, that's a good line. I'd stick with that."

"You're impossible." Catlin couldn't resist a giggle.

"His bad driving sure saved you from an onerous task. Kind of strange about heading to the mountains with his secretary at night, don't you think?"

"The HR Director said they were going to a late meeting."

"What did the secretary say?"

"I didn't ask her. She looked awful. I feel sorry for her."

"If she was involved with John, I do too."

Catlin was silent for a moment, reflecting on the power of insight. "A few weeks ago I would be grieving for John and mad at you for saying that. Now I don't feel anything for him and agree with you."

"It's great to be able to be completely honest with you again. I always felt like John was in the way of that and I had to be careful about what I could say to you."

"It'd be easy to blame him, but it's my fault for letting him control me. I hope I don't fall into that trap again."

"You can count on me to nag you if you do. So are you going to his office tomorrow?"

"I think so. I'm curious what kind of things he left."

"Me too. Be sure to share with me."

"I will. Thanks. I'll be back to work soon."

"Take some bereavement leave. I won't tell anyone you don't need it."

Catlin giggled again. "If I go to hell for laughing about this, it's your fault."

"A very smart person I know said everyone grieves in their own way."

"That does sound good."

"So stick with it."

They hung up, laughing.

23

The next morning, Catlin dressed in black, though it wasn't her best color, and waited in the gleaming law office lobby for Brad Gipson. *I forgot how fancy this place was*, she thought. *I'm glad I wore my patent leather pumps.*

When Brad came out, he apologized for the delay and shook her hand awkwardly. "Uh, could you come into my office? There're some things I'd like to talk with you about, besides John's stuff."

Surprised she wasn't just handed a box, she replied, "Okay."

"Want any coffee or water?" he asked as she settled into his guest chair.

"No, I'm fine, thanks."

He pushed a small box across his desk to her. "Here's what John had that isn't company stuff. Not much."

"Apparently not." She rifled through the short stack of papers, raising an eyebrow at the Zion brochure.

"Great hiking there. Didn't know John was into that."

"I didn't either."

"Uh huh." Brad's attention had already shifted to a leather-bound book he pulled out of his desk drawer. "Anyway, I wanted to talk about the Wilson case with you."

"The Wilson case?"

"Right, Amy Wilson's diary. I thought you knew about that case."

"No, why would I?"

"I just figured John would've asked you to help, you being so good at research and all."

"The case involves historical research?"

"Yeah. It's like this. The historical society got the diary in a donation with a bunch of other papers and photos. Caregiver found it when he cleaned out his client's closet after she'd died. The old lady didn't have any relatives, you know, that kind of deal. County's public administrator had no luck finding family and disposed of the estate. So anyway, this long-lost nephew turns up, says hey that's mine, I'm in the direct family line, give it back. But the society says, no way, we got it fair and square, and how do we know you're not some faker tryin' to take it."

"Is the diary valuable?"

"Sure yeah. Goes back to the late 1800s. This Amy Wilson chick was something else. Hooker made good by marrying the sheriff, becomes a mom, great stuff. You'd like reading it."

"You've read it?"

"Yeah. Both parties agreed it'd be okay, us being a prestigious law firm, you know. It's supposed to be under lock and key but John let some of us go through it. He'd kind of hit a dead end. Oh—sorry. Anyway, so he showed us. That's why I thought you'd seen it before too."

"No, he never mentioned it."

"Huh. Well, it's my case now. Partners split up his load through the firm. Work goes on, sad but true."

"Sure."

"So here's the thing. When they dropped this Wilson diary on me, I said can I get some outside help, and they said okay."

"You want me to help?"

"Yeah. Take it home and read through it. I got some info on the LLN too."

"LLN?"

"Long-lost nephew. If you can connect him to Amy, the historical society said they'd give the diary back. What do you say? Up for it? I mean, I know you're grieving, so I totally understand if you don't want to get into it."

She reached for the book—or did it reach for her? "Everyone grieves in their own way. I think it would help to work on this." She sensed echoes of simple joys, and where Carolyn's book had enticed, the diary welcomed her as an old friend.

"Cool. Much appreciated." He pushed a button on his phone. "Liz'll work up the agreement with you." He nodded to the pretty young woman who appeared promptly at his door. "Let's meet again in a couple days, and you can tell me what you think. Sound okay?"

"That sounds fine." She put the diary on top of John's papers in the box and shook Brad's hand. "Thank you for entrusting me with the diary. I'll be very careful with it."

"I know. See you soon."

When she got home, she started reading the diary right away. "I can't believe I'm getting paid to do something so fun," she told Packard. Knowing she had to read with the purpose of finding Amy's family, she skimmed the entries with pencil ready to note all names mentioned.

The diary started with a short entry.

July 1868—Hot. The streets are filthy. But the house is very fine. Elegant. Josephine says the men are gents. I get a day to recover from weeks on the stagecoach, and then must get to work.

"Josephine!" Could it be the same madam?" She skipped through until she saw another name.

March 1869—A new beauty joined us today. Molly is demure and from good family. She swears she will only stay here a short time, the trip from Maryland having used all her funds. I remember making the same promise.

"Hey, Molly is one of the girls in the census list!" She kept reading through the year of sporadic monthly notations until a new name caught her eye.

March 1870—Molly's cousin arrived today. We watched them embrace in the street and Josephine asked how shall we tell these lovelies apart? James said nothing as usual. But from his expression, he already knows.

May 1870—I should hate her. As beautiful as Molly, but vivacious where Molly is reserved, laughing when others are quiet. Catherine can change the plainest dress to the latest fashion in less than an hour with her needle and thread. I said I envied that and she told me but dear Amy, you can change a simple potato into a delicious meal and that is a far more useful skill. Laura said she had the cleanest undergarments thanks to her skill with soap. Emma said it was she who Josephine relied on to count the money. We all agreed that was a very useful skill and the house rang with our merriment.

"This is too much to be coincidence. Molly, James, Laura, Emma, and Catherine." She wrote down the names and the comments. Catherine could sew, Amy cook, Laura wash clothes, and Emma count money. "Did they give the census taker those professions as a joke?" The revelations in subsequent entries hit her like waves as she sped through the rest of the diary.

February 1872—Tears today. James placed Molly's trunk on the carriage and drove her to Madam Beth's, a sober house to the south. We all but one waved good-bye. Catherine was in the garden, weeping how can she leave me when I came so far to be with her? I held her close and said nothing. Sisters come and go in this town. But the men keep coming and we stay busy.

December 1873—I am glad to be favored by a kind man. Walter is steady and works always for the good. Catherine takes pride in being the best in our house, but we learned today that beauty has its price. Josephine is not happy to banish the Judge. What else can she do when he damages her most valuable goods? Either way she loses money. Catherine cannot work for weeks and we will have to work all the harder to make up for it. She promised to sew new gowns for each of us. A fair trade.

July 1874—Walter said Josephine was mad to let Judge Wellingbrook back into the house. He told her to never let him near me. No fear of that, it is Catherine he wants. Or wanted. Why is she so sad? I am glad he is dead, such a cruel and heartless man. Walter wanted me to comfort her, but Josephine refused to let me see her.

July 1874—A dark day. Sisters come and go, but Catherine is one I will miss. I wish I could have talked with her before she took poison. Now James is in seclusion and Josephine is red-eyed. She is bringing a new beauty to the house before announcing the loss. Work goes on. At least I have Sampson. A grand name for such a little dog. Walter says Sam should be enough. Sam it is.

September 1874—I thought Josephine would live forever. How can she be gone? The whole town is in mourning. The most important men arranged a fine procession. Walter convinced Father McIntyre to let her be buried in the churchyard. He said giving her a plot is the least the church could do as they had no trouble taking her money to care for the orphans all these years. Money we earned on our backs, I told him. But I don't begrudge her the ceremony or final resting place. She was a good mother to us all. James promises to be a caring brother. He wants me to help with the business and spend less time upstairs. Walter agrees as long as he is still served.

October 1874—Walter is furious with Daniel. Called him a foolish love struck dunderhead with no more sense than a cat has for mathematics. He gave the note to the newspaper and worked alone for the burial. When I said I would dress him Walter shooed me away, saying he was like a brother and would take care of him like he was his own. James is very down, to my surprise. I would say there was no love lost between those two but of course there was—Catherine.

March 1875—If James wants me to help with the business he should let me see the accounts. He says banking was always his work for Josephine and if I want to do more for the house I can go to the kitchen or back upstairs. Walter says to leave him be. He runs a good house and if some money is being set aside for James' own use it is fair enough.

December 1879—I caught James reading a letter with the strangest mix of emotion on his face: surprise, anger, joy, and finally he whispered one word—granted. I turned away and left without a sound. I do not know who could write and make our ever-stoic brother feel so, but it is his business. Walter said it is a fine thing in a woman to let a man be and rewarded me with a tender kiss.

September 1880—I have never seen James so moved. He thought no one saw his happy tears reading another mysterious letter, but I did. I said nothing. I would not betray his secrets even if I knew them.

November 1880—I broke my promise to let James be. The whole house could hear his sobs and all the girls were so frightened that I had to ask him what was wrong. He swore me to secrecy except for Walter. Then he told me an amazing story. Both lovers have been alive all this time! I thought— well! Walter has some truths to confess to me about Daniel. In the next moment I learned Daniel had just died and Catherine was dying. It was like that terrible sadness years ago. James said he will tell me more when he returns with the baby and made me vow to care for our house and the child if something happened to him.

December 1880—Such a joyful Christmastime with a baby in the house! It is hard to say who is fussing most over the beautiful little girl, James, Walter or me. James has promised to tell me everything in due time. But for now we are happy and busy.

March 1881—James is very weak and wasting away before our eyes though he is still strong enough to force the doctor out of the house with a glare. He has drawn up his papers and I have agreed to the arrangement. Walter said he will love the child of our friends the same as his own if he ever had any. He gave me such a look that my heart jumped. James smiled from his deathbed and baby Samantha Lynn laughed.

April 1881—Emma swore she heard rustling in the basement last night. James said it was rats and fell back asleep. He is near done. I would be surprised if he sees the next morning. I am tired too. Running this house is hard work. I have lost my appetite for it and only want to care for the baby. When I said as much to Walter he said many a madam would pay good money for such a fine establishment and it was high time I became a respectable woman. How so I asked him. By marrying a respectable man he said. But are there any to be had in this town I said. We laughed at the jest. It is well known that there is no man more respectable in Denver than Sheriff Wilson. I asked him *what will people say about his choice of bride. He said he did not give a hoot and they will probably say he is a lucky man to get a rich wife.*

April 1881—We buried James next to Josephine. Walter is straining his friendship with Father McIntyre, but the donations never faltered so the good priest could not refuse his request. This summer we will ask another favor. We want him to christen Samantha Lynn as our own after we marry.

June 1881—A happy time. Walter was correct. It was easy to sell the house to new hands. Our wedding was simple and beautiful. I am a wife and mother.

July 1881—What a surprise I got when I shook out Samantha Lynn's christening gown! It is too small for her now, of course. I will save it for another infant. James must not have looked through the baby clothes or he would have found his letters to his Dearest C. I knew his precise handwriting from the books. I do not know where her letters are. One of many things James never told me. These letters are part of my girl's history so I will keep them for her and tell her all I know when she is old enough to understand.

July 1883—Samantha Lynn has a brother. She is not yet three and already a little mother. She wants to hold baby Benjamin. I must watch or she will try to lift him from the cradle when he cries.

September 1885—So tired. Though she is still too young I gave the letters to Samantha Lynn. Walter will have to explain who her mother and father are. But for now she

knows the letters tell a special story meant for her and any
daughter she may have.

That was the final entry. Catlin took a deep breath. She
felt like she had been underwater, immersed in another
world. The diary spanned seventeen years, and she couldn't
imagine how it would make much sense on its own, just like
the letters. She was the first person to have all three pieces:
the diary, letters from James, and the book of letters from
Carolyn, which she realized was Catherine's assumed name.
Now she knew why the book editor couldn't find any docu-
mentation on Carolyn. Or on Jack Rayburn, who apparently
was Daniel Hayden. So the editor was right about them being
lovers. And Josephine Muget was Catherine's mother in a
professional sense. The bookstore owner would be interested
to know his great-grandfather's name appeared in the diary,
confirming he died in a parlor house. But Adam Wellingbrook might not appreciate Amy's comments on the Judge's
personality.

As fascinating as the story was for her own ancestry,
Catlin knew she needed to concentrate on proving or disprov-
ing the nephew's connection, since that's what she was
getting paid to do. "Too bad I can't make a case to keep the
diary. I have the letters that Amy gave to Samantha Lynn. But
the nephew's blood line would be through Benjamin."

She opened the folder of information on the nephew that
Liz had given her before she left the law offices. He had sent
several e-mails and a letter to express his claim. It was
unfortunate that he had lost track of his dear great-aunt

Samantha when he moved to Portland after his parents died and that the county didn't try harder to find family. He didn't realize she had moved from Colorado for a warmer climate and learned about her death and the disposition of her estate only when a friend noticed the article about the diary in the historical society's newsletter and called him.

His great-aunt Sam was the daughter of Benjamin Wilson, only son of Walter Wilson, a sheriff in early Denver. She was named after Benjamin's adoptive sister, who ran away from home in 1899 to elope with a man unacceptable to the family, causing great distress to Walter, a widower since 1885. Benjamin's daughter never married. She kept house for her parents and inherited the family home in the 1960s when they passed away. She gave the family Bible and other papers to her favorite great-nephew on his fifteenth birthday, saying he reminded her of her brother. On that occasion, she showed him the diary and promised it to him after her death. He would share the family items with the historical society when they returned the diary to him. He enclosed a genealogical chart tracing his family history and expressed hope for a mutually satisfactory resolution to the situation.

Based on John's notes, conversations with the great-nephew, Eric Wilson, had not gone well, and the law firm's requests for copies of the papers and relevant pages of the family Bible had been refused. John was convinced Eric was a fake who had picked up a few key names from old newspaper articles and made up everything else.

After a few hours tracking names in the census, Catlin was convinced of exactly the opposite. Walter Wilson, head of household and a widower, was in the 1900 census with his son Benjamin. In 1910 and 1920, Benjamin had a wife, son, and daughter at the same Denver address. In 1930, the last census accessible by the public, only Benjamin and his daughter Samantha were at the house. The other names in Eric's chart also checked out in the census records. Catlin figured anyone could construct a chart, but Eric's story also matched the diary and the book of Catherine's letters.

"I wonder what kind of papers he has," she said to Packard. "Maybe there's something about the missing sister."

That might be a good way to approach Eric, she thought. She'd be honest and tell him why she was reviewing the diary but also tell him about her potential family connection. She sent off an e-mail, stood, and stretched.

"How about a visit to the dog park while we wait? You haven't been there in a long time."

Packard barked and danced around her.

"It sure is good to have you back, Bumblebutt. Should I bring the Frisbee?" She pulled it from the backpack and held it in front of him.

He snatched it from her hand and trotted to the front door. He turned toward her and woofed.

"Okay! Looks like you're ready."

Once at the park, she took it easy with the throws, reminding Packard he was just back from the dead. But she still had to fake a toss and quickly hide the Frisbee in the back-pack to get him to stop.

"You're definitely back to normal," she told him on the way home.

She figured it was too soon but checked her e-mail anyway.

"Hey, Eric replied already!" She clicked the message.

He wrote, "Hello Catlin—I'm glad the historical society has found a pleasant representative. The attorney they were using was obnoxious, IMHO. It'd be great to explore family ties. I have some materials you'd find interesting. Can we talk? My contact info is below. Hope to hear from you soon. Best regards, Eric."

"Should I call him now? What do you think?"

Packard barked.

"Right. If not now, when? I'll go for it."

Eric made her feel instantly comfortable when she introduced herself. His voice was warm and friendly. He sounded excited about the possible family connections, and told Catlin several times how much he appreciated her researching the diary for the attorneys. He said he had been planning on flying down the next week to visit the historical society, and they agreed to meet for lunch.

"Bring your family information. I'll show you mine if you show me yours," he said, laughing.

"You were right. I'm glad I called him," Catlin told Packard when she hung up. "He sounds like a really nice person."

She hummed while she compiled a report for her meeting with Brad Gipson. She summarized the family connections, referenced the census data, and made copies of the census sheets she had printed from Ancestry.com, carefully highlighting the lines with Eric's family members.

"It'd be good to copy the important pages of the diary and highlight the key information so Brad and the historical society people don't have to flip through the whole diary to verify what I'm saying," she said to herself. "I wish I didn't have to give it back so soon. I may find out more after I meet with Eric, but then I couldn't double-check anything."

She touched the leather cover regretfully like one would touch a friend who would be leaving soon and be greatly missed. She looked from the diary to her home office copy machine and back to the diary.

"I'd be doing everyone a favor if I made a copy of those pages for me too," she said. "I wouldn't have to bother Brad or the historical society later, and I could be totally sure about Eric's connections." She smiled brightly and loaded a fresh stack of paper into the machine.

24

A week later, Catlin waited outside Urban Solace, her favorite neighborhood comfort-food restaurant, watching each unaccompanied male walk by.

This is like a cross between a blind date and a business meeting. He sounded so nice on the phone; I wonder what he'll look like. Not to be judgmental, but I hope that's not him. Studded belt, chains, and a nose ring are too much metal. Please don't be that smoker. Whew. That's a great suit and he's so handsome. Oh well, his partner's a lucky guy. Oh my god, who wears checkered shorts and flowered shirts anymore? Honestly, I thought we were all past that.

"Excuse me. Catlin?"

"Eric?"

"Yes, hi."

"Hi." She smiled into earnest brown eyes. Her subconscious flickered over tousled hair, open smile, upright stance, runner's build, pressed khakis, and a label-free polo shirt. Click. Approved.

She realized he had been conducting a similar survey as his smile widened and he said, "Great to meet you. I hope you weren't waiting long."

"No, I just got here."

"Shall we get a table?" He held the door open for her.

"Two for lunch? Inside or outside?" the hostess asked.

"Outside, definitely. They have a great patio," she told Eric.

"Good deal."

They sat at a metal table and immediately slid utensils aside to make room for the books and papers they wanted to share.

"This is so exciting," she said.

"It is. You never know where research will lead, but it's great when it leads to new friends." He raised his water glass to her. "Hey, I hope you don't mind, but I asked my friend who told me about the diary to join us later. He's a history geek too, especially the Old West. Some guys never stop playing cowboy."

"Sure, it'll be nice to meet him."

"But we don't have to wait to start. Here's a copy of the agreement between James and Amy."

"Wow. Okay, here's the book of Carolyn's letters. Except that wasn't her real name, and Jack Rayburn wasn't her husband's real name either."

"Jack Rayburn?" Eric stopped mid-reach.

"Right. They knew each other before but changed their names. That's in Chapter 12."

Eric grabbed the book and flipped toward the end. "My friend is going to be very disappointed to hear his storied ancestor's name is an alias."

It was Catlin's turn to be startled. "His ancestor is Canyon Jack?"

"Yeah. Always tops my sheriff tales with his legendary buffalo-hunting–wagon-train-leading great-cubed grandfather. Who was Jack really?"

"His name was Daniel Hayden. The editor described him as a rancher-gunslinger."

"Aw shucks, no kidding? He wasn't a low-down, lyin' horse thief?"

"Doesn't seem like it."

"Figures. Out-machoed again."

The waiter appeared, and they ordered lunch.

Eric read the end of the book while Catlin examined the agreement.

"James Seeley and Amy Van Buren—those are the names in the foreword," she said.

"Samantha Lynn is the baby's name in the agreement," Eric responded. "At least she didn't change her name. Too bad you had to give the diary back to the attorneys. I never got to read it in detail, but I thought Amy mentioned other names."

Catlin grinned. "I probably shouldn't have, but I made a copy of the important parts before I returned it, just in case." She pulled out a stack of clipped paper from her tote and placed it on the table.

"Why Ms. Davis, aren't you the clever one?" Eric reached for the pages but Catlin held up her hand playfully.

"Ah ah wait. What do you have in trade, Mister Wilson?"

"And she's a smart negotiator. Hmm. I'll see your diary and raise you a photograph." He put a picture in an ornate frame in front of her.

"Who is it?"

"That is my great-aunt's namesake and could be your great-great grandmother, Samantha Lynn."

"She's lovely."

"According to Aunt Sam, her father treasured this photo of his sister. Kept it locked in his desk. She found it after he died. Samantha Lynn broke everyone's heart when she ran off. Walter never spoke of her again and didn't let anyone else either. Benjamin tried to find her after Walter died, but it was too late to pick up her trail."

"Somehow, she passed the letters from James on to the baby who was my great-grandmother, though."

"The letters Amy found?"

"Uh huh." Catlin showed Eric the page copied from the diary. "See? James wrote letters to 'My Dearest C' and Amy gave them to Samantha Lynn."

"Aunt Sam always told me if I found the keeper of those letters I'd find long-lost family."

Catlin blushed at his intense gaze. "Well, cousin, I'll call your photograph with a packet of letters," she said, and brought out the ribbon-tied bundle.

"Whoa. You are magic, you know that? My hands are actually shaking. You better unwrap those."

"Sure." She pulled the ribbon and unfolded the first letter.

"The handwriting's the same as in the agreement. Must be James."

"And look at the last letter in the book of Carolyn's letters."

"Same there too. I imagine you've studied both sets and they make sense?"

"They coincide, but not everything makes sense. Carolyn writes beautifully, but she changed other people's names, too, and wasn't ever clear about why she was on the run. From Amy's diary, her real name was Catherine."

"Catherine what?"

"I don't know. I haven't found anything that says."

Eric turned to the foreword. "Here's Daniel Hayden faking his death with the help of the sheriff."

"Walter Wilson stopped him from committing suicide; that's what Carolyn wrote. And Amy wrote about Walter dressing Daniel alone for burial."

"He probably loaded rocks into the coffin while Daniel made his getaway. Fantastic! And here's our food. Good time for a break."

Catlin nodded and put the letters back in her tote. They moved the other papers aside and dug in. Talk turned to work, food, and weather. *What a nice guy*, she thought. *How relaxing to have a conversation with no hidden agenda. To be free and let the relationship unfold, whether he'll be a passing acquaintance, lasting friend, or more.*

"I'm thinking about extending my visit a few days," Eric said. "Give the historical society a little more time. I'd like to take the diary home with me."

"What will you do while you wait?"

"Got any suggestions?"

"I'm the last person to ask, I'm such a stick-at-home. If it weren't for my dog, I'd never leave the house."

"It's hard to believe no one is taking you out on the town."

"I was engaged for several years, but that recently ended."

"Uh oh, I hope I didn't put my foot in my mouth here. Are you sad?"

"No. I mean, he died in a car accident, so I could be sad, but we had some issues and were headed to break up anyway, but I hadn't done it yet because my dog was sick and then Packard had a miraculous recovery and, that very night, John crashed into a tree." Catlin took a deep breath. "And that's why I got to read the diary and so it's why we met. It's cosmic." She beamed.

Eric laughed. "I don't understand, but I'm definitely intrigued." He glanced toward the doorway. "We'll have to table that discussion for a bit, though. Canyon Jack's descendant has arrived, and I need to harass him unmercifully now that I know my ancestor saved his ancestor's ass."

He stood and waved his friend over. "Catlin, I'd like you to meet . . ."

She turned in her seat. "Neil!"

"Hey Cat! Great to see you again! Oh, and you too, buddy." He grasped Eric's hand and slapped his shoulder.

"I'd like to say the same but I have the feeling I'm going to be sorry I invited you here. Guess I'll play the schlep and ask the classic question, how do you two know each other?"

"I supervised a construction job in her neighborhood," Neil started.

"Where you left without saying good-bye," Catlin continued. "And then we met again at an awards banquet."

"Where you drove off and never called to tell me how Packard was doing."

"I know, but he was diagnosed with cancer and I couldn't think about anything else. Then John was in a car crash." She stopped at the aghast look on Neil's face. "I guess that was kind of abrupt."

He sat next to her and took her hand. "I'm so sorry, Cat, I had no idea. Are you okay? I know how tight you two were."

Catlin noticed with surprise that his eyes were brimming with emotion. "It's sweet of you to be so concerned. I didn't think you cared that much for John."

"I meant Packard."

"Oh. Packard's good. My vet is totally amazing. He saved him when things were looking very grim."

"That's great!"

"But John was killed in the accident."

Neil's smile broadened until the signal arrived from his brain that joy wasn't the most appropriate response. He tried to morph his face into a look of regret. "Uh, I guess the wedding's off, then."

Eric slammed his glass of iced tea on the table and turned away, napkin over his face, choking with laughter. "You take the cake. Try to show a little sympathy, man."

"It's okay," Catlin said. "That seems to be the standard reaction."

"Any dessert here?" the waiter asked.

Neil nodded. "Suddenly, I'm in the mood for cheesecake."

"Yum, me too."

"Make it three," Eric sighed.

While they waited, Eric explained the family lines and interrelationships. Neil read the last chapters of Carolyn's book and the parts of Amy's diary Catlin pointed out to him.

"Incredible. What a small world . . . then and now."

"How did your family line continue?" Catlin asked him.

"It's sketchy. My mom got pretty frustrated trying to trace the Rayburns. Family legend says Canyon Jack came out of nowhere, leading wagon trains. Great-great-great grandma swore they got married in 1878 on the trail before the baby was born, and she kept the name, but you know how paperwork could get lost in those days. If there ever was any. She moved in 1885 when she got word a sheriff from Denver was looking for her, married a Prescott who adopted the boy, and the rest is history."

"Hold on there. I don't remember you ever telling me the part about a sheriff looking for your great-cubed grandmother," Eric protested.

"Nobody wants to think their granny was a criminal."

The waiter brought the cheesecake, decorated with slices of kiwi.

Catlin delicately removed the fruit.

"Don't like kiwi?" Eric asked.

She wrinkled her nose. "Too many seeds. Oh my god—seeds! That's it!"

"It's just a garnish, cousin. No need to get upset."

Catlin grabbed Carolyn's book and opened it to the last letter. "Look what James wrote. 'I wish that I could carry out your request to find the half-seed sown by your beloved. But alas, that duty I must bequeath to another.' He probably asked Amy to do it. I bet Walter was looking for Jack's child because Amy asked him to when she died."

"Ironically, that's what made granny move away," Neil said. "Your people were all over my people, man."

Eric shrugged. "Don't forget, if it weren't for Walter Wilson, you wouldn't be here. Your great-cubed grandfather would have killed himself for love."

"True enough. His Catherine must have been something special."

"I'm sure she was beautiful," Catlin said. "Look at this picture of her daughter."

"Strong family resemblance." Neil said it lightly, but as he looked into her eyes, past and present shifted along a metaphysical fault line, and he thought he heard piano music. He tapped on the framed glass to bring himself back to reality. "What about your family line?"

"Similar frustration for my mom in her genealogy hunt. My great-grandmother was left at an orphanage in San Francisco with the packet of letters but no name. She was adopted by the Cadwaladers, a wealthy couple who named her Elizabeth, and the rest is her-story."

"Do you have any pictures of her?" Eric asked.

Catlin nodded and reached into her tote. "Here's her wedding picture. She was twenty-four."

Neil laid the photo of Samantha Lynn next to it. "You're definitely a whatever their real name was."

"That's poetic phrasing," Eric snorted. "You're definitely a whatever?"

"That's the mystery, though, right?" Catlin said. "I don't know the real family name of any of them, all the way back to Catherine."

Neil tapped on Samantha Lynn's picture again. "Sometimes, there are notes on the back of photos." He looked up at Eric. "How attached are you to the frame?"

"Hey, that's from the turn of the century. What're you thinking about doing?"

"Minor surgery." Neil pulled a Swiss Army knife from his pocket. "A couple of careful slices, and all could be revealed."

"Or there's nothing on the back and it's ruined."

"Also possible. But if a frame is more important to you than Catlin finding her true roots, I'm sure she understands, right, Cat?"

"Umm. Sure, I know how valuable family heirlooms are." She tried to sound completely respectful and not agonizingly curious.

"Oh all right." Eric threw his hands in the air. "Try not to cause too much collateral damage."

"No worries. These hands are steady as a rock. You know I've done this before. Nurse, prepare the operating table, please."

Catlin shook out a clean napkin and spread it on the table.

Neil placed the picture face down and studied his knife. He pulled out the scissors, laughing at Eric's alarmed look. "Just kidding." He selected an appropriate blade and cut a fine line along the edges of the frame.

They all held their breath as he teased the backing off and collectively exhaled in disappointment at the blank surface underneath.

"Nothing. Dang. Sorry, cousin," Eric said.

"Don't give up so fast," Neil said, peering closer. "That's not the back of the photo. It's a separate piece of paper," he continued, sliding the flat of the blade under and lifting a folded note out of the frame. "Nurse, would you like to read the message from the past?"

Catlin looked at Eric, who nodded.

"Absolutely you should do the honors," he said.

She unfolded the note and read aloud, "Darling Brother, How I miss you! Tell Papa he was right, if he will listen to a word from me. I find myself nearly alone in a heartless city.

Nearly alone, for I hold in my arms an innocent reminder of poorly chosen love. Already invisible, I shall vanish, leaving my life and family letters with the child. God will choose her name and fate. But my heart has named her for my mothers, in the hope that true love shall prevail. Amy for the mother who raised me and Catherine Porter for the one who bore me. Farewell, may we meet again in heaven. Your loving sister, Samantha Lynn."

"There you have it, cousin. You've found your family connection! Neil was right, after all. Now you can start looking for Catherine Porter."

Catlin stared at the note and slowly shook her head. "This is unreal. I've been looking for Catherine Porter for months. I thought she was someone completely different, and it turns out she was the same."

The men exchanged a look and a shrug.

"That makes no sense at all," Eric said.

Catlin nodded. "I know. All the books I read said she committed suicide."

"History's a joker sometimes," Neil said, folding his knife. "Why were you looking for Catherine Porter?"

"Her story was sad but typical of the time. I wanted to fill in the details, make her a real person who mattered. I bought Carolyn's book when I was researching for Catherine, kind of as a diversion."

"Turns out the book was an important clue. Like I said when we sat down, you never know where research will lead, cousin." Eric paused. "But I guess we're not related except through adoption. Maybe I shouldn't call you cousin."

"It's nice," Catlin said. "I like it that you do."

"Me too," Neil said. "Family relationships are real nice."

Eric frowned. "You are related, you know. You have the same great-cubed grandfather."

Neil waved his hand. "Distantly related, very distantly."

"We're all related like in the past," Catlin said. "Daniel and Walter were friends like you and Eric. Benjamin and Samantha Lynn had family history like Eric and me. And Daniel and Catherine were—uh . . ." She stopped, face flushed.

"I like how you're connecting the dots, Cat. We should explore the picture a lot more thoroughly after Eric flies home to Portland. When are you headed out, buddy? I'd be glad to take you to the airport."

"Yes, I can see you'd be delighted to drop me off as soon as possible. But we had more family memorabilia to share today."

"No problem. I'm a firm believer in past as prologue. And this time, I think time is on my side. I've got to get back to work, but let me know if you need a ride." Neil took Catlin's hand. "May I call on you, Ms. Davis?"

She nodded, afraid that words would come out in a breathless squeak.

He kissed her fingers. "See you soon," he whispered, more huskily than intended. He cleared his throat. "How long are you staying in town?" he asked Eric.

"I've got a meeting at three with the historical society's executive director and attorney. Depending on how that goes, I may leave tomorrow." Eric shrugged at Catlin's look of surprise.

"The offer for a ride still stands. I'd like to hear what they say."

"Fine, fine. I'll call you tonight."

They shook hands, and Neil left.

"The cheery whistle is a bit much," Eric said.

"Maybe he's a happy person."

"No, he's rubbing it in, but I'm used to it. I've been losing out to him since junior high."

"You've known Neil since then?"

"Yes, I have. And no, I'm not going to spend the afternoon telling stories about him." Eric hesitated. "Maybe I'll tell a few. So you know what you're in for." He grinned wickedly. "But first I need to write all these connections down while they're still fresh in my head."

"Good idea. Here's some paper." Catlin pulled a tablet from her tote.

"The girl who has everything." Eric gave a little sigh, picked up a pen, and started drawing lines and brackets, filling in names as he spoke. "Okay, at the top we have Catherine Porter and Daniel Hayden, AKA Carolyn Parker and Jack Rayburn. They marry and have Samantha Lynn."

"Right. Who is adopted by Amy Van Buren and Walter Wilson after Catherine, Daniel and James Seeley have all died," Catlin said.

"My family branches from Amy and Walter's son Benjamin," Eric continued as he filled in more lines and names. "Ben and his wife have a daughter named Samantha who is my great aunt, and a son who is my great grandfather."

"Catherine's daughter Samantha Lynn runs away and has a baby who is left at an orphanage and becomes Elizabeth Cadwalader, my great grandmother." Catlin pointed to the page and Eric added more lines.

"Neil's paternal line branches from Daniel too, after he had assumed the name Jack Rayburn." Eric started another line at the top of the page. "We don't know if he actually married Neil's great-cubed grandmother on the trail before he found out that Catherine was still alive."

"He knew he had fathered a child, but that wasn't enough to keep him from marrying Catherine. She must have been his soul mate." Catlin sighed. "That part of Carolyn's book was so romantic."

"Uh huh." Eric tapped on the page with his pen. "Is that everybody?"

Catlin nodded. "Everybody who's family. There's one other weird connection, but it doesn't have a place on the chart."

"What's that?"

"The judge that Amy talks about in her diary, Judge Wellingbrook. I got Carolyn's book from his descendant, who has a bookstore downtown. The Judge could be my ex-fiancé's great-cubed grandfather."

"Do you know that for sure?"

"No. But I guess it doesn't matter now anyway."

"It doesn't seem like the people in that family line are an important part of the story."

"No, they're not," Catlin said cheerfully.

25

"Isn't it amazing how things work out?" Catlin asked Packard that Saturday. "I thought I'd be making final wedding plans now. Instead, I'm going on a date. Life can change directions fast." Irony evaporated as she selected the perfect sun dress for a casual dinner and walk on the beach. "Neil picked the place so you could come too, isn't that nice?"

Packard woofed.

"I thought you'd like being included. You'll be a perfect gentleman, won't you?"

He sat and raised his paw.

"That's sure to impress. Good boy. Want to wear your bandana?" She held the cloth in front of him.

He shook his head.

"Right. It's informal. No need to overdress." She slipped on heeled sandals and a vintage cardigan. "All set. Now we wait for . . ."

The doorbell rang.

"Neil."

Packard raced down the hall.

Catlin followed, breathing deep yoga breaths to calm her pounding heart. She motioned for Packard to sit and opened the door.

"Wow," Neil said. "You look great."

She twirled and curtsied. "Thank you."

They gazed into each other's eyes until Packard barked.

"Excuse me, sir. You're looking very fine too." Neil reached down, and Packard lifted his paw for a shake.

Catlin laughed. "Come in while I get his leash."

"Okay." Neil stepped inside, admiring the old-fashioned warmth of the furniture and art.

"Nice sketches," he said when she returned. "Your work?"

"No, those are by an architect friend. A bunch of us went on a cycling trip in France years ago."

"Sounds like a good way to see the countryside."

"It was fun. Do you ride?"

He shook his head. "Not bikes. I've always been more partial to horses. I like something live under me." *Jeez Neil, try to be a little more subtle before she runs screaming from the room.*

"I've never gone horseback riding. We used mules on the digs in Mexico."

"Big difference, trust me. There're some good stables in south county near the border. Want to try it next weekend?"

"Uh huh." Catlin smiled giddily. *Oh my god, we're making future plans. Keep calm, don't blow it.*

Packard tugged at the leash in her hands.

"Somebody's hungry," Neil said. "Shall we head off?"

At the sidewalk, Neil opened the truck door, and Packard jumped into the extra cab behind the seats as if he'd been riding there since puppyhood.

Neil gave a hand to Catlin and waited while she settled in before closing the door.

"He's such a gentleman," she whispered, watching him walk around to the driver's side.

Packard licked her cheek.

"Yes, just like you."

The silver-haired restaurant owner greeted them heartily. "Aloha, old friend. Welcome back. I see the gods have finally blessed you with a beautiful *wahine*. And companion," he added, nodding to Packard. "Cool dreadlocks, ancient one."

"Is Packard an old soul?" Catlin asked.

"He is. As are you, Light Child. Born to give love and spread joy. What you're doing with this *haole* is a mystery beyond my powers to discern."

"Cut me some slack, Wayne. I'm trying to make a good impression," Neil sighed. "Where's your aloha spirit?"

"All in fun, *brah*, all in fun. Come to the patio. Everything is ready."

He led them to a table at the end of an expansive wooden deck that faced the beach. Votive candles flickered in the soft breeze. A weathered blue bottle held a single orchid. Indistinct conversations of other diners and the brush of waves at low tide hummed in the background. He pulled out a chair for Catlin and gestured to Neil. "What do you think?"

"Perfect. *Mahalo*."

"Kona Longboard for you?"

"Sounds good. Want a beer, Cat? It's *da kine*. Brewed on the Big Island."

"*Da kine*?"

"The best."

"Okay, I'll try it."

Wayne nodded. "Two Longboards and a bowl of water, coming up."

The waitress brought their drinks and took their order.

They toasted the sunset with a clink of long-neck bottles.

"Here's to the past that brought us here, the present we're enjoying, and the future to come," Neil said.

"That's beautiful." She took another sip and looked around. "This is a great place. Have you been friends with Wayne a long time?"

"I met him about ten years ago on one of my first jobs here. He does construction management in what he calls his spare time . . . when he's not at the restaurant."

"What have you been working on this summer?"

"A big water line in north county. Great change from sewers. We're almost done."

"Do you have the same crew? They were so nice."

"Yep. Francisco and Bill are working as hard as ever."

"But Bobby left."

"He's still with the company. Altman's building a freeway interchange outside of Phoenix. It wasn't his choice. We have to go where the work takes us. Greg doesn't pay us to be picky."

"Like being a military brat."

"Yeah. I plan to stick around, though. There's plenty of work here."

"That's good."

"It is." Neil reached across the table and covered her hand.

She smiled and breathed a contented sigh, watching his eyes in the candlelight, feeling his touch infuse her body with a thrumming heat.

They didn't move until the waitress brought their entrees along with a plate prepared especially for Packard.

"I love chicken teriyaki," Catlin said.

"Try the mahi mahi, too." Neil slid a piece to her plate.

Enthusiastic slurping emanated from under the table.

The waitress returned and asked, "How is everything?"

"Ours is excellent, and his is gone." Neil pointed to the floor. "The ancient one is a pretty speedy eater."

Catlin laughed. "That's a good sign. It was very scary when he didn't want to eat."

"I'm sorry you both went through that. I hope you don't mind me saying I'm glad everything turned out the way it did."

"Almost everyone is, except John's parents. Nancy helped me see the light before the accident happened. He wasn't very nice to me."

"It's called abuse."

"I understand that now. It wasn't so clear when I was in the middle of it all. I guess that's how manipulative people get their way. They create confusion and self-doubt."

"Don't doubt yourself. You should only spend time with people who tell you how amazing and beautiful you are."

"That should narrow the field."

"That's the idea."

After dinner, Wayne escorted them down the back steps to the beach. He handed Catlin a gardenia blossom, "With the blessings of aloha for a special night."

They took off their sandals, leaning on each other and laughing as they wobbled across the loose sand to the water's edge where thousands of tiny moons glistened in the swells.

Catlin lifted the gardenia to her face. "It's so fragrant."

Neil bent closer. "Yes, you are," he said, cupping the flower and her hand in his. He tucked the gardenia behind her ear, caressed her cheek, and gently tilted her chin.

Their lips merged while the waves shimmered around their feet, receded and returned, receded and returned.

On her front porch, she moved eagerly into his arms again, anticipating a lingering good-bye. But Packard scratched on the door.

"Looks like someone wants in," Neil said.

"Actually he wants out. Want to come in for a bit? I need to let him into the backyard."

"Sure." While she was gone, he looked closer at the photographs in mirrored frames clustered on a side table. A handsome couple in black tie posed by a vintage Mercedes. A gray-haired woman with steely eyes sat in a chair with happy birthday balloons floating over her head. Catlin, wearing cutoffs and a tank top that set him drooling, cradled a curly brown ball of fluff.

"Hard to believe Packard was ever that small," he said.

"I know," Catlin said, coming up behind him. "He was the cutest puppy. Except for all the things he ate. When he grabbed something, he'd rather swallow it than give it back."

"Like?"

"Underwear, gloves. I learned not to leave things lying around."

"Ever see them again?"

"Oh yes, but not in any usable condition."

"He seems mellow now."

"He is. I keep my best shoes in their boxes, though, just to be safe."

They laughed.

"Sorry he can't come along when we go riding."

"That's okay. Tonight was a special treat for him. And me," she added.

"Me too." He pulled her close.

Catlin caressed his face and traced delicately around his ear. She smiled when his eyes closed on a quick intake of breath. "I like a man with sensitive ears," she said. "What else do you like touched?"

"I think it's about time you found out." He slipped his hands under her sweater and pushed it off her shoulders.

She dropped her hands to let it fall and then dragged her nails up his forearms and over his biceps. She shifted her hands to his hair as he tightened his arms around her.

In another heartbeat, their lips joined like two fire lines, and their minds swirled.

The light from the gas lamp angled through crystal prisms
and danced along the brocade wall. Piano music and silvery
laughter filtered through the oak floor. Daniel slid his hands
down Catherine's back. She arched against him and whispered, "You can drop those guns on the chair, cowboy."

He leaned back to look in her eyes, brilliant green and
drowsy with desire. "What guns?"

Catlin blinked. "That was some kiss. Did you hear piano
music?"

"Yeah, I was thinking your neighbors have pretty old-
fashioned taste. Kind of weird to be coming from below,
though."

"Uh huh. Last time I checked, this was a one-story house.
Did I say something about guns?"

"You told me to drop them on the chair. I've only got one
weapon, but you've sure got me thinking about using it."

She trailed her fingers along the trimmed beard while
gazing into his eyes. "Why am I so drawn to you? We don't
know each other yet and I can't stop wanting to be close.
Logic says we should slow down. But kissing you was like
being transported. I was in a different world."

"Catlin, it feels right to be with you. I don't want to go to
another world. I just want to go down the hall." He tilted his
head with a look that was both tender and sly. "But if you
want to slow down, I can do that."

He took her right hand and turned it over to kiss the
palm. He nibbled at the mound below her thumb and slipped

his tongue between each finger, taking his time, holding her gaze, finally kissing each tip.

She drew his hand to her lips and sucked his middle finger, watching his eyes cloud with need, feeling her own yearning.

He clasped her hands, pulled them away, and leaned in to kiss her again, turning at the last moment to lick gently at her ear and work slowly along the side of her neck. His lips slid lower, and his hands skimmed lightly upward. He brushed the straps of her dress off her shoulders, echoing her moan.

"Let me," he whispered, scattering soft kisses. "Now." Coming back to her mouth, he let his control slip, felt her open to his tongue, yield her body to his stiffening against her.

"Perfect fit, don't you feel it?" He dropped his hands and crushed her to him.

She gasped, "Closer. Please. I can't get close enough to you."

With an incoherent cry he swept her up, buried his face in her as she curled around him. In a slow-motion dream walk, he carried her to the bedroom.

He set her down by the brass bed and unzipped her dress, happily watching it float to the floor. "Nice choice of underwear," he said, caressing her bare breasts.

She kicked off her shoes and fell back onto the bed. "You are way overdressed," she said, pulling him in.

He knelt over her and let her unbutton his shirt, although he would have just as soon yanked it off over his head, buttons be damned.

She ran her hands over his chest and shoulders. "Mmm. You're not afraid to do the heavy lifting, are you?"

"I just carried you here, didn't I?" He dropped down to cover her mouth before she could protest and sank into the coverlet with her, skin on skin. "Tell me. Tell me what you want, Cat." His kisses and hands shifted lower; he pulled away black satin and inhaled the scent of her softest skin.

Her gasps matched the rhythm of each sip he took of her. Every place he touched was burning, and she was breathless at the thought of what else he could do. She reached down and cupped her hand over his tightening jeans. "I want everything. All of you, on me, in me."

Denim flew off; nothing lay between them except heat and desire. She thought she might explode when he slipped his fingers inside, achingly slowly, and pushed his palm against her. She was the shore to the waves of sensation he created, retreating and pressing again and again. So close to release, she groaned, "Now. I can't wait."

He watched her eyes close as he slid inside, felt her tighten around him and then open to take him deeper when she linked her legs over his back. Everything he was merged with her. And became someone else, somewhere else.

Daniel whispered, "It's been so long," against her throat.

Catherine moved her hips slowly, the way he liked.

He loved to watch her face while he took her where no one else could. The desire to have her all to himself filled his heart; the knowledge that he would soon have the wealth to do it filled his body with power. He kissed her urgently, increasing the pace.

Her breath quickened. She arced upward and cried out, "Ohmygod that feels so good!"

Neil came back to himself as she throbbed rhythmically around him.

"Oh my," Catlin said, still breathless. "That was fantastic." She smiled with wicked innocence. "Your turn."

He knew he would become addicted to that look. "I'm not sure I caught it all. Let's see it again from a different angle." He rolled, scooping her with him to reverse positions without losing contact.

"Smooth move."

"Uh huh. Swim meets are won in the flip turn. Why don't you sit up for your second lap?"

"Umm . . . I've never . . . tried that before."

"Then you're in for a treat." He pulled her knees forward and she pressed against his chest to straddle him.

"It feels different up here," she said, eyes widening.

"I'm handing you the remote, sweetheart. You take control."

The smile never left her face while she experimented with angles and pace until she buckled over him, panting in overwhelming pleasure. She arched back and tossed her head to wring out one last sensation. "Mercy. That could get habit forming," she said, collapsing onto his chest.

"Everything about you could get habit forming," he said. "May I take the last lap?"

She nodded.

He rolled her under him again, reclaiming the initiative with ferocity. Free to fly, he dove hard and fast into her surrender until, just before the end when the crash was inevitable, he slowed enough to draw out the finish to their mutual cries of satisfaction.

He pushed off of her reluctantly.

"You're incredible," she said when she regained her breath.

"I appreciate the compliment. Three laps a personal best for you, then?"

"Oh yes."

They relaxed in the afterglow as moonlight filtered through the curtains.

He leaned on his elbow. "So, are you getting up early for church?"

She giggled. "No. I've kind of lapsed."

"I see. Lapsed Catholic? Your soul could be in trouble."

"Lapsed Episcopalian. We only get in trouble if we eat our salad with a dessert fork."

"I'm always doing that. Lucky I'm a lapsed lapsed or I'd be doomed to hell."

"Don't you believe in anything?"

"I'm considering Unitarian. I like their message."

"Which is what?"

"I have no idea. That's what I like." He touched her cheek. "Seriously, do you want me out of here before breakfast?"

"Somehow I think it would take through breakfast to say good-bye. Would you like to stay?"

"I would." He dropped down next to her and smiled as she curled into him with a happy sigh. "So what's for Sunday breakfast at your place?" he said, stroking her hair.

"Cheerios."

"Perfect. A girl after my own heart."

Later, Catlin tiptoed to the back door and let Packard into the bedroom. "Are you okay with Neil staying the night?" she whispered, bending down.

He licked her nose.

"You always have the right answer."

Neil woke in the morning to a tongue delicately exploring his fingers. "Mmmm," he said. "Let's pick up where we left off. I'm game." He opened his eyes to a liquid golden gaze. "Whoa. Hello, ancient one."

"I knew my hair would be a mess," Catlin mumbled.

He turned over. "Not you, sweetheart. You are beautiful and amazing, even first thing in the morning." He pulled her into his arms. "Especially first thing in the morning." He nuzzled her neck and skimmed his hands along her body. "Like I was saying, let's pick up where we left off."

Her self-conscious worries about morning breath, eye goop, and ratted hair flew out of her head along with every other thought except his absolute maleness—calloused hands, muscled weight, and, most particularly, that warm insistent form rising against her belly.

"God, I want to be inside you again," Neil whispered.

"Please," she moaned.

"Well, that was a very moving Sunday service," Neil said. "But I guess we need to get out of this bed before it's too late for brunch, let alone breakfast."

Packard huffed from the floor.

"You're right. We're usually at the park by now."

"Speaking of parks, I have softball practice at noon."

"Time to get back to reality," she sighed.

"Until next weekend." He kissed her gently. "Do you know where my jeans ended up?"

Finally dressed and fed, they said good-bye. She waved from the porch, Packard sitting by her side, until Neil's truck turned the corner. "Could this be the start of happily ever after?" she asked.

Packard looked up at her and barked.

"I hope so too."

26

Catlin woke and rolled over quietly. She turned back to look at Neil, who was snoring contentedly, as she slipped out of bed. She smiled and padded downstairs to the living room, drawn to a rosy light glowing in the corner. She watched as the amorphous shimmer coalesced into a pretty girl dressed in white with a pink bow in her curls.

"Hi. What's your name?" Catlin asked.

"Sa-MAN-tha Lynn," the little girl chirped.

"And how did you get here, Samantha?"

"Samantha *Lynn*."

"Okay, sorry. How did you get here, Samantha Lynn?"

"God sent me."

"Really."

"Yes." Samantha Lynn nodded, curls bouncing. "It's almost time."

"Time for what?"

The girl giggled, hands over her mouth. Then her wide green eyes turned toward the staircase. Catlin followed her gaze.

Neil thumped down the last few steps and called out sleepily, "Sweetheart, are you okay?"

"I'm fine. I was just talking to Samantha Lynn." Catlin gestured to the corner and stared. A flowered ottoman sat empty. Moonglow lit the room with pale light. She shivered.

Neil wrapped his arms around her. "You're cold," he murmured. "Let's go back to bed. It's too late to be on the phone anyway. Tell your friend you'll call her tomorrow."

Catlin melted into his warmth. "Sure," she said, and leaned against him as they went upstairs.

The next morning, Catlin laughed out loud. "Packard, you wouldn't believe the crazy dream I had. Oh my god, I bet if Neil knew I had us all cozy in a big house and him saving me from ghosts, he'd die of embarrassment."

She wasn't sure what her ghost child meant it was time for, but she did know it was Monday and time to go back to the office. It felt like she had been gone for years; she didn't even know what projects she'd be working on.

"What will you do today?" she asked Packard. "Inventory the squirrels and birds? I'll expect a full report when I get home tonight."

She hoped the day would start slowly, but Nancy whisked her toward Michael's office the minute she walked in the door.

Mark waved and called out, "You can thank me later," as she was hustled along.

"What's going on?"

"I don't know," Nancy said, "But Michael told me he wanted to talk with both of us as soon as you got here."

Michael looked up from two stacks of paper when they came in. "Ah. Catlin. Welcome back. And condolences. Keeping busy's good for grief. We've got lots going on; that's the good news. So have a seat, ladies."

"Are there some new projects?" Nancy asked.

"Two brand new projects. Just found out late Friday. Catlin, you get the lead on whichever one you like. Ready?"

She nodded.

"Okay. Project one is a document for a road widening with possible archaeological issues, right up your alley. Very interesting, good budget, solid team. The client is the Regional Transportation Agency's environmental department."

Nancy's eyes narrowed. "The RTA . . . wait . . . isn't that Oliver Spencley's group?"

Michael shuffled his papers. "Yes, but . . ."

"You said you'd never sell your soul to that bastard. You know how he treats consultants. He'll make you do all the free work getting a project set up and then fire you for no good reason except to feed his twisted ego. What were you thinking?"

Michael shrugged. "It was Mark's idea to go after it. I figured it was harmless, get him used to losing proposals, take him down a notch. I didn't think we had a chance because we don't have any experience with the RTA."

"It didn't occur to you Oliver might be looking for fresh meat? Half the firms in town won't answer his calls, he's been so abusive," Nancy chided.

"Fine. Catlin, if you don't want to take this one, Mark can run it," Michael said.

I just escaped from an abusive relationship and no way am I doing that again is what she wanted to say but, instead, asked, "What's the other project?"

Michael pulled the second stack of papers closer. "This might suit you better anyway. Project for the Bureau of Land Management. Federal document for an access road extension with Native American involvement. BLM people are very professional, even Nancy would agree, right?" He looked over at her.

Nancy uncrossed her arms. "They are a great client."

"Is it in the east county?" Catlin asked.

"Nope. This is the best part. It's in Colorado near Denver. You can go out there for a month and get it done. They want the environmental assessment written by someone who'll work in their office, and then they'll handle the permitting themselves. Perfect, right? Get you out of town for a while, good break from sad memories."

Catlin's throat tightened. "A month?"

"They want it done there. Fastest way, over-the-shoulder review, all that. They want to start next week."

"Are you worried about Packard?" Nancy said. "I can take care of him. And I'll make sure Michael doesn't set you up in some dumpy motel." She leaned over and touched Catlin's arm. "Are you okay?"

Catlin nodded and then shook her head, tears in her eyes. She covered her face with her hands.

Nancy gestured toward the door with her thumb.

Michael said, "I'll let you two talk about it," and scooted from the room.

"Catlin, what's the matter?" Nancy asked when the door closed. "Is Packard all right?"

She nodded, and lowered her hands enough to look at her friend. "I had a date this weekend," she choked.

"Ohh. And you're worried he'll lose interest?" Nancy laughed. "Sweetie, I'm sure whoever it is will want to pick up right where you left off when you get back. It's not like you gave it all away on the first date."

Catlin's eyes filled with fresh tears and she hid her face again.

"You didn't! You scamp!" Nancy chuckled. "Confession. How many times?"

Catlin held up three fingers, hands still in front of her face, and then switched to four.

"Oh my. And who is this phenom? Anyone I know?"

"Uh huh."

"Here's a Kleenex. Don't make me do twenty questions."

Catlin wiped her eyes. "Neil," she whispered.

"Ooo, the way you say his name gives me chills. How did you hook up?"

"It was incredible . . ."

"So I gather, but I meant how did you meet him again?"

"No, the coincidence was incredible. Well, the other part was too." Catlin giggled. "Anyway, it turns out he's friends with the guy who claimed the diary."

Nancy's eyes grew wider as Catlin continued the story.

"I knew you two were meant to be. I love it when I'm right."

"Nancy, don't you see? I can't go out to Denver right now. It's too soon for a break. We need more time together. But I can't work for the RTA either." She shuddered. "I've heard too much about that guy. He's the devil."

"If you want to keep working, you'll have to decide. I personally think Mark should reap the rewards of his marketing effort. He's been too sheltered."

"How do I tell Neil? What if he thinks I don't care or that I didn't have a good time? What if he feels rejected and dumps me? What if someone else comes along and he forgets about me?"

Nancy sighed. "I don't know about what ifs. I do know you have to be honest and you have to be clear with him."

"What do you mean?"

"Tell him what's going on, why you're making the choice. Tell him what you want to happen when you get back. Ask if that's what he wants too. And be ready to accept his answer without recriminations."

"You make it sound easy."

"It's not. But thinking you know what's on his mind and adjusting your message to that is a road to disaster. C'mon, where's that spine? What are you going to do?"

"Go to Denver, I guess."

"Do you want me to take Packard?"

"No, but thanks. I'll drive him out to my folks. He won't mind a month in Palm Springs. It's cooling down now."

"Don't worry. This is just an interruption. You've got your whole life ahead of you."

"Thanks, mom."

By the time Neil called on Wednesday, she had what she wanted to say well rehearsed. But it seemed like he had his own concerns.

"Would it be okay if I came over? I need to talk to you," he told her.

"Sure." She hung up, thinking she had been worried about the wrong scenario; he wanted to break it off, probably because she was too easy. She sat on the couch moping. "Why did I let myself get carried away?" she cried.

Packard howled.

"It's your fault, you know. If you hadn't scratched on the door, we would have stayed on the porch."

He sat and raised his paw.

"I'm sorry, that wasn't fair." She got him a Milkbone. "I won't blame, and I won't get needy. I had a great time. If he's done, he's done."

The doorbell rang.

"I hope he's not done." She took a deep breath and opened the door.

"Hey, Cat." *She looks upset, she knows something's wrong. Crap.*

"Hi." *I'm not going to be all smiley and pretend everything's fine. I'm a big girl and I'll take it like a man.*

"How's my buddy?" Neil said, stepping inside.

Packard flopped onto his back, tail wagging like a crazed metronome.

They both bent over to scratch him.

"Pavlov's dog gets his revenge," Catlin said. "The trainer is the one who gets trained."

"Guess he's got me trained, too," Neil said. "Look, I'm sorry to sound so serious on the phone. Saturday's not going to work out, and I wanted to tell you face to face."

"It's okay. The weekend isn't going to work for me either."

"Oh. Maybe this won't be such bad news, then." *She's backing off; I knew I shouldn't have come on so strong. What was I thinking?*

"I'm sure it will be fine." *Just hit me already so I can slam the door and cry my eyes out.*

"It's work." He looked down at his hands.

"I understand." She crossed her arms.

"There's a new project." *This is not going well. Where's the reset button?*

"I totally understand new projects." *He's stealing my lines. If he's making this up he'll never believe me when I tell him about Denver.*

Packard barked and jumped onto the couch.

"What do you think you're doing, Bumblebutt?" Catlin scolded. She hurried over and pulled him off. "Sorry, he never does that."

"Maybe he's trying to tell us something."

"That dogs should be allowed on the couch?"

"No, that we should sit down and talk." He put his hands on her shoulders. "But first let me say what I should have said before anything else." He kissed her deeply. "Hello. It's great to see you."

"It's great to see you too." She looked up, and to her annoyance, started to cry.

"Hey, hey, sweetheart, everything's going to be fine." He wrapped his arms around her and they settled on the couch. "I'll only be gone a month. I have to get the job started right until they bring in a local foreman." He wiped the tears from her cheek.

"You're leaving town?" She sniffed.

"Just for a month."

"That's perfect."

"It is?"

She nodded. "I have to leave town for a month too. The agency wants their document written in their local office. It was that project or one for an abuser worse than John. I had it all figured out how to tell you, but then I was afraid you wanted to break up because I was so easy."

"No way. Guys don't break up with girls because they're easy. That's an old wives' tale."

"Is it?"

"Sure. Old wives tell it because they're jealous about what easy girls are getting." He whispered the last part in her ear and she giggled.

"Besides which, you're not easy," he assured her. "You are beautiful and amazing." He kissed her to reinforce the message.

"Where are you going?" she asked him when she could talk again.

"Denver. New water supply pipeline."

"Denver! Oh my god."

"You been there?"

She shook her head. "No, I'm going there for my project."

"Really? When?"

"Next week. I'm taking Packard to my folks in Palm Springs this weekend and then driving back to catch a flight on Tuesday. What about you?"

"I'm putting the camper shell on the truck and driving out starting Friday. You got a place to stay set up yet?"

"No, my boss is arranging it, and Nancy's pressing him for something better than a budget motel on the outskirts of town."

"Here's a crazy idea. The company has an apartment in the city. Two bedroom, two bath. That's where I'm staying. We could share. Strictly legit. Your boss would save rent, and we could buy the big box of Cheerios. Everybody wins."

"Well . . ."

"Even better, I could drive you and Packard to your folks and then we backtrack through Vegas and head up to Denver."

"You're volunteering to meet my parents?"

"I am."

"Are you sure?"

"Yep. I'm not scared. Remember, we're related. It'll be like visiting family."

"And you'd be okay spending the night there? I can't show up, push Packard out the door and leave the same day."

"Absolutely. I'll stay in a motel if they'd rather."

"No, there's plenty of room at their place."

"Excellent. I'll be on my best behavior. Scout's honor." He held up three fingers and grinned.

Her mother sounded pleased when Catlin asked if Neil could stay.

"Your helpful foreman is bringing you? Lovely. Shall I prepare one or two guest rooms?"

"Uhh . . ." Catlin hesitated.

"One it is. We look forward to meeting him, darling."

Nancy gave the plan the girlfriend seal of approval. "Go ahead, play house. It's a great idea. With two bathrooms you can observe his bad habits and not have to deal with them. If it doesn't work out, you can always get a hotel for the remainder and then fly home."

Michael was the most enthusiastic of all, upgrading her rental car to a compact as a reward for "negotiating free accommodations."

She didn't remember the trip to her parents' ever going so fast. They sang old car songs, told bad jokes, and commented on the scenery. Packard performed his usual navigational duties, letting Neil know where to stop. When they got to town, she directed him to the Hacienda.

"Wow," he said, driving through the gate. "Didn't Nancy Sinatra own this place once?"

"No. Next block over."

"Suddenly, I'm nervous about getting my forks mixed up."

She laughed. "Don't worry. You'll do fine."

Her parents came out and greeted him warmly.

Predictably, her father's first question was, "So, Neil, do you play golf?"

"Only in the loosest sense of the word. Mostly I hit on the range."

"What's your best score?"

"One time I shot a seventy-two . . ."

"Respectable."

"On the front nine," Neil continued. "The back nine didn't go as well."

"We can hit a bucket or two after lunch," Luther said, slapping him on the shoulder. "See if you're trainable." He laughed.

Catlin and Amanda rolled their eyes, and they all followed Packard into the house.

The men looked grim when they returned from the range.

Amanda asked, "How did it go?"

Luther said, "It's not a game for everyone."

Neil shrugged and winked at Catlin.

"But this boy's a natural," Luther announced with a broad smile. "You'll have to figure on staying longer when you come back so we can get on the course."

"I hope the fairways are wide," Neil said. "Otherwise, home windows and passing cars better look out."

That night, Neil came out of the shower in the guest suite to find Catlin plumping pillows against the headboard, a book on the bedside table.

"What've you got planned, here?" he asked.

"I thought we'd read a little before going to sleep."

"Hmmm. Are you afraid of making too much noise in your parents' house?"

"I, umm, you know . . ."

"Say no more, I have the perfect solution." He hopped into bed, sitting up against the pillows. "C'mere, sweetheart." He pulled her onto his lap facing him and said, "Be vewy vewy quiet," in his best Elmer Fudd voice.

"What are you doing?" she whispered, wrapping her legs around him.

"Shhh. I'm hunting wabbits." He held her tighter.

"Where's your shotgun?" Her eyes lit up. "Never mind."

"That went well," Catlin said, still misty at saying good-bye, as they drove off the next morning.

"Yeah. Your dad's a good guy."

"More important, my mom thinks you're a good guy."

"I'm glad. Seems like she could be a tough judge."

"I'm paying attention to her opinion these days."

"As well you should. Moms matter."

She looked at him with a sunny smile and settled back to enjoy the ride.

27

They were drawn to funky diners where the waitresses called them "honey" and asked if they were newlyweds. They stayed in weathered motels with individual cabins that were well past their prime but seemed to appreciate visitors all the more for it. On a side road outside of Grand Junction, they snuggled in the camper with the tailgate down, in sleeping bags Neil zipped together, watching the stars and moon arc across the sky.

"We'll be in Denver tomorrow," he said.

"A different adventure."

"Are you nervous about setting up shop?"

"No . . . maybe a little."

"Don't worry. I'm completely housebroken, and I can cook."

"You can?"

"Yep, *can* being the operative word. If it's in a can, I can heat it up."

"We might get tired of soup every night."

"There's always Top Ramen."

"I'm not sure that's technically food. It's just as easy to fix a salad as it is to eat something with no nutritional value."

"Mmm, wabbit food."

Catlin was giddy in her first report to Nancy after getting settled in the apartment. "It's going great," she said.

"Yes? Any bad habits rearing their ugly heads?"

"I think he leaves the cap off his toothpaste, but we're using separate bathrooms, so that's not a problem."

"I hope you're not using separate bedrooms."

"I'm using the other bedroom for my clothes. It's like having a huge dressing room."

"I'm experiencing closet envy. Have you done any sightseeing?"

"Not yet. We're going to explore the old red-light district this weekend. Some of the houses have been turned into museums."

"That sounds fun. Now we should talk about work for a minute so I can justify the call to Michael."

"The project's fine so far. How's everything at your end?"

"It's good. Mark thinks you made a huge sacrifice so he could have a project management experience and he's everlastingly grateful."

"That's nice."

"He hasn't had any meetings with the client yet. Just wait until Friday. Okay, that's enough work talk. Tell me more about your housemate."

When Nancy called on Friday evening, she was the one who could barely contain herself. "I hope I'm not interrupting anything, but Catlin, you're not going to believe this!"

"Good news?"

"If bad things happening to bad people is good news, then it is."

Catlin laughed. "Okay, I'm interested."

"I don't know if I should begin with the punch line or tell this chronologically. I'll start by saying Mark has had an epiphany. He's moving to Bali to become a photographer."

"What? You're kidding."

"That's the least of it. Ready?"

"Go ahead."

Nancy cleared her throat. "Once upon a time there was an evil king . . . No, here's what happened, according to Mark. The first meeting for the road-widening project was this morning. Everybody's very pleasant, off to a good start, getting into the technical issues. Several project managers are there from the department because they're not sure about schedule and who will end up running it. Suddenly, Oliver bursts in, totally pissed off because they began without him. He starts ranting about procedure, demands to know what Mark has been doing, threatens to fire our company and his own staff, indiscriminately spitting at the entire room. Mark is stunned into silence."

"Oh my god."

"I know. Then Oliver clutches his chest and starts panting. Mutters something like 'pain, oh shit,' takes two steps towards the door and collapses on the floor."

Catlin gasped. "He had a heart attack?"

"Right there. Mark expects someone to jump up and start resuscitation, but the whole table just sits like zombies. Mark told us he shouted, 'Doesn't anyone know CPR?' and Silvia says, 'Oliver said the class would be a waste of time.'"

"Is Silvia the mean one or the one who's depressed?"

"Catlin, they're all mean and depressed. That's what selling your soul does to you. Anyway, it doesn't matter. They're all his minions. Shall I continue?"

"Please do."

"Where was I? Oh yes, Oliver is convulsing. Mark looks around for the conference room phone and can't find it. Minion One says Oliver had it removed from the room because one time it rang when he was talking. By this time, Oliver is still. Mark says someone should call 911 on their cell, and Minion Two says they're not allowed to have cell phones at meetings. 'Can't you run to your office, then?' Mark says, and they all look down at Oliver, who is lying in the doorway. Minion One gets up and steps over him to go make the call. The rest of them collectively shrug and file out, stepping over him without a glance like he was some unfortunate stain on the carpet."

"Leaving Mark alone?"

"For hours. No, the paramedics came pretty fast after that."

"Then what?"

"Mark says he has a new respect for our public safety workers. They were totally professional and efficient. They did their best, but in the end, Oliver left on a gurney under a sheet. One of the paramedics told Mark it was clear he had been gone within a few minutes, but they never second guess, always give it everything they've got."

"And Mark saw the whole thing? No wonder he's trauma-tized. Is he serious about moving to Bali?"

"He already resigned. Michael told him to think about it over the weekend, but Mark said, 'Life's too short to work with mean people,' packed up his personals, and left."

"Whew! That could have been me at the meeting. Looks like Mark was the one who made a sacrifice."

"You never know which choice will change your life. Things still lovey dovey in Denver?"

"Uh huh. We're headed out to dinner. Call you later?"

"Sounds good."

Neil listened with wide eyes to Catlin's retelling after they were seated at the steakhouse. He ordered fish and a salad when the waiter came. "Maybe we should find the nearest park with jogging trails," he told her. "And check out the fitness center at the complex."

"Those are all good ideas," she agreed.

On Saturday, they set out to explore the old town, hand in hand. They admired the architecture and stained glass of the renovated buildings. Catlin bought some postcards at a gift shop, resisting other trinkets. They found the row of brick houses that had formed the core of the red-light district along a tree-lined street.

"They look pretty ordinary, considering what used to go on behind those walls," Neil said.

"I know. The one in the middle is the museum. Let's go inside."

The sleepy-eyed docent in the entryway barely glanced up as she handed them a brochure, saying the tour was self guided. "Feel free to wander," she told them.

Neil became engrossed in the cases holding pistols, knives, and other weaponry. Catlin studied the photographs along the walls leading into the parlor, where a crystal decanter sat on a sideboard beneath a large mirror.

When Neil followed her, the parlor was empty. He stood by the sideboard and took a closer look at the decanter, its leaded glass patterns reflecting in the polished wood. Sensing movement, he looked into the mirror and smiled at a young couple in period clothes who stood facing each other, the woman's hand at the man's lips. He turned to watch the reenactors, but they had vanished.

"What the . . . ? Oh, I get it. Trick mirror. Good one." He faced the mirror, tilting his head at different angles, but couldn't catch the image again.

He walked out of the room to find Catlin and saw her mounting the stairs, one hand on the banister and one holding her sack daintily in front of her. She walked slowly, as if reluctant to reach her destination.

"Wait for me," he called, but she ignored him and continued up the stairs. He climbed the steps and turned back on the landing when the piano started playing. A tall man sat on the bench hunched over the keys, tapping out a familiar tune. "Catlin, that's the song I heard at your house," Neil said. "Dang, where did she go?"

He hurried up the stairs and down the hall, checking each room. He found her in the last room on the right. She was standing by the ornate brass bed, mesmerized.

"This bed is like yours," he said, coming up behind her. The memory of their first night rushed over him, the salty scent of her hair, her dress crumpled around their feet, her skin glowing in the candlelight, his pistols close at hand. "This place has me thinking strange thoughts," he said, shaking his head. "What are you staring at, sweetheart?" He spun her towards him, and recoiled at the fear and horror contorting her face.

"Can't breathe," she croaked in a voice he didn't recognize. She gasped futilely for air.

Neil grabbed the paper sack from her hands, dumped out the postcards and held the bag over her face, pushing her onto the bed. "Inhale," he commanded. "Now exhale. Inhale. Exhale. That's my girl. Nice and slow. Everything's okay."

The docent came into the room, chiding, "Folks, that's original furniture, we don't allow—oh, panic attack?"

Neil nodded.

"That happens sometimes." The docent sat next to Catlin, regarding her intensely. "What did you see?" she asked.

Catlin lowered the bag and took a deep breath. "A vicious fat man. Shouting and snapping some kind of whip."

"Ah. He's a long-time occupant. Not many have seen him. Most people just sense an unpleasant chill in the room."

"What do you mean, occupant?" Neil said. "Are you saying Catlin saw a ghost?"

"That's a common term. You might also say a spirit, although it's actually lingering energy from emotionally charged events. Some people are more attuned to it than others. What did you see?"

"Nothing in here," Neil said. "Just the couple in your trick mirror in the parlor. And the piano player."

"There are no tricks to the mirror, but it's been in the house since the beginning so it has reflected many couples, I suppose. The piano player is quite popular."

"Is this a regular gig for him?"

"You might say that. Tall man in a dark coat?"

"Right."

"He's one of the spirits most frequently seen. Did you hear music?"

"Yeah," Neil said slowly.

"An auditory experience is not as typical."

"Meaning?"

"Generally that ghost is seen but not heard." The docent smiled at the shock on Neil's face. "You may be more attuned to the spirit world than you think." She patted Catlin's hand. "But if you're sensitive to negative energy, you shouldn't stay in this room. Come across the hall. It's everyone's favorite."

Neil kept his arm wrapped around Catlin as they entered the sunny room with red brocade wallpaper.

"All our visitors love the challenge of this room," the docent said. "There's a hidden doorway to a secret stairwell. I offer anyone who finds it a free reading at my studio." She handed Neil her card.

"What kind of reading?" he asked.

"Tarot cards, palm, past-life regression. Whatever the client chooses. People seem to know what they need."

Catlin walked to the corner of the room while the docent chatted, moved aside a stack of hatboxes and touched the latch she knew she would find. Dutch doors sprang open, revealing a dark stairway.

"Oh my, such a clever girl," the docent said. "I don't do many free readings, I can tell you." She trotted over and shut the doors before Catlin could start down the stairs. She put her hands on Catlin's shoulders and looked deeply into her eyes. "Come back," she said firmly.

Catlin blinked. The room came into focus. "Hi."

"Hello, dear. You two have had an interesting visit, but you should both get some fresh air. Your husband has my card. Please call me soon and make an appointment. It's on the house, as it were. He'll explain." She shooed them downstairs and out the door.

"That was one bizarre experience," Neil said as they walked away. "Like a twisted Disney haunted mansion."

"Uh huh."

"Are you okay? Seems like you got attuned to the bad ghosts."

She shook her head. "Can we sit for a minute? I still feel weird." They found a bench. "I wasn't just attuned in that house. I was there."

"Sure you were there. Oh, you mean like you'd been there before?"

"No. Like I was really there with that awful man. He was yelling at me, threatening to hurt me. And then I felt this crushing weight on my chest, and I couldn't catch my breath."

"That was the panic attack, Catlin. Hey, you know what? Maybe you were thinking about what Nancy told you about that guy yelling at your co-worker. You felt the negative energy in the room and put it together with her story about what happened yesterday."

"You're saying I made it up?"

"No, I'm saying you're a sympathetic and imaginative person. That's part of what makes you so beautiful." He leaned over to kiss her but she pulled back.

"This was real."

"I totally understand. I thought the piano player was real too. Maybe it was a trick, or maybe the docent lied; it's part of their spooky experience bit to have people pop in and out while she's pretending they're ghosts."

"But you didn't see anything in the room when we were there together. I did."

"That's a little harder to explain." Neil took the brochure from his back pocket. "I never read this thing; maybe they bill it as a haunted funhouse."

Catlin stared into space, hands in her lap.

He started reading out loud, "Built in the late 1860s, blah blah, first owner Josephine Muget, who operated it as a parlor house until her death in 1874, followed by James Seeley and then Amy Van Buren . . . These names sound familiar."

Catlin, startled from her fugue, snatched the brochure from his hands. "Josephine! Duh! James and Amy! Remember Eric's family diary?"

"Oh yeah, right, right."

"This isn't just a parlor house, it's *the* parlor house! I thought I'd have to search the city directories to find it, but we walked right into it. It's cosmic!"

Happy to see her smile again, Neil hugged her tight. "So Catherine Porter lived there too. I bet that's why the experience was so intense for you. Family memory. That fat guy could have been an unhappy customer."

"Or mean. He had this little whip in his hands and meant to use it."

"Little whip? Like a riding crop?"

"I guess."

"I saw one in a case in the house. Some guy left it there when he went out feet first. Apparently the widow didn't want the memorabilia. Anyway, all this creepiness has got me hungry. Want to have lunch?"

She nodded.

That night, Neil could sense Catlin needed to feel secure, so he held her until she fell asleep, although that wasn't his first choice as the way to end the day, the images of their first time still fresh in his mind. *Funny about other images like pistols and candlelight getting mixed in*, he thought. *Maybe Daniel and Catherine are playing family memory games with both of us.* He smiled as he drifted off, thinking, *this is our chance to make a peaceful life together.*

An hour later, he bolted upright at Catlin flailing and gasping for air in another panic attack. He switched on the light and raced for the sack she had left in the living room.

"Nightmare?" he asked when she calmed down.

"The fat man. He said it was my turn this time and was chasing me through the parlor house. He meant to kill me."

"I'm sorry we found the house. It's like that guy has it in for you."

"Or Catherine. Maybe she spurned him."

"Could working girls do that in those days? Didn't seem like they had much choice about customers."

"No, I guess not. I wish he'd leave me alone. Whatever happened isn't my fault." She folded the bag and put it on the bedside table.

"I wonder if it would help to learn what happened between them. The docent seemed to know a lot about the house's history."

"I don't want to go to that place again."

Neil got the business card from his wallet and brought it back to bed. "We could call her and make an appointment to talk at her studio. You won a free visit, remember? How did you find the door latch, anyway?"

"I don't know. Everything got foggy for me as soon as we walked into the house."

"It may be a come-on to build clients for . . ." he glanced at the card "spiritual counseling by Margaret Star Gazer, but we can't have you waking up with panic attacks every night."

"Especially with such a terrible person in my dreams."

"I have an idea for how to make sure somebody else is in your dreams," he said, putting the card aside and caressing her cheek.

"You always have such excellent ideas."

28

Neil called the docent Sunday morning and confirmed an afternoon appointment. "She can see us today," he told Catlin. "She seems eager to talk with you."

"That'll be good." Though she had slept soundly the rest of the night, the feeling of evil pursuing her remained, and she resented the invasion into their joyful world.

"Meanwhile, want to go see what the fitness center has?" he said.

"Sure."

They changed into workout clothes and lost themselves in the weights and machines at the bright, modern facility. They swam in the pool, enjoyed the Jacuzzi, and had a late lunch of smoothies and wraps. By mid-afternoon, Catlin felt back in the present and ready to challenge the past.

Margaret's studio was a tiny wood-frame house with a steep roof. Brocade curtains hung in the windows, and thick wool carpets covered the hardwood floor. Shelves heavy with books and oriental knickknacks lined the walls.

"Welcome, my sensitive friends," she greeted them. She gestured for them to sit on the couch and faced them on a tapestry stool. She took both their hands and scanned their palms, saying, "Mm hmm, mm hmm," as she looked back and forth.

Neil rolled his eyes, but Catlin seemed serious, so he decided to play along and hold his comments for later.

"I was premature in saying you were married, but no matter. Destiny will out. I see compatibility and commitment and a determination to get things right this time."

"This time?" Neil interrupted.

"Oh yes. You have been together before, haven't you sensed that?"

He shrugged.

"No echoes from the past, images of earlier times intruding into the present?"

"We found out recently that we have a common ancestor in Daniel Hayden, and that the relationship between Daniel and Catherine Porter, who's in my family line, started in the parlor house," Catlin said.

Margaret raised her eyebrows at the names. "So you are linked to the early tragedies of the house. No wonder there was such an uproar."

"For us?" Catlin asked.

"No, for the spirits after you left. Some were delighted to see you again, but one in particular was furious. I am sure you know which one."

"The fat man," Catlin said.

"Yes, Judge Wellingbrook was especially agitated."

"Judge Wellingbrook is the fat man? He died in the house, didn't he?" Catlin remembered Amy's story and what the bookseller told her.

"Most decidedly. Heart attack according to the newspaper reports of the time. But . . ."

"But newspapers can be wrong?" Neil said.

"But the spirits don't lie," Margaret said. "Violence leaves a powerful footprint. The energy of the room is too negative for his to have been a natural death. The story is that Catherine Porter committed suicide the next day, and that would also have left a telltale sign, but her spirit is not here."

"How do you know?" Neil said.

Margaret shrugged. "I know." She leaned back and studied them a moment. "As do you." She smiled. "I have a great interest in the early history of the house too. I am a descendant of Josephine Muget. Her spirit is here and uneasy with unfinished business. Let's share what we know, for your sake." She touched Catlin's hand.

"My sake?"

"Yes. You are in danger, dear. The past can stretch its claws farther than we think. You called me today, why?"

"My experience in the house was so vivid, and then I had a bad nightmare and another panic attack last night. The fat man was trying to kill me. He said it was my turn."

"He was a dangerous man and is a malevolent spirit. We need to find out how your ancestor crossed him. But first, what else do you know about Catherine and Daniel?"

Catlin and Neil told her about the letters and Amy's diary.

Margaret exclaimed, laughed, and sighed at the revelations. "Amy was rumored to be the sweetest of the first girls," she said. "Her room is the one with the secret doorway, but it's the warmest in the house. And your story explains a lot about James. I see now why he played the piano for you," she said to Neil.

"Why? He wasn't a fan of Daniel's."

"No, but he failed in his duty to Catherine to tell Daniel about the plan after Josephine died, even though he tried to talk with Daniel. He must have blamed himself for Daniel's suicide and Catherine's grief for many years." Margaret turned to Catlin. "He reconciled with Catherine, as we know now from Amy's words. I sense only joy from his spirit at your presence."

"So where do we go from here?" Neil said.

"Ah. Now I think it's time to discover why Catlin is so closely connected to the early days of the house."

"How do we do that?" Catlin asked.

"Are you open to a past-life regression, dear?"

"I guess so. What's involved?"

"I put you in a relaxed hypnotic state where you can access the stories of your previous lives. It's perfectly harmless and has given many people insights that have greatly benefited their present condition. Would you like to try it?"

"Okay. Can Neil be there?"

"Yes, of course." Margaret looked at him. "Just be careful not to go under too."

"No worries. I'm immune to the power of suggestion."

"Yes, I saw that stubborn streak in your palm." She smiled.

They moved to a back room for the past-life regression.

Comfortable on a massage table under a sheet and blanket, Catlin settled back and began deep yoga breathing, concentrating on soothing music and Margaret's lulling voice. She closed her eyes under the herbal eye pillow.

"Become aware of the table supporting you," Margaret said. "Let yourself relax into the force of gravity and release all tension. Become aware of your toes feeling relaxed. It feels good and safe to let go. Feel your ankles relax. Now your calves. Listen to the music and breathe."

With every breath, Catlin let go a little more and relaxed her body, following Margaret's voice as each part was named, moving upward to shoulders, out along arms to fingers, up to the crown of her head, and over to her eyes and lips. She was aware of the flow of air in and out, conscious but content to let the outside world slip away behind the patternless music and unseen voice.

"Now imagine you are standing at the beginning of a staircase with a beautiful wooden railing," Margaret said. "And when you are ready, start to go down the stairs. You are safe and feel comfortable descending the steps. With each step down you are more and more relaxed."

In her mind, Catlin moved downward, letting her fingers glide over the smooth handrail.

"Finally, you reach the bottom of the stairs. In front of you is a long hallway. It is well lit, and you can see many doors. Are you in the hallway? Do you see the doors?"

"Yes."

"Behind each door is a past life. Begin walking along the hallway and look at the doors. Do you see a door that attracts you?"

"Yes."

"Stand in front of the door. What does it look like?"

"It's beautiful. Beveled glass. A dark wood frame. Heavy, very grand."

"When you are ready, open the door." Margaret paused. "Have you opened the door? Are you inside?"

"Yes." Catlin smiled at the scene in her mind.

"Where are you? What do you see?"

"I'm in my house. It's big. The furniture is velvet and mahogany. A marble staircase leads to the second floor on two sides."

"Do you live here?"

"Yes. My family is rich."

"Can you see yourself here?"

"Yes. There's a mirror in the entryway."

"What do you look like? How are you dressed?"

"I'm pretty. I'm wearing a beautiful blue dress and full petticoats. My hair is long and thick."

"What are you doing?"

"I'm getting ready for a party. My friends are coming."

"How old are you?"

"I'm fifteen. It's my birthday party."

"Can you see anyone else in the house?"

"Yes. We have servants and tutors. My governess is here. My cousin has come for the party."

"Can you see your cousin?"

"Yes. She's pretty, just like me. Some people think we're twins."

"How do you feel about her?"

"Oh, we love each other," Catlin said earnestly.

"Like sisters?"

"More."

Margaret smiled. "I can see that. When you talk about her, your face lights up with love. Now allow yourself to age five years. Are you still in the house?"

"No." Catlin frowned.

"Where are you now?"

"In another big house. It's busy and noisy."

"Do you live in the house?"

"Yes. And I work here."

"How did you get there?"

"I took a train and a stagecoach. It was a long ride."

"Did you want to leave your home?"

"No. But my cousin left and I missed her."

"So you followed her?"

"Yes. She's in this house too. She said the work was easy. I'm happy to be with her again."

"What is your job? What do you do?"

Catlin shrugged under the blanket. "Anything the men ask."

"Ah." Margaret hesitated.

"Mostly they're nice. Mother tries to look out for us."

"Your mother is here?"

"That's what we call her. She's not our real mother. She runs the house."

"Is she the madam?"

"Yes. Madam Joey. She's the boss."

"Her name is Joey?"

"Josephine. We're all her girls. But she loves me the most."

"Why is that?"

"Because I'm the best." Catlin smiled proudly.

Margaret chuckled. "What is your name in this house?"

"Catherine."

"Excellent." Margaret nodded and shared a look with Neil. "Allow yourself to age a few more years. Are you still in this house?"

"Yes. But my cousin has gone to a different house. She wanted to be someplace quieter. Everyone has forgotten her."

"Have you forgotten her?"

"No. I miss her a lot. But it's hard to see her."

"Do you have other friends?"

"Yes. Amy is my friend. I have a dog. And someone else." Catlin beamed.

"Someone is special to you?"

"Yes, he's very special."

"Is he in the house?"

"Whenever he can be."

"Does he love you?"

"Oh yes. He wants to marry me." Behind the eye pillow, Catlin's eyes filled with tears.

"Why are you sad?"

"Because we can't marry," she sighed. "His social standing is critical to his work. I would ruin his plans."

"Let yourself age a little more. Now what is happening?"

"No, no, everything's gone wrong!" She tossed her head and her hands fluttered.

"Breathe deeply and relax," Margaret soothed. "Your subconscious loves you and won't reveal anything you are not capable of handling. Step back and observe. What is happening? What do you see?"

"I'm in a room, standing next to a bed. An awful man is lying on the bed."

"What is the man doing?"

"Nothing. He's dead."

"How did he die?"

"I killed him. But I made it look like he had a heart attack," she answered calmly. "I stabbed him in the ear with a long hatpin."

"All right," Margaret said slowly. "Why did you kill him?"

"I couldn't let him live. He killed my cousin. He beat her to death with his whip."

"Wouldn't he have been punished?"

"No. He was a judge, an important man. She was nothing. Hardly anyone knew she'd been killed. He would do the same to me, or worse."

"Worse?"

"He threatened to scar my face with the whip if I didn't become his exclusively." Catlin was silent for awhile.

"What's happening now?"

"I'm in the basement. I'm afraid. But mother says her plan will work. The sheriff never liked the judge, and he's worried about me. No one saw James bring my cousin's body to our house. We'll use her to save me. So many lies," Catlin sighed. "I wish Daniel had been here to protect me."

"Who is Daniel?"

"My love."

"Where is he?"

"Away, seeking wealth. He doesn't know what's happened."

"Who is James?"

"A house guardian. He's like a brother."

"What is your mother's plan?"

"She'll dress my cousin in one of my gowns and say I committed suicide. They'll bury her with my name."

"What will you do?"

"Ride away into the night with James. He'll pretend I'm his sister and help me find work in another town." Again Catlin fell silent.

"Now where are you?"

"Another basement. I'm someone else. I have a different job."

"What is your job now?"

"I wash clothes. It's some kind of hotel. It's hard work. I'm waiting."

"What are you waiting for?"

"A letter from Josephine. She'll tell Daniel what happened so he can come for me. Everything will be all right then."

Margaret looked at the clock on a side table, and whispered to Neil, "She's been under long enough. It's time to bring her back."

Neil nodded.

Margaret said, "Let's leave this life for now. Go back through the door and into the hallway. Walk to the stairs. Are you at the foot of the stairs?"

"Yes."

"When you are ready, start climbing the stairs. It feels good to go up the stairs. You are relaxed. Become aware of this room. You are comfortable. You are aware of the music and the blanket. I will count to five, and when I get to five, you will awake, taking all these memories with you into the present. You will be comfortable with these memories; they will not upset you. One," she counted. "Breathing deeply, you are relaxed and listening to the music. Two, you feel the table under you. Three, becoming more aware of your surroundings. Four, you are ready to awake and be present, you are totally relaxed and feeling fine about all your memories. Five," Margaret finished, and took off the eye pillow.

Catlin opened her eyes.

"Are you here?" Margaret asked.

"Yes. Wow," Catlin said, thinking back.

"Indeed. You truly were Catherine in this previous life. That explains the intensity of your experience in the parlor house yesterday, and why the spirits have been so animated by your presence. You are working out some interesting karma."

"If Catherine killed the judge, then does that mean Catlin killed him?" Neil said. "Is that why the fat man is after her?"

"But Catherine had good reasons," Catlin protested, sitting up and pushing off the blanket. "He killed her cousin and wanted to abuse her."

Margaret leaned back in her chair. "Revenge and self-protection are strong motivators. Such actions don't come without a price, however. And there is Daniel to consider."

"What did Daniel have to do with it? He wasn't even there," Neil said.

"Exactly."

"That goes for Mother Josephine, too, then." Neil pointed at Margaret. "She aided and abetted."

Margaret nodded. "No one is free of karma."

They all sat silent while the gentle music played in the background.

"Assuming my story is the truth, how does it help us now?" Catlin asked. "It's not going to make the fat man less mad."

"Correct," Margaret said. "Knowledge isn't action. We have to take the next step." She tapped her fingers against pursed lips. "I wonder if an intervention would work."

"Intervention?" Neil said.

"Yes." Margaret sat up straighter. "What do you do when you have wronged someone?"

"Me?" Neil shrugged. "I usually avoid them until we've both forgotten about it."

The women laughed.

"The spirits have nothing but time," Margaret said. "You can't outlast them. If you are to find peace in this life, avoidance isn't an option. You need forgiveness."

"How do you get it?" Catlin said.

"Just like in this life, if you want forgiveness from someone, you have to apologize. And make amends if possible."

"We're talking ghosts here," Neil said. "How do you say I'm sorry to something that doesn't exist?"

"There are many techniques for dealing with the spirit world. I like the direct approach. Go to their turf, call out to them, say what needs to be said, and listen to their response."

"Like a séance," Catlin said.

"Yes." Margaret said. "Like that but without the candles."

"Why no candles? Too spooky?"

Margaret shook her head. "Fire code."

"Shucks." Neil laughed. "Can't we at least shine flashlights in our faces?"

Catlin frowned. "You're talking about us going back to the parlor house?"

"That's right. We have to go to them." Margaret stood up.

"It was very scary yesterday. If Neil hadn't been there I might have choked to death."

"That's another important message for the Judge to hear," Margaret said. "This time you are not alone."

Neil helped Catlin off the table. "When would we have this spookfest?" he asked.

"Tonight. The house was entirely too active this morning. One woman almost fell down the stairs in her hurry to leave. This must be settled quickly. A little haunting goes a long way."

"Tell me about it," Catlin said.

They planned their strategy over dinner at a nearby café.

"I still don't see why Catherine should apologize to the Judge," Catlin said. "Didn't he deserve to die?"

"The chain of violence has to be broken," Margaret responded. "More violence only strengthens negative energy. The question for you, as Catherine's reincarnation, is whether it was your role to enact that justice."

"Okay. He killed my cousin."

"That is her journey, dear, not yours."

"But I don't have any cousins."

Margaret shrugged. "Don't worry. Karma has a way of finding the right person for the job."

"Well, he did threaten me."

"Think back to your experience as Catherine. Could you have survived the night safely to take alternate action later? Perhaps enlist the help of James or others?"

Catlin closed her eyes to remember. "Yes," she sighed. "Catherine had fooled him into thinking she had submitted to his will. I realize something else, too. As cruel as he was, the Judge loved her; that's why he wanted her all to himself."

Margaret nodded. "Those are good insights to keep in mind. But when we go tonight, I suggest we begin with an easier task than the Judge—Daniel and James."

"Huh?" Neil looked up from his manicotti.

"We need James completely on our side. We should make sure he and Daniel are reconciled," Margaret told him.

"Hey, the best man won. I don't think Daniel should have to apologize for getting the girl," he said.

"No, but Daniel could have prevented the cascade of tragedy if he had responded to James and learned about Catherine's escape."

"So I have to be the first one to say I'm sorry?"

"I understand it doesn't seem fair. Think of it as obtaining another arrow in your quiver to defend your lady."

"I guess knights in shining armor need all the arrows we can get. But if I'm supposed to be the Lone Ranger, shouldn't it be silver bullets?"

Margaret smiled. "Those are good too."

29

They approached the museum well after closing time. Yellow light from a single lamp in the entryway shone under the hooded windows on the ground floor, but the upper floor was dark.

"We can't switch on any lights," Margaret whispered. "No one is supposed to be in the building after hours." She unlocked the door.

Neil straightened his shoulders and walked inside.

Catlin gulped and followed.

Margaret came in and locked the door behind them. "Remember what I told you, Catlin. Don't wander off alone. It would be too easy for your mind to slip into their world. You must stay in the present. All right, let's start in the parlor."

Catlin said, "Does this floor always creak and groan so much?" as they crept past the display cases.

"No," Margaret replied.

"Something's different about that case," Neil said, pointing. "The riding crop is missing."

Margaret frowned. "Not good, not good," she muttered.

Catlin turned back to face her. "Was that . . . ?"

"Judge Wellingbrook's whip, yes. I don't like it that he has grown strong enough to move items in our world."

Neil said, "*You* don't like it? Catlin and I are going to hate it."

"Quite possibly. Hurry."

Scant light reached the parlor. The furniture crouched around them on clawed feet ready to sprout talons. The mirror, which should have reflected the lamp in the entryway, showed only inky darkness. They stood in a circle, holding hands.

"Josephine Muget," Margaret began. "I come in love as I do every day. I bring visitors with the power to right old wrongs. We ask for your blessing in our search for forgiveness tonight."

They waited. Crystal prisms swayed on the lamp in the corner.

"Your turn," Margaret said to Neil.

"James—"*I sound like a girl*. Neil dropped his voice an octave. "James Seeley. I come as a descendant of Daniel Hayden, with humility and respect, to apologize for his wrongs to you. I acknowledge your love for Catherine. I thank you for protecting her when I foolishly abandoned her. I apologize for ignoring you when I should have sought your help. I am sorry my pride and selfishness caused you grief. I ask for your forgiveness."

Margaret nodded in approval. Catlin squeezed his hand.

Three keys sounded on the piano, and then the full chord resonated in the room.

"Is that good?" Neil whispered.

"I'm not sure yet," Margaret said. "Catlin, you should speak to him too."

Catlin cleared her throat. "James Seeley. I come as a descendant of Catherine Porter and the current receptacle for her soul. I honor you and thank you for your protection and generosity. I apologize for not treasuring your love as the precious gift it was. I am sorry my impetuous act of revenge caused so many problems. I ask for your forgiveness."

A Mozart sonata began to play. The music stopped. The image of a tall man in a dark coat shimmered in the mirror; he smiled and bowed. The mirror went black again.

"So far so good," Margaret said.

They dropped hands.

Neil wiped his palms on his jeans. "Too bad that wasn't the hard part." He touched the back of his neck. "Is a window open?"

Catlin shivered and rubbed the goose bumps on her arms. "I hope so."

Margaret said, "Not everyone is as careful about closing up as I am," and stepped away to check behind a velvet curtain. "The younger docents get distracted, and . . ." She turned back in alarm.

Something was tapping on the sideboard. The sound intensified to a heavy drumming and then became a mind-numbing pounding that jolted the decanter off the edge. Glass spewed in all directions. Vicious shards defied the laws of gravity and flew toward Catlin like guided missiles.

Neil jumped in front of the spray and tumbled to the floor with her beneath him, tucking her head into his shoulder.

"Josephine! James! Will you allow your house to be violated? Will you allow your loved one to be attacked?" Margaret cried.

The pounding stopped.

Twin swirls of chilled air scooped up the glass; the decanter reformed on the sideboard and twinkled in the dim light as if it had never moved.

"I'm gonna need fresh shorts if this keeps up," Neil said. "Are you okay?" he asked Catlin.

"I think so," she said.

He stood and pulled her upright. "You cheerleader types probably never got tackled."

Catlin pushed the hair out of her eyes. "No, that's another first."

"Stick with me, sweetheart. Nothing but the best of times."

Margaret rejoined them. "The Judge must be angry that we haven't addressed him yet. Even so, I think it would be useful for Catlin to make peace with Josephine before we go upstairs."

"Upstairs? Can't we call him down here?" Catlin said.

"He's certainly present." She rubbed her hip.

"The intervention will be most effective where the negative energy was originally created. That's Catherine's room. First Josephine, though."

They held hands again.

Catlin took a deep breath. "Josephine Muget. I come as Catherine Porter to apologize for taking such rash action and not seeking your help instead. I am sorry I wasn't here to comfort you at your death and honor your life. I ask for your forgiveness."

The house was quiet. The lamp in the corner remained still.

Catlin looked at the staircase, wondering how she would find the courage to go up, and noticed a light glowing on the bottom step like in the dream she had about Samantha Lynn. She let go of Neil and Margaret and walked to the stairs.

"Wait," Neil said. He glanced at Margaret, and they both followed her.

Catlin stopped in front of the staircase, watching as the translucent form of a woman in full skirts flickered into view. "Oh, Josephine," she said, hand on her heart.

"Child, I forgive you," Josephine said. "I regret I placed money before love and did not protect you. Do you forgive me?"

"Yes." Tears ran down Catlin's cheeks.

"Trust me now, and we shall face the Judge. It is time he left this house forever. Come." The apparition turned and floated upward.

"Here we go," Neil said, and reached for Catlin's hand, but she had already started up the stairs.

"She's gone over," Margaret said. "This may have to be done in their world. It's not my first choice but perhaps it's necessary."

Neil glared at her. "There'll be some real bad karma between you and me if anything happens to Catlin."

"So grows the chain," Margaret sighed.

They hurried up the stairs.

Neil passed rooms filled with men and women in various stages of undress. He heard boots thudding to the floor and bedsprings groaning, high-pitched squeals and low moans. The next sound chilled his blood.

Catlin screamed. The unearthly shriek reverberated through the house.

Neil sprinted to the end of the hall as the door to Catherine's room slammed shut and the lock clicked. He blew out the lock with three shots of his pistol and kicked in the door with the heel of his leather boot.

"Let go of her!" he thundered to the Judge.

Wellingbrook brandished his whip, keeping his other hand twisted in Catlin's hair where she knelt, whimpering, at his feet. "Alas, the hero returns too late," he sneered. "You'll not have her again. When I free her soul from this shell I'll have complete power to impose my will in your world and dominate in mine." He ignored Josephine's transparent fists flailing ineffectually at his arm. "We made a bargain, madam, leave me!" he shouted. He sliced through her with his whip and she disappeared.

"You're forgetting who has the gun," Neil said, taking aim.

"No, you're forgetting who's already dead." Wellingbrook laughed and yanked Catlin up in front of him.

"Why are you hiding behind a woman if you're so immortal?" Neil still held the gun high.

"I like having her close. Her fear tastes delicious; her pain feeds my soul." He tightened his grip in Catlin's hair. "Why do you think that your weapon is real?"

Neil hesitated. In that split second of doubt, the whip slashed his arm. The gun vanished.

"Ah, how pleasurable to see my rival's blood. I'm out of practice or I would have hit bone." Wellingbrook lashed out again, but Neil danced back and the whip whistled through air.

"Catlin, wake up," Neil said as he sidestepped another blow. "C'mon, sweetheart, I need your help."

"You cannot evade me forever," Wellingbrook snarled, swiping at Neil's face. "Eventually, you will tire, but I have all eternity."

"All eternity to do what? Be hated by everybody? That's no life—or afterlife. I feel sorry for you if all you've ever tasted from a woman is her fear and pain. You're missing out, my friend."

Did he imagine Wellingbrook's form wavering for a moment?

"Hasn't a woman ever given herself to you willingly with love?" Neil asked, deliberately softening his voice while he ducked. "That's so sad." He could see the braided handle of the whip through Wellingbrook's hand. "I'm sorry."

The iron grip on Catlin's hair loosened; her eyes cleared. She jumped out of the Judge's grasp and turned to face him. "Isaiah Wellingbrook. I come as Catherine Porter to apologize for taking your life. I am sorry I didn't choose a different path when many were possible. I regret that my hand violently stopped your journey. I ask for your forgiveness."

The Judge stood motionless, whip held high, his eyes wide. "A different . . . path," he repeated. "My first wife," he said to Neil, who had put his arm around Catlin.

"What?" Neil said.

Wellingbrook lowered his arm. "My first wife gave herself willingly with love. She died in childbirth."

"Then what are you doing here, man?"

"What indeed?" Wellingbrook stared at the whip in his hand. Finally, he sighed, "Cruelty filled the void in my heart. Perversion silenced whispers of love." He raised his head, gray eyes intent on Catlin. "My desire for revenge has spanned more than a century. I exerted my influence from son to son through generations. They do my bidding without knowing. Awakening your awareness of your past was the best I could achieve with the Wellingbrook line."

Catlin gasped. "Carolyn's book!"

Wellingbrook nodded. "It brought you here." His face hardened to an evil pride. "The McKenzie line proved to be more malleable and imaginative. I was content to have my descendant exact my revenge, but his efforts recently failed, thwarted by a sacrifice I failed to anticipate."

"So John was a Wellingbrook descendant," Catlin said. "I thought he was after Packard, not me."

Neil frowned. "I figured that guy was bad news from the beginning. How was he a Wellingbrook?"

"The bookseller told me the Judge's second wife was a McKenzie and she took back her maiden name when she returned to Boston with their young son. I wonder who made the sacrifice. Oh my god!" Catlin thought back to a wan face in a hospital room. "Could it be Angela? I thought there was something else she wanted to tell me about the accident. She said John dropped his cell phone but maybe she—"

Wellingbrook shouted, "Enough!" and raised his whip.

Neil pulled Catlin tighter as she cowered.

Wellingbrook intoned, "Let it be finished! Catherine Porter. I apologize for my hateful actions. I am sorry that you and your descendants have suffered at my hand. I regret all of the violence that grew from my influence. I ask for your forgiveness."

"Granted," Catlin whispered.

The whip fell to the floor. A thin mist rose toward the ceiling and disappeared, leaving Catlin and Neil alone in the moonlit room.

He touched her face. "Catherine Porter. I'm sorry I thought pursuing wealth was more important than being with you. I love you."

She smiled. "Daniel Hayden. I'm sorry I thought other people's values were more important than our life together. I love you, too."

They kissed, long and slow, spanning time, pulling the past into the present.

They broke apart at a fierce pounding.

"Oh no," Catlin said. "I thought he was gone for good."

"Open the door!" Margaret called from the hallway, hammering on the door again with her fist.

Neil let her in. "You missed all the fun," he told her. "Where were you?"

"You ran ahead of me in the hall, and when I got here, you had gone inside the room. Why did you lock the door?"

"I didn't. The Judge did. I kicked it in after I shot out the lock." Neil ran his hand over the undamaged wood and brass. "You've got some maintenance plan here. Everything fixes itself."

Margaret looked at his arm. "You're bleeding. We should tend to that right away. What happened?"

"Had a tussle with the Judge. I've got to learn to keep my focus."

Catlin picked up the riding crop from the floor. "I apologized to him. We think he's left the house."

Margaret closed her eyes to sense the room. "The negativity is gone. He's at peace. Where's Josephine?"

"Things got too intense for her," Neil said. "Maybe she'll come back now that the house is clear of pesky varmints."

"All the spirits may rest easier," Margaret said.

"In that case, you can hire a real piano player for atmosphere," he said.

Margaret laughed. "We'll consider it."

30

The next morning, Catlin woke in the apartment, snuggled next to Neil. "That was one wild dream," she said to herself, pulling her hair back. "Ow!"

Neil opened his eyes. "You okay?"

"Uh huh. My head is sore." She sat up. "My hip hurts too." She peeked under the covers. "Those are interesting colors," she said, pushing off the blankets to show him her bruise.

"I'd like to say I'm not responsible, but I know I am," Neil said. He kissed the spot gently. "We wore more padding in high school." He sat up next to her, grimacing when he placed weight on his arm.

She looked at the bandage. "Oh my god, did all that really happen?"

"Yep, we had our first drunken brawl." He laughed at her shocked face. "You know I'm kidding. Yes, we battled the forces of evil last night and conquered them with love. Unfortunately, it's Monday, and we have to get to work. Did the Lone Ranger have a day job?"

"I don't know, but I think normal work will be a good thing. I'll let the past stay put for a while."

"Sounds like a plan. If we've recovered by this weekend, maybe we can go horseback riding."

"Our second date at last." She smiled and kissed him. "Whose turn is it to make coffee?"

They reveled in normalcy, sharing chores, working out together, and sightseeing on the weekends. On their last Friday evening in Denver, they visited Margaret at her studio to say good-bye. She told them that Josephine and James had taken to appearing in the mirror as if it were a new trick they found amusing, but Catherine's room remained peaceful. "Some people say they sense the warmth of new love," she said. "You created good karma that will always be with you."

On the trip home, they stopped in Moab for several days to explore Arches National Park and stayed in Springdale to hike the trails in Zion. When they arrived in Palm Springs, Packard leapt up to lick their faces and then hunkered down to sniff Neil's sneakers.

"Don't get too fascinated by those," Neil said warily.

"Maybe he senses the spirit world," Catlin said. "Aren't they the shoes you had on when we did the intervention?"

"For the most part."

Luther slapped him on the back. "We'll have to get you outfitted with real shoes for the golf course. Let's stop at the clubhouse tomorrow, my treat."

Amanda said, "Now, Luther. Not everyone wants to play as much as you do."

"It's only eighteen holes. Good man-to-man time. The shoes are a gift for taking care of my daughter and putting that beautiful smile back on her face." He hugged Catlin. "You look wonderful, honey. Have a good time in Denver?"

"Uh huh."

"We want to hear about it, but you've had a long day getting here, so let's get you settled tonight. We can play tomorrow by ear," Amanda said, and hustled everyone inside.

The men left late the next morning to bond on the golf course. Catlin relaxed with her mother in the den, Packard at her feet, and relayed everything about the trip.

"That's an incredible story," Amanda exclaimed, listening to the experience in the parlor house. "Do you think Neil is Daniel's reincarnation?"

"I don't know. He didn't do a past-life regression. He said he's immune to hypnosis."

"This life is what really matters. He seems devoted and protective."

Catlin knew what was coming next.

"Are you two serious, darling?"

"We haven't talked about that."

"There's no hurry. But if you are, or do get serious, I want you to know your father and I would be very happy to welcome him into the family." Amanda stood up and kissed Catlin on the cheek. "Lunch?"

Neil laughed when Catlin asked him how the golf game went. "The good news is that I didn't smash any windows and nobody got hurt. I got a birdie on one hole, unfortunately."

"Isn't that a good thing?"

"Not for the duck."

The following afternoon, Neil carried Catlin's suitcases into her house while Packard raced around the living room and down the hall.

"Home at last," she said, opening the back door for Packard, who threw himself onto the grass in a frenzy of snorts and rolls.

Neil laughed at the sight. "I may do the same when I get back to my own bed."

"I guess we both have a lot to catch up on before Monday," Catlin sighed.

"We do," Neil said. "And I'm not looking forward to doing laundry all by myself."

"Oh I see. You'll just miss my help with chores?"

"There's only one thing about you that I'm going to miss until next weekend," he said, pulling her into his arms.

"What's that?"

"Everything."

He called her a half hour later to let her know he had arrived home safely and missed her already. They agreed to talk Sunday night.

Determined not to mope, Catlin busied herself with grocery shopping and cleaning the house. She reinstituted her standard routine on Sunday, chatting with neighbors on the way back from Frisbee in the park with Packard. She called Nancy in the afternoon and tried not to watch the clock until evening in anticipation of Neil's call.

"Want to go back to Wayne's on Friday?" he asked her on the phone that night. "I wouldn't mind a first date reprise."

"That'd be nice. But it's too cold for the deck."

"Right. Packard will have to stay home. Bundle up, and we'll walk on the beach after anyway."

"Okay."

Friday couldn't come soon enough. They almost settled for Catlin's leftovers instead of dinner out, they were so excited to be together again. But they calmed down and enjoyed their date, talking about the week's events over dinner and a brisk walk on the beach.

The chilled air made pulling him into her bed especially delicious, cuddling next to him afterward especially cozy. And the heat in between was as overwhelming as always.

"I shouldn't complain," Catlin told Nancy over lunch a few weeks later. "But after being so close in Denver, it feels like we're going backward."

"Do you want to move in together?"

Catlin shook her head. "I don't want to just live with him."

"Maybe you're so used to being engaged you're still in that getting married mindset. He could be in a different place. You need to relax and give him time."

"It's hard to be patient when the life I want is within reach," Catlin said. "I miss being with him. We talk every day, but it's not the same. When we're together, I feel happy and secure. I mean, I know I'm a capable person, but things are easier with him there because he believes I'm capable. I think we can accomplish more together than by ourselves. Plus, he's supportive of my writing. He thinks it's great that I want to be published."

"Have you told him about your inheritance?"

"No. That'll be a happy surprise someday. He's not into material stuff, anyway. He says quality time with me is what matters most to him. He makes even the mundane fun. We trade whose place we stay at on the weekends and help each other with laundry, chores, and cooking. It's not that I want to *get* married; I want to *be* married. To him."

"You are such a goner over him. You never talked like that about John."

"Who's John?"

Neil took her Christmas shopping in his neighborhood's quaint downtown when she said she wanted to find a vintage gift for her mom. After wandering through the antique stores, they lingered in front of an old-fashioned bridal shop on a side street.

I wonder if I'll ever need one of these, Catlin mused, gazing at the display window.

"You know, you'd look good in white," Neil said, kissing the back of her neck.

"Umm, champagne would be better," she said, eyeing an opalescent satin gown with brocade bodice. "I'm a spring."

"Sure, champagne." He draped his arm over her shoulder and pulled her closer. "But beer for the boys. Spring is good. How about April? Our softball league doesn't start until May."

"April showers bring May flowers." She giggled as he nuzzled her ear. "I always liked May."

"That'd work too. Bobby will be back from Phoenix and can cover second base for me for a few weeks."

"He got a lot further than second base with Nancy. She'd look pretty in the blue chiffon." Catlin nodded toward a flowing dress in the corner of the display. "It's the same color as your eyes." She smiled up at him, reflecting how looking at him still fused all her brain cells.

He returned the smile and lifted her left hand to his lips, tenderly kissing each finger.

"What are we doing?" she asked dreamily, eyes half closed.

"I think we're planning a wedding, sweetheart," he said, grasping her hand in both of his as he knelt on one knee in front of her. "Catlin, will you marry me?"

"Oh my god," she squeaked, tears glistening. "I don't know what to say."

"Then I'm in big trouble down here." Neil smiled. "It's a one-word answer, Cat. I was hoping it'd be easy."

"Oh!" She shook her head. "I'm sorry." She pulled him up toward her and said, "Yes," fervently. "Yes yes yes!" she shouted to the people on the street watching, and everyone applauded.

Neil spun her around on the sidewalk and then kissed her until they were both dizzy.

"Will you kiss me like that after we're married?" she asked, stroking his cheek.

"Every blessed day, I promise, come hell or high water."

"Then I'll always be happy."

"If you're happy, I'm happy."

They kissed again, and the world stopped one moment longer as past and present conjoined to create a new path for two well-acquainted souls.